"You've been monopolizing my thoughts."

Josh's deep murmur was as hypnotic as the warm fire crackling in the grate. He gently tugged at the clip that held Ellie's topknot, and her hair came tumbling down with a silken whisper.

"In what way?" She looked up at him solemnly, her eyes wide, her body quivering at his nearness. In swift answer his mouth was on hers, plunging her into the dark turbulence of desire.

"*Every* way," he finally whispered raggedly. "And I'm not sure if I like that." With a trembling hand he stroked her back, leaving a blazing trail. "But I do know I want you...."

THE AUTHOR

Leigh Roberts used her public-relations background in writing *Siren Song*. She also borrowed one of her fantasies—singing in a rock-and-roll band. Still undiscovered by a major record label, this delightful author lives in California with her husband and two young sons.

Books by Leigh Roberts

HARLEQUIN TEMPTATION
20—LOVE CIRCUITS
55—SIREN SONG

HARLEQUIN SUPERROMANCE
81—MOONLIGHT SPLENDOR

These books may be available at your local bookseller.

Don't miss any of our special offers. Write to us at the following address for information on our newest releases.

Harlequin Reader Service
P.O. Box 52040, Phoenix, AZ 85072-2040
Canadian address: P.O. Box 2800, Postal Station A,
5170 Yonge St., Willowdale, Ont. M2N 6J3

Siren Song

LEIGH ROBERTS

Harlequin Books

TORONTO • NEW YORK • LONDON
AMSTERDAM • PARIS • SYDNEY • HAMBURG
STOCKHOLM • ATHENS • TOKYO • MILAN

Published April 1985

ISBN 0-373-25155-6

Printed in Canada

1

ELEANOR MARTINSON PEERED anxiously through the windshield of her car, trying to discern the boundaries of the narrow pavement through the rain that sheeted between tall redwood trees. Though it wasn't yet the middle of the afternoon, the rain deepened the forest's shade into an impenetrable gloom. She had flicked her headlights on half an hour ago, when she had turned off the highway onto this narrow twisting road into the heart of the hills above California's Santa Clara Valley. She heard the soft slurp of mud under her wheels and felt the little car lurch as it left the pavement momentarily. With all her heart, she wished she hadn't come.

It had been sunny when she left Santa Cruz that morning. The storm hit when she was halfway to La Honda. There was no thunder or lightning; that wasn't the way of rainstorms in California's coastal areas. Instead there was the steady downpour of rain, sometimes little more than a trickle, sometimes in cloudburst proportions.

Right now it was coming down in a spate, obscuring her windshield, making it hard to see driveway openings along the road. She blinked her headlights to the Bright setting and slowed even more.

The house ought to be somewhere along here, she thought. She had already come the prescribed three and a half miles from the scattered buildings that made up the small town of La Honda. But now the wind was gusting, blowing rain in angry tatters across her field of

vision. She almost missed the mailbox leaning drunken-
ly on its half-collapsed fence post, heralding rutted,
muddy tracks that led deeper into the forest.

She skidded to a stop, backed up and turned into the
drive, checking the number on the mailbox. This was
the place. A faint sigh of exasperation escaped her. She
had heard of Joshua Blackmun's penchant for solitude.
But it was highly inconvenient, when she needed to see
him, that he wouldn't leave his mountain aerie.

The little car plowed through standing water in the
ruts of the driveway, while Eleanor used one hand to
ease the tense muscles of her neck. Driving in the rain
always made her nervous. Perhaps the weather would
clear before she finished her business and was ready to
go back to Santa Cruz.

The car suddenly stopped dead and she sighed. All
she needed was to get stuck in the mud. She gunned the
engine a bit without success, and decided to leave the
car there. The house was in front of her; she could see a
light some distance ahead. She'd simply have to slog to
it without a raincoat or umbrella.

When she opened the car door it was nearly torn from
her fingers by a violent gust of wind. Using all of her
considerable strength, she struggled out of the car and
slammed the door, taking the full force of the gale in her
face. Buffeted by wind and water, she staggered toward
the dim, distant bulk of the house, unable to find a path,
her smart, expensive shoes burying themselves in the
mud with each step.

Instinctively, she clutched her thin cotton jacket
closer. It was no real protection, but it offered the illu-
sion of comfort against the storm. The jacket and the
sleekly casual pants that matched were not really up to
November, even in California. But it had been so warm
that morning—she hadn't realized she would be the next
thing to drowned before nightfall.

She gained the precarious shelter of a small front porch and hammered on the door. Vaguely she realized she was shivering, drenched by her brief exposure to the elements. The wind stopped momentarily and she could hear footsteps from inside the house, then another sound behind her—an ominous creaking noise. Puzzled, she moved to the edge of the porch, peering past her car.

The wind swept down in sudden fury, sending branches dancing, tearing angrily at the tattered leaves on some walnut trees. The creaking noise intensified. With a reverberating crash, a massive oak tree near the juncture of driveway and road slowly tilted and fell, its outer branches barely missing Eleanor's car.

Still gaping at the ruins of the tree in stupefied astonishment, Eleanor didn't realize that the door of the house had opened until a dry voice spoke. "Whoever you are," said Joshua Blackmun behind her, "you could have gotten my attention without felling my tree."

She turned at the sound of his voice. He was lounging in the doorframe, gray eyes coldly amused. "It almost hit my car," she whispered, hardly aware she was speaking. "If I'd come along five minutes later it might have hit *me*."

"A hard fate even for an autograph hound," he replied, his face showing little compassion. His words brought Eleanor out of her shock. She wrenched her mind away from the vagaries of nature and gave her full attention to the man before her.

Her first impression was that he seemed surrounded by an aura of power, of energy, unexpected in someone who'd been retired from projecting that kind of excitement for three years. His rangy frame was more than six feet tall—the right size, she thought inconsequently, to go with her own five feet ten inches. And he looked older than she'd expected. But of course she'd only seen him once, when he was performing. From the audience, anyone on a stage would look different.

One of the lean, wiry ones, she found herself thinking. His shoulders were broad under the worn blue chambray shirt, his muscular chest tapered into a slim waist and narrow, powerful hips. Realizing that she'd been scrutinizing his body as if he were a slab of meat, she lifted rueful hazel eyes to find him still busy with a scornful assessment of her. She could not resent it, since she'd done the same thing, but she knew she failed to present her usual cool, immaculate image. Her hair was in dark, wet wisps around her cheeks and down her back, and her clothes were plastered damply to her strong, Amazonian body. She raised her chin and tried to assume control of the situation.

"I'm not an autograph hunter, Mr. Blackmun," she said briskly, her clear voice showing no sign of her rising displeasure. "My name is Eleanor Martinson. I left a message with your answering service that I would be driving up to talk to you this afternoon. Didn't you get it?"

His eyebrows lifted. "So you're the one who's been pestering me lately. No, I didn't check with my service today." He looked past her at the wreck of the tree blocking his driveway. "There's no point in telling you to leave, unless you've got a chain saw in your car. I suppose you'd better come in."

She inclined her head graciously. "Thank you," she murmured politely, clenching her teeth to keep from shivering. Her wet clothes had become unbearably cold and clammy; she could think of nothing but a hot toddy and a roaring fire. But from the sample she'd had of his hospitality, she was unlikely to get much consideration from Joshua Blackmun.

From the outside, his place had looked like one of the small, shabby ranch houses that were scattered throughout the Santa Cruz Mountains. But the inside had been extensively remodeled. He stood in the doorway as she walked past him directly into a living room that must have occupied a dominant part of the home's space. It was long and expansive, with a soaring, skylit ceiling and a huge fireplace at one end, from which a vigorous blaze illuminated the room with leaping flames. On one side French doors opened onto a rain-drenched deck with a view of pearly, cloud-wreathed hills.

The furniture was comfortable without being pretentious; it consisted of a couple of overstuffed chairs and sofa, a round oak table and a modern wood-and-leather rocker drawn up to the fire. One corner was a veritable music store, with a baby grand, an electric keyboard outfit, several guitar cases set neatly against the wall and a couple of smaller cases for violin and mandolin on top of the piano.

Eleanor made straight for the warmth of the blaze, shivering uncontrollably as she held her hands to the heat. Her shoes squished moistly on the hearth, and she glanced back in dismay at the muddy trail she'd left across the faded colors of an old, hand-hooked rug. "Sorry," she managed through chattering teeth.

A short laugh escaped him. "You are a mess, aren't you?" he said, a note of reluctant amusement warming his husky voice. "I'll get a towel." He turned at the doorway with a mocking smile. The hint of a drawl in his words was deliberately intensified. "Why don't you-all just take off your shoes and stay awhile?"

Alone in the living room, Eleanor groped for the shreds of her self-possession. Under other circumstances, her plight would strike her as funny. But faced with Joshua Blackmun's unfriendly attitude and the awkward problem of being unable to leave until the tree was cleared away, she could find nothing to laugh at. She had expected his antagonism to some extent, and she had been prepared to deal with it in her usual competent, tactful way. The tree was a completely unforeseen and unwanted complication.

She turned slowly in front of the fire, grateful for its heat, noticing that a cloud of steam had already begun to rise from her clothes. With difficulty she stripped off the sopping jacket. The light sweater she'd worn under it was too wet to afford much warmth, and her pants were still plastered against her legs with dampness.

Joshua came back into the room carrying a thick terry towel. "I called the road crew and reported the tree down, but the phone went dead before they could say when they would be out." He tossed her the towel. "Give me that jacket. I don't want it dripping on my floor."

He vanished again, reappearing as she finished toweling the worst of the moisture out of her hair. She ran her fingers through the still-damp brown strands, combing them off her face, and then forgot about them. Her hair had been carefully cut to need very little in the way of maintenance, a boon after swimming or jogging. She wrapped the towel around her shoulders like a shawl and tried to suppress her shivers. They weren't altogether because of the cold, she knew. She was nervous, and that wasn't like her.

Joshua came and propped one arm along the mantel of the rough stone fireplace, directing a keen, assessing glance at her. "Well," he remarked, "you don't look quite so much like a drowned rat. What did you want to see me about?"

She faced him steadily and realized that he was making her feel nervous. She pushed that knowledge away. "You know what I want, Mr. Blackmun," she told him, a faint note of reproof in her voice. "You've had two letters and a phone call from me. All this could have been avoided if you'd just cooperated earlier."

His expression changed, the spare planes of cheekbone and jaw taking on hardness. "I don't cooperate with any form of publicity." There was menace in his words. "Peter knows that."

She shook her head, summoning a tolerant smile. "If that's the case, why did Peter hire Randolph Public Relations to promote your new album? Believe me, Mr. Blackmun, Peter is expecting large-scale success from this album. That won't happen without the right kind of promotion."

He bit back an angry retort as another shiver escaped her. "You'll catch your death of cold if you stand around in those wet clothes," he said brusquely. "I'll show you where you can change."

She hesitated, dubious, and he seized her arm impatiently. "Come on," he continued in a gentler tone. "You're getting my floor all wet." Bemused, she found herself propelled out of the living room into a small bedroom. Joshua left her there for a minute, returning with a long velour bathrobe and another towel. "You should congratulate yourself," he said with another mocking smile. "You're the first woman who's been allowed to wear my bathrobe in some time." He closed the door gently behind him before she could answer.

It was just as well he did. She knew it would have been impolitic to make a sarcastic retort when she was there to coax him into behaving reasonably about the promotion schemes. Just the same, she spent several moments thinking up a couple of scathing replies.

Hastily she shed her clothes, sighing in relief as the warmth of the thick velvety velour met her chilled flesh. Her underwear was damp, too, but the thought of Joshua Blackmun catching sight of it if she hung it to dry was simply too disquieting. There were mud splashes on her stockings, and her shoes were caked with mud. Barefoot in the burgundy-colored robe, she gathered up her clothes and shoes and slipped out of the room.

The bathroom was right next door; her jacket, dangling carelessly from a hanger, was already dripping into the bathtub. She squeezed as much moisture as she could from the pants and sweater and hung them over the shower rail. Still carrying her shoes, she went in search of a place to clean them.

She was in the kitchen wiping the mud off them when he reappeared. He sent an ironic glance to the teakettle she'd put to boil on the old gas stove. "Making yourself comfy, I see."

It was an unkind remark and she flushed. "I thought perhaps we could discuss business over a cup of tea. If that's too civilized for you—"

"Oho.... So the lady has claws after all." He didn't seem put out by her brief flash of anger. His eyes raked up and down her with unwilling approval. "You're a big girl, aren't you? My robe almost fits you."

It was true. The sleeves were too long and the hem touched the floor on her—she thought it would probably reach him midcalf—but otherwise the robe fit quite well. Perhaps it fit too well in front; if she moved too suddenly, the lacy top of her camisole showed. She tightened the belt, feeling a return of that inexplicable tension, although it had nothing to do with his comment. She had long ago decided that, although not slender like a model's, her tall, well-rounded figure represented a very acceptable ideal of womanhood.

The teakettle hissed and Joshua motioned her politely toward the waiting teapot. "Please, make yourself at home," he said, the mocking note back in his voice. "Who knows how long you'll be staying, after all. Perhaps if they turn the power back on you'd like to do some of my laundry."

She sent him a level gaze. "You don't need to make

this any more unpleasant than it is. Besides," she added, straight-faced, "my laundry would naturally come first. *Is* the power off?"

He nodded, his lips almost smiling. Suddenly she wanted to provoke him to smile; she wanted to see what such an expression would do to the brooding, craggy depths of his face. She wrenched her mind around to the problem at hand. "Perhaps you'd care to join me in a cup of tea," she said politely, carrying the teapot over to a small pine table in the windowed dining area that overlooked the same deck the living room did. "If you'd bring some cups, maybe we could come to some sort of understanding about the promotion for your album."

She set the teapot down and looked at him. For a moment their eyes clashed, then he opened a cupboard and collected two mugs, bringing them to the table. "You certainly are single-minded." There was faint disapproval in his voice.

"I didn't come all the way up here and nearly get smashed by a tree for social chitchat," she reminded him briskly. There was a pad of paper and a felt-tip pen on the table. She turned over the first two pages to find a clear sheet, and took up the pen.

"This is more or less what I had in mind," she began. "My briefcase is in the car, and I'm not going back into that to get it." She sent a nod toward the window, where the rain still lashed against the glass. "I planned a two-pronged campaign involving both the print media and TV. We can start off with some interviews in San Francisco." She named three important music critics and rushed on before the storm she saw gathering on his face could break. "Peter's received a number of requests for you to appear at benefits: one for the San Francisco cable cars, another for a mental health clinic and a third for a children's hospital. Naturally you wouldn't be the only performer—several other local big names are going

to appear." She rattled off some names and was gratified to see his expression change. "Would you be interested in appearing?"

"I'll have to think about it," he muttered. She plowed
ahead.

"Peter was also thinking about a tour, nothing long or
exhaustive. Six cities, perhaps. No buses, no big backup
section. Just you and a couple of musicians and a mini-
mal crew." He looked thunderous. Eleanor dared a persuasive smile. "Come on, admit it," she said coaxingly.
"You're dying to get back onstage. The applause, the
feedback from an audience—don't you feel the need to
validate the work you've been doing with some public
exposure?"

For a moment she thought he would explode. She
maintained her friendly, cajoling expression and was re-
warded by his reluctant smile. "You think you're pretty
acute, don't you?" His voice was a growl, but she heard
the humor behind it and allowed herself to relax a little.

"I used to work exclusively with musicians," she admitted. "For a lot of them, that's the sole force that
drives them. Applause, adulation, groupies...." She
made an involuntary gesture of distaste.

He pounced on that momentary revelation. "And you
don't like that? I'd have thought, since you're responsi-
ble for whipping up the frenzy of adulation, you would
approve of it. Sells lots of records, you know," he added
sarcastically.

Eleanor sat up straighter, keeping her voice level with
an effort. "I no longer have to work with those people,"
she said quietly. "The Randolph agency wouldn't be
handling you if that was the sort of promotion you
wanted." It wasn't strictly true, but he didn't need to
know that. "And this silly fuss you're making shows
that you're not in it for the publicity."

"Silly?" This time he did explode. "You're damned

right I'm not in it for the publicity. I don't know what possessed me to agree to record another album. God knows I don't need any part of the hype and the phoniness that go hand in hand with success in the recording industry."

He surged to his feet and paced angrily around the small alcove. Eleanor felt too big, as if she occupied too much space. But she sat calmly, her feet still crossed in front of her despite the danger from his heedless motion.

"So why are you doing it?" She kept the inquiry calm. And she was interested in his reply. The news that the reclusive Joshua Blackmun was set to record a new album on a nearly unknown Santa Cruz record label was bound to generate a great deal of interest and publicity. The man must have known that.

He stopped pacing, arrested by her unexpected question. "I don't know exactly why. When Peter mentioned recording for him...suddenly I was ready for it. I've been laying down some tracks with my home system, but it's not the same as being in a studio with good backup and excellent quality audio." He shook his head. "Peter doesn't do hard-core PR on his other artists. I didn't realize he was going to see me as so exploitable."

She met his angry stare coolly. "All publicity isn't exploitation. Lucky for you, Peter hired the Randolph agency. Strictly a class act, I can assure you."

He laughed shortly and resumed pacing, not so violently as before. Ellie let her gaze wander to the French window.

The rain, she noticed, was over, and a weak light attempted to break through the clouds that veiled the distant hills. She thought hopefully that if the road crew arrived to clear away the fallen tree blocking Josh's driveway within the next three hours, she could still make it home before it was fully dark. She brought her attention back to Josh, trying to regard him dispassionately as she sipped her lukewarm tea.

He had paused in his pacing and stood rigidly by the French window, one hand braced against the frame, staring in brooding silence at the mist-shrouded shapes of the hills. His face looked older than the picture she dredged up from memory, which was a composite of newspaper and magazine accounts of his career and her own observations from the one concert she'd attended.

There was no trace of the motorcycle accident, although some press stories at the time had implied he was disfigured for life.

She recalled the blaze of publicity that had bracketed that accident three years ago—the reports of a public quarrel with his current love interest, Vivienne Santos, a sultry well-known singer with a predilection for turning men into pretzels. Then had come the near-fatal crash, the long weeks in the hospital, the announcement that Joshua Blackmun was going into seclusion despite the frantic efforts of his record company, which had been successfully putting him through the superstar mill.

After the first year, there had been only sporadic mention of his activities by tabloids avid for news of anyone who didn't want to be news. And Joshua Blackmun went to great lengths not to be news. Aside from the occasional surprise gig at nightclubs in Palo Alto and Woodside, he maintained a low profile both musically and personally. His album for Peter Macguire's small, Santa Cruz-based label, Trax Records, would be his first since the crash.

Her thoughts were interrupted by a sound—a low, moaning whimper. Josh whirled around and took in her startled gaze with a sudden shout of laughter. "No, that wasn't me wallowing in self-pity," he said with the return of his mocking manner. "And it wasn't a ghost or anything. Sounds like Bertha's about to give birth."

He strode out of the kitchen and down the hall to an open door across from the living room. The room he entered, with Eleanor close on his heels, was obviously his bedroom. The headboard of the bed was made of hickory saplings bent into baroque curves and swirls. Instead of a spread or comforter, there was a huge faded old Navaho blanket, its fringes just touching the floor. An armoire hulked in one corner, and a whole wall was covered with the louvered doors of a huge closet.

One pair of these doors was open, and Joshua crouched between them, speaking in a soothing voice. At first Eleanor didn't even see the German shepherd lying on a tumble of silver-gray towels inside the closet. But the dog whimpered again, and Josh spoke to her quietly, running a soothing hand around her ears.

Eleanor didn't come too close. "Is this Bertha?"

Josh's voice matched her own, calming tone. "This is Bertha. She's never had puppies before."

Perching cautiously on the foot of the bed, Eleanor regarded Bertha's golden-brown, slightly apprehensive eyes. Another low whimper escaped the dog's throat. Eleanor found herself smiling reassuringly. Suddenly there was a tiny mewling sound—a puppy had arrived. Bertha looked around curiously and approached the glistening little body with her inquisitive muzzle. Remembering stories about dogs that eat their young, Eleanor tensed.

After sniffing the puppy thoroughly, Bertha began licking the little bundle all over, her expression suddenly, ridiculously, complacent. Josh sat back on his heels with a satisfied grunt and Eleanor felt uncontrollable laughter bubbling up inside her, a mixture of the exhilaration of witnessing a new life beginning, and a sudden, inexplicable happiness.

"Look at her," she sputtered. "She looks like...she looks so smug! Hey, Bertha, c'mon. Lighten up! Other dogs have done it right, too!"

Josh turned and watched Eleanor as she sat on the foot of his bed, doubled over with the attempt to stifle her laughter. He tried to look stern, but the edges of a smile were there. "This is no time to be laughing," he admonished her. She gestured back toward Bertha and he turned quickly. "Whoops, here comes another one."

"It's two," Eleanor pointed out, controlling her mirth. Bertha licked over a larger surface, magnificently impartial as to which puppy she tended. The first one was squirming and burrowing its way to her belly. "Aren't they cute, but so strange! Like little rats."

Josh sat beside her on the bed. "The finest blend of shepherd and setter," he said firmly, regarding his dog with a fond gaze. "Bertha's going to be a great mother. My God, is this another puppy?"

The puppies came sporadically for the rest of the afternoon. Josh spared a moment from the scene of parturition to root out a bottle of champagne and a battered ice bucket from his pantry. Eleanor foraged in his kitchen, coming up with cheese and crackers and a couple of ripe pears. They picnicked on the bed, offering bits of cheese to Bertha and finding a wide range of conversational topics that always seemed to come back to Bertha's amazing productivity.

"My brother's English setter once had twelve puppies," Eleanor told him as they watched the goings on in the closet in fascination. "Luckily he belonged to a marching band, and most of the members wanted one. What are you going to do with them all?"

"Maybe this is the last one." Josh looked hopefully at the seventh puppy. Bertha had lost her look of satisfaction and began to assume a harried expression. A row of little bodies, their fur already beginning to fluff up a bit, wriggled at her side, nursing ecstatically.

Eleanor swirled the bottle of champagne in its ice bucket. "This is cold. D'you have glasses?"

The eighth puppy arrived during their first toast, offered grandiloquently by Eleanor. "To the furtherance of life on earth, no matter where it occurs!"

The second toast, "To moderation in litter size for all dogs," was proposed by Josh.

Eleanor countered, shooting him a meaningful look, with, "Here's to a visit to the veterinary clinic for Bertha, and a life of carefree enjoyment for Irish setters ever after!"

Josh didn't seem to hear as he filled her glass from the half-empty bottle. Turning toward her as they sat on the foot of the bed, he gave her a look of searching, tentative exploration. Eleanor met his gaze squarely, her defenses down. The awareness of him that had plagued her since her first moment in his house blossomed into something powerful and compelling. With a suddenness that took her breath away, she realized that it would be very easy to get involved with this man. Far too easy.

"Here's to having the unexpected happen," he said softly, seriously, lifting his glass toward her. She was caught in the mesh of his gray-blue eyes. They were almost like tweed, she thought dreamily, and the expression in them sent a sensation through her that she felt she'd been subconsciously waiting for, wanting, during her entire twenty-nine years.

His face was so close, and she realized that she swayed toward him as he moved to take her glass and set it carefully on the floor with his. He placed one arm behind her on the bed, and then she was leaning against him, her body flowing toward his in an involuntary reaction to the summons in his eyes. Part of her thought, *This is crazy, this is madness....* But something deep and primitive that she had never acknowledged was answering his unspoken question by raising her lips to meet his.

The first kiss was tentative, tremulous, but intensely

affecting to Eleanor. The softness of his lips took her by
surprise, and their gentle pressure seemed too slight to
account for the explosive gyrations of her heart. Their
lips parted, and she stared bewilderedly into his eyes
and was captured by the flame that smoldered there.

The second kiss was a plunge into deep, passionate
waters. His lips lost their softness and moved aggres-
sively on hers, challenging her in a wild, sensuous duel.
His tongue found hers and twined with it roughly, ex-
citingly. She slid her wet lips against his and moaned
when his hands moved along her shoulders, around her
back, pausing under the heavy weight of her breasts.
She felt silky warmth on her fingers and realized that
they were buried in his hair, holding his mouth to hers
with all the strength she could muster.

The heat and passion of her own response stunned her
and took her by surprise. Conscious thought was super-
ceded; she knew only that what was happening felt
good, felt right. Under the soft velour of the robe she
wore, her body cried out for the inflammatory touch of
his hands. When he parted the robe over her breasts, she
regretted that she'd left on her camisole. Fabric was an
impediment she could have done without.

Josh's hand moved blindly over the fine white cotton,
seeking a way underneath. Moaning with the fever of
her desire, she arched into his hand, heedless of the bar-
riers still between them. He found her nipple and fingered it gently erect, then moved to the other one. The
sensation was electric; Ellie moved restlessly beneath
him. It wasn't enough. . .even when his mouth replaced
his hand, sucking and nipping gently through the thin
cloth, she still shifted impatiently.

His hands moved under the robe, discovering the
smooth flesh between her camisole and silky bikini
underwear. He trailed his fingers along the edge of the
panties, then over them, sliding down between her

thighs. His touch was a mere brush of fingers, lighter than a breeze, but its effect on Ellie was devastating. She gripped his shoulders mindlessly, her whole being centered on the unbelievable flood of sensation he loosed in her. The waves of stinging heat were taking her higher, higher...she wanted, she needed....

He tore his mouth away from her breast. He rolled over, leaving them both stranded, gasping, on the faintly abrasive surface of the Navaho spread.

Eleanor's lips ached for Josh's touch. She wanted to draw his head back to hers, to let her hands roam across his body with leisurely, amorous intent. The very wantonness of her desire suddenly shocked her into sitting up abruptly. Josh's bathrobe fell open, and the air was cool on the damp fabric, causing her nipples to swell even more and her breasts to harden with excitement. His eyes dropped to her breasts and came back hot and hungry. She pushed her hair behind her ears and tried hazily to collect her thoughts. Too sudden.... She let her lashes veil her eyes until he turned away and she could watch him unregarded.

He was sprawled on the coverlet, his face curiously blank. Now that the heat was dying a bit within her, Eleanor could hardly believe that she had acted so recklessly on such short acquaintance. She felt the sickening lurch of stomach that comes after doing something irrevocable and foolish. She had never given in to impulse so strongly with any other man—not even with Garrison during the brief years of their marriage. But Josh wouldn't know that. She lashed her already smarting self-esteem by imagining his thoughts. "Cheap celebrity-hunting bimbo," was the most charitable thing she could come up with.

She jumped to her feet, trying to tuck the bathrobe more decorously around her. She flung up her head and dared Josh's stare. "That shouldn't have happened," she said flatly.

His eyes had not, as she had feared, turned contemptuous, but his expression was unreadable. "Why not?" he asked equably. "Are you celibate?"

Exasperation was preferable to the embarrassment she'd been feeling. Gratefully she let it flow through her. "Not at all," she replied coolly, although it was the next thing to true. "I'm also not...impulsive." To forestall the retort she saw on his lips, she added hastily, "And I don't believe you are, either."

He digested that for a moment, frowning. "All right," he said finally. "Neither of us is impulsive. Where does that leave us?"

The sound of a chain saw ripped through the air. Eleanor moved over to the window, which overlooked the driveway, and peered out. The sun was westering, and she wondered hazily how long they'd lain on the bed, kissing with the hot impatient fervor of teenagers. The thought sent a rush of fire to her cheeks. "They're cutting away the tree," she said, not looking at him. "Hope my clothes are dry."

She hadn't heard him move, but his warm breath on her neck was a warning before his voice sounded almost in her ear. "Stay all night." The words were abrupt, almost harsh, but underlying them was strong emotion. She turned slowly and studied him. He met her scrutiny full on.

"You're already sorry you said that," she whispered at last. He look startled, then rueful.

"The first thing you've got to learn," he said, taking her shoulders in a hard grasp, "is that you never tell me what I'm thinking." He pulled her closer and she went pliantly into his arms, unable to resist the lure of that fire-lipped, sensuous mouth as it covered hers. "The second thing," he murmured, his lips moving against hers in a way that sent flames licking through her, "is that you never say no." For a moment she was lost as their mouths fused together, coaxing from her a flood of response that left her weak. But only for a moment.

She regarded him gravely as he ended the kiss. "No," she said with reluctance.

He stiffened. "What did you say?" There was no outrage, no demand in his voice, only a half-felt plea that was as hard to resist as a baby's cry.

"I said no. I'm not going to stay the night. I'm not even going to stay the evening. I'm going to put on my clammy clothes and walk out the door and drive away before I get caught in another storm." They both knew she wasn't talking about the rain.

He let his arms drop. For a long moment they gazed at each other. The chain saw whined again, and he drew her impatiently away from the window. "If that's the way you want it," he said slowly. She watched as he glanced into the closet. Bertha had evidently finished having puppies. She lay with half-slitted, slumberous eyes while her new offspring clambered around her.

Then Josh was examining Ellie in a slow, devouring way. "If that's what you want," he said again, this time with a lazy smile curving his lips, "then I'm sorry for you. Because you're already caught, lady. This particular storm is not going to be over until it thunders." He touched her tousled brown hair and let his hand trail down her cheek. "And the rain comes down."

She stood immobile as his hand moved around the curve of her neck. His voice thickened. The fire in his gaze made her helpless to turn away from it. "And when the rainbow comes...ah, lady," he murmured, his fingers gliding down the globe of her breast and going around her waist to gather her close, "then we'll both be glad we stuck around." He pressed one more kiss on her unresisting lips, sweet and tender, before letting go and turning briskly away. "So let's see if your clothes are dry, Ms Martinson. And then you can convey my wishes in the matter of publicity to Peter."

Eleanor watched as he strode from the bedroom. "Yes," she said faintly. "Of course. Whatever you say, Mr. Blackmun." She passed her fingers over her swollen lips. Maybe on the long drive down Highway 1 she could figure out just what had happened. Shaking her head, she moved toward the door. It certainly had been a client interview to remember. She pushed aside the unwelcome thought that it had been more than that, and went to put on her clothes.

2

THE WHITE SAND SPARKLED beneath Eleanor's flying feet in the early-morning light. High above, like scraps of paper flung to the wind, sea gulls wheeled and tossed their restless wings. The storm-scoured sky was bright blue, decorated with fat, harmless white puffs of clouds.

Eleanor drew the cold salty breeze deep into her lungs, taking an abstract pleasure in the pounding rhythm of her legs, the easy way her body moved over the hard-packed sand. She sidestepped piles of sea wrack with the absentminded grace of long practice. When she neared the pier she began the long plod up through dry sand to the pedestrian path that edged the beach. Her early-morning run followed the same course every day: through the sleeping town of Santa Cruz, down to the beach, along the edge of the water for a couple of miles, and then back up by a different route along the hilly streets to breakfast and a shower.

Usually the exertion acted as a form of meditation, emptying her mind of all but the sensation of running, freeing her from conscious thought until she emerged, glowing with health and vitality, ready to start out for work. Today, however, her feet and the rhythm of her breath seemed to spell out a name over and over: Josh-ua Black-mun, Josh-ua Black-mun. She slowed to a walk at the bottom of the hill leading to her home, but even then her pounding heart echoed the name. In an effort to distract herself from it, she looked around appreciatively, allowing herself to see her surroundings with newly aware eyes.

The road curved steeply up one of the hills that ringed the town. It was lined with redwood and oaks, and the graceful, now-bare branches of flowering plums. The houses that perched precariously along the road were older, a mixture of Spanish stucco and tiled roofs cheek by jowl with rambling, shake-sided ranch homes.

Her house was at the top of the hill, where the road dead-ended in a turnaround. It was one of the ranch houses, an old one, its haphazard outlines and mossy shingles giving it an organic, "grown from the ground up" look. Her apartment was over the garage, which was attached to the hillside only by a bulging, over-grown retaining wall.

She was on her way up the steep outer stairs that led to her place when a door opened in the main part of the house. Her mother's sleep-tousled head poked out.

"We didn't know if you got home safely last night," she began, her brown eyes blinking owlishly. "That was some storm."

Eleanor paused on the stairs and used her sweat shirt to blot some of the moisture from her forehead. "It certainly was," she agreed, glad for some reason that her face was hidden. Although her mother never pried, she was an acute observer, and Eleanor didn't want to encounter that probing stare. "A tree came down over the road and kept me from getting home when I'd planned."

Her mother's eyes widened, but she refrained from comment. "Dad wanted me to remind you that it's Group tonight. Do you want to come to dinner?"

Eleanor assented after a hasty mental review of her own refrigerator's barrenness. Her mother's head vanished with a farewell remark, and Eleanor finished mounting the stairs to her apartment.

The rooms over the garage had originally been added

as rental accommodations for students from the nearby University of California. They were vacant when Eleanor had returned from Los Angeles five years ago after a disastrous marriage. At that time the little apartment had offered the security of home that she craved; she had never intended to stay in it for as long as she had. But her parents, though loving and supportive of all their children, had made no attempt to pull her back into the role of dependent daughter. Their own busy lives as teachers at the university and their firm belief that everyone was entitled to privacy had made the arrangement so relaxed that Eleanor had never gotten around to finding another place to live.

With an unaccustomed feeling of detachment, she let her eyes sweep around the living room. Though her furniture was the cast-off variety often found in low-rent housing, fresh-flower-spattered upholstery and bright graphics on the cool, cream-colored walls gave an elegant but inviting impression. She had built the low bookcases herself, and had paid to have the small but functional fireplace installed. The only out-of-place note was her ruined shoes, lying on the bright green carpet where she had toed them off last night. She picked them up and went on into the bedroom.

The room was small, not much bigger than the low platform bed that had been her second carpentry project. Wide casements opened onto a view of the town, with the ocean sparkling beyond. She had hung soft white rice-paper shades at the window to avoid obscuring that view, and the rest of the room, with the severe lines of the bed and the functional white stacks of drawers, had a faint Asian flavor.

Eleanor tossed the shoes in the closet on her way to the tiny bathroom. An invigorating shower washed away the initial fatigue of her morning's exercise, imbuing her with a sense of vitality that was reflected in her brisk but graceful movements. She dressed quickly in a soft wool frock with wide dolman sleeves and a bold slash of coral accenting the asymmetric closure.

Backing her little car out of the garage, she noticed with distaste the mud splashes on the fenders, left by her encounter with Josh's rutted driveway. That meant five dollars to her youngest brother Robbie, who was always hard up for money but not as thorough at cleaning cars as he was at collecting payment.

Eleanor was the third of her parents' progeny. Alice, her thirty-six-year-old sister, lived near San Francisco with her engineer husband and two children, and taught mathematics at a junior college. Thirty-three-year-old Ken was in Arizona, teaching computer science at the university in Phoenix. But Eleanor had never succumbed to the lure of the academic community that embraced her parents and her older siblings. She'd left college after receiving a bachelor of arts degree and moved out to try her wings in Los Angeles, where an enthusiastic young woman with a more or less useless background in literature stood a better chance of finding work.

Dodging down a side street to avoid a mini traffic snarl, she frowned as the thought of Los Angeles intruded in her reverie. She was finished with all that. Her life now was more satisfactory than she'd ever thought possible: work she enjoyed at the Randolph Public Relations agency; good times with her friends.

Nevertheless she couldn't help contrasting the drive through Santa Cruz's sun-drenched, cheerful streets with commuting through the soulless, traffic-filled boulevards of Los Angeles. There was a lot to be said for surroundings that were conducive to keeping down the stress quotient of daily life. She didn't blame Joshua Blackmun for not wanting to have his peaceful existence shattered by the full focus of media scrutiny.

The Randolph agency was located in an old Victorian cottage near the Pacific Garden Mall. Eleanor admired the neat pots of calendulas that flanked the front door as she parked her car in the driveway and walked briskly up the path. Gena Randolph came out of her office when Eleanor entered, interrupting her greeting to Marigold Parker, who sat at the reception desk in what had been the cottage's living room.

"Well?" The brightness of Gena's voice didn't quite conceal a note of anxiety. "How did it go with the great star?"

Eleanor directed a searching look at her boss. Gena was a petite, immaculate blonde, older than Eleanor by six or seven years and generally inclined to be casual and lighthearted about the business she had run since her husband's death.

Gena wasn't usually so wound up about client interviews, trusting Eleanor's ability to smooth all the tangles and keep things moving. In fact, lately Eleanor had begun to feel a little resentful at the way Gena assumed she would take on all the functions of a partner, including a lot of paperwork, without receiving either the title or the pay.

She tried to steer her boss discreetly into her own office, a former back bedroom. Gena wasn't going to like what she had to say. But Marigold crowded into the small room with them, her dark, intense eyes sparkling with lively interest. She exclaimed in her most dramatic tones, "Please, you have to let me hear. I've had a crush on Joshua Blackmun since 'Let the Lady Decide' came out." She heaved an immense sigh, tossing back the bright apricot curls that framed her face. "That song was the story of my life that summer," she explained solemnly.

Eleanor shrugged and sat in her old wooden desk chair. The casters shrieked as she pushed it back and propped her feet on her desk, ankles crossed casually. Gena, with a disapproving look at Eleanor's long, shapely legs, perched in the comfortably shabby client's chair before the battered golden oak desk. Marigold remained standing in the doorway, where she could keep an eye on the phone.

"It's no epic grist for your mill," Eleanor warned Marigold. The receptionist wrote romances, and was waiting with baited breath for response from a major publisher on her current effort. "Joshua Blackmun is warped from all that seclusion." She glanced at Gena. "He is very much opposed to any form of publicity or promotion. I don't know if he'll even agree to a benefit performance, let alone a tour or the interviews Peter wants."

Gena shifted restlessly in her chair. "He's got to agree," she said, the strained note prominent in her voice. She glanced meaningfully at Marigold, and the receptionist slowly withdrew, closing the door after her with obvious reluctance. Gena leaned forward in her chair and tapped Eleanor's desk for emphasis. "This account for Trax is very, very important to me, my dear. I don't want to lose it."

Eleanor looked away from Gena's drawn face. "Peter is not just a client, he's also a personal friend. He wouldn't take his account away if we were unsuccessful on one project."

"We can't take that risk," Gena said vehemently. "He sees this album as the breakthrough he's been waiting for. I don't think he'll hesitate to dump us in favor of one of the big PR firms if we mess up."

Eleanor lowered her feet to the floor with a thump. "I'm not messing up," she said indignantly. "I don't know what you want me to do, Gena. If Blackmun doesn't want publicity, I can't force him to do interviews. And neither could any high-powered city firm. It looks to me as if Peter will have to accept Blackmun's feelings on this subject."

Her boss sat back in her chair, a defeated slump to her shoulders. "Well, that's that," she muttered. "It means the end of everything, that's all."

"That sounds more like Marigold than you," Eleanor remarked, trying to mask her alarm with gentle jocularity. "What's the melodrama about?"

"I can't keep my head above water if I lose Peter's account," Gena said starkly. "I've been on shaky ground since Harold died." Harold Randolph had begun the agency; he'd been the one to hire Eleanor when she'd come back to Santa Cruz five years ago. Three years later he was dead, stricken by the wheeler-dealer's nemesis, a heart attack. Gena had assumed control after her husband's death. "He had gambling debts—lots of them," she went on succinctly. "And I admit I've made some expensive mistakes. I was never cut out to be Ms Executive."

Eleanor interjected a soothing denial, but Gena waved it away impatiently. "You don't need to waste your tact on me. I'm not much good at this business and we both know it. I was happy working in that gallery, but I naturally assumed it would be better to take over the agency than to sell pictures for someone else."

She glanced down at her slender, well-manicured hands. "I was wrong. I'm a failure here. I want to sell the agency and buy an art gallery that's available in the mall. But I won't be able to get a good enough price unless this deal with Peter really takes off. Joshua Blackmun's album could put Trax on the map. And then we'd be very valuable to Trax, and the agency would be worth more—a lot more." She stood up and leaned across the desk, her small, usually lively face tense. "I'm counting on you, Ellie. Make a go of it for me. It's my last chance."

Bemused, Eleanor stared after Gena as her slender form swept through the door. Gena had laid it on the line with a vengeance. The implications of the speech were still percolating through her when Marigold threw the door open.

"What's the bee in *her* bonnet?" The receptionist's eyes were bright with suppressed curiosity. Marigold often proclaimed that a writer must know all the secrets of human nature; certainly she never stopped trying to find out all the secrets she encountered.

Unwilling to gossip about the state of the agency and still stunned by Gena's revelations, Eleanor could manage only a mystified shrug. "It's Group tonight," she said, changing the subject. "Are you coming?"

Marigold nodded eagerly. "There's a scene in chapter 5 that just doesn't hang together. I'm hoping the Group will come up with something."

"Oh, boy!" Eleanor rubbed her hands together gleefully. "I'd better get on the phone and call the others. No one will be absent if they know you're reading one of those steamy chapters."

Marigold blushed with pleasure. Eleanor's father, as an adjunct to his job of teaching literature at the university, hosted a writing group every other month in his living room. The Group contained a stimulating mixture of students, former students, members of the community and even a few people who drove long distances to attend.

The members shared an enthusiasm for writing and a delight in constructive criticism of one another's work that rarely produced rancor. The writing ranged from intense, modern poetry to autobiographical reminiscence. Although she rarely contributed anything, Eleanor had grown up with the Group and loved attending the meetings. Every person had a story to tell that he or she was passionately interested in, and that passion made all the stories interesting to Eleanor.

Marigold wandered away to answer the summons of the telephone, and Eleanor was left to chew her pencil in solitude. Gena's revelations had taken her by surprise; she was just beginning to see the implications. If she didn't manage to handle Joshua Blackmun satisfactorily, the Randolph agency was likely to go under, and her job along with it. If she did, the agency would be sold, and the new owner might or might not be someone with whom she could work. Either way, her options seemed limited.

For a moment she wished she had capital, or some kind of business experience, or both. With money, she could have bought the agency herself; with business sense, she might have been able to borrow enough. But like Gena, Eleanor wasn't interested in the business aspects. She was good at the work she did—damn good, she told herself stoutly. But record keeping, wages, bookkeeping—all the minutia of making a business run smoothly—didn't seem stimulating enough to shoulder the burden. She dismissed the idea of somehow buying the agency for herself, and thought instead about ways to succeed in publicizing Josh's album without his active cooperation. Frowning, she pulled the telephone toward her and dialed Trax Records.

Peter Macguire's record company was located in a former lumberyard, and while she waited for someone to answer the phone, Eleanor pictured the benign chaos that always reigned there. Finally a breathless male voice spoke. "Trax Records. Peter speaking."

"Don't you have someone to answer the phone yet?" Eleanor asked teasingly. "It's very unprofessional to answer it yourself. Where's your presidential dignity?"

Peter's deep laugh came rumbling through the receiver. "At least it's no one important on the other end. How are you doing, Ellie? Seen Josh yet?"

"Hasn't he called you?" Eleanor had expected Peter to

be informed of his star's refusal to cooperate with publicity. "Maybe his telephone's still out of order." She plunged into a narrative of her adventure of the day before, discreetly omitting the parts that didn't involve Trax. Peter was a good friend, but she had no intention of letting anyone know how close she came to being swept off her feet like any teenage groupie looking for a fame fix.

When she had finished, Peter was silent for a moment. "I expected something like this," he confessed finally. "Josh mentioned to me that the whole Los Angeles 'star-maker machinery' was repugnant to him, and that's the main reason he agreed to record for me. You'll just have to convince him that we aren't trying to exploit him. Doing a few interviews and a benefit or two isn't going to kill him."

"Try and convince him of that." Eleanor thought of the way Josh had kept her bewildered, off base, before and after the kiss. "I'm not sure I'm the right person to handle him."

"Of course you are, Ellie. I have confidence in your persuasive abilities. I don't care what means you use, so long as you deliver him to the press at suitable intervals."

Peter's voice was careless, and Eleanor was surprised to find herself shocked. "Peter, the guy has really suffered. I don't know if it's wise to reopen that whole can of worms."

There was another pause. Peter spoke, a new note in his voice. "What's this? Did you fall for the well-known Blackmun macho allure? Ellie, don't tell me—"

"Don't be absurd," she said hurriedly. "We hardly exchanged a civil word once he found out who I was. I was just thinking that the last time he got fed up with the music business, there was a very traumatic incident. I wouldn't want you to precipitate something like that again."

Peter laughed. "Not much chance. Josh has his act together now. The worst he'll do is storm down here, curse me up one side and down the other for being a callous bastard, and take his record away." His voice changed. "I don't really want that to happen, Ellie. I'm counting on you."

Eleanor hung up the telephone with a bleak expression. Now there were two people throwing the whole sticky mess into her lap and blithely assuring her that she could handle it. The sense of well-being she'd started the day with began to fade. Muttering to herself, she pulled her card file of media people toward her and began to telephone.

She worked steadily through the day, phoning contacts, setting up meetings, beginning the paper trail that would, hopefully, culminate in articles and press reports that would whip up interest in the forthcoming album. Still turning over the merits of various plans in her mind, she left the office at five-thirty and drove through the streets with absentminded competence.

It wasn't until she'd reached her apartment and confronted her near-empty refrigerator that she remembered her mother's invitation to dinner. She changed into faded blue jeans and a bright red sweat shirt and twisted her hair into a careless knot. On an impulse, as she passed through the living room she pulled Joshua Blackmun's latest album from the long row of alphabetically filed records on the shelf beneath her stereo system.

The front cover was an undersea fantasy in rich, stylized colors showing strange fish and mollusks frolicking with a narwhal, that misunderstood marine mammal whose single pearly, luminescent tusk, when found by superstitious medieval mariners, gave rise to the legend of the unicorn. The album was titled *Narwhal*, and the first track, as Eleanor remembered, was a rhythmic,

strangely moving combination of rock guitar and sea
chantey. The lyrics were tight, compressed, but con-
veyed the sense that the singer felt himself, like a narwhal, to be transformed by some sinister influence into
the semblance of a myth for a credulous public to gape
at.

Instead of playing the record, Eleanor turned it gently
in her hands. There was a picture of Josh on the back
cover. She knew instinctively that he didn't like pictures
of himself on his albums. The photographer had captured the look of lean, energy-focused authority that
was the essence of Joshua Blackmun, the performer.

Although she attended many concerts and club dates
in the course of her work with musician clients, the
memory of the one concert of Josh's she had been to was
fresh in her mind, as was the unsettling effect it had had
on her.

He had come striding onto the stage, his big Fender
Stratocaster clutched confidently in one long-fingered
hand, and followed by the backup band, who played an
eclectic mixture of instruments including saxophones,
fiddles, mandolins and rhythm bass. Settling the guitar
strap around his neck in one quick, automatic gesture,
Josh had stared challengingly at the crowd.

"Hello," he'd said in that gravelly voice that could
soar so unexpectedly in a ballad. "The band and I would
like to give you a little invitation." Then he'd roared
into "Sweet Home Chicago," sending the audience a
surge of electric energy that he hadn't let falter all evening, even when he'd discarded the electric guitar for an
acoustic one and played, alone, a series of earthy,
pleading blues songs. Though she'd seen many first-
class musicians perform, Eleanor had never responded
so basically as she did to Josh's music.

As she stared at his picture on the back of the album,
she conjured up the man himself so that the two images

merged, fusing into Josh, a real person, not a well-known musician, who disturbed her thoughts more than was good for her.

She crammed the album back onto the shelf and jumped to her feet. There was no reason to dwell on that interlude upon the Navaho bedspread. In the future, she must tell herself that their brief contact was for working purposes only. From bitter experience, she knew that as lovers, musicians were poison.

She opened her front door to go down to her mother's kitchen. On the little landing she called her porch, leaning with negligent grace against the railing, was Josh.

She felt her face go blank as she stared at him, a thousand sensations flooding her. Unseeingly she took in the details of his appearance—his lean, rangy body in snug-fitting, faded jeans and work shirt. The smile barely curving his mouth. The mouth itself, with a thin upper lip and full, sensuous lower lip that spoke of interesting conflicts. His eyes, lazy, tweed gray, their expression both knowing and—was it possible?—uncertain. Those big, long-fingered hands she'd noticed from the audience, presenting her with a waxed paper wrapped bundle of roses, stems still wet from the florist's bucket. "For you," he said, the smile deepening. "Hope you got home okay."

"Yes," Eleanor said, her social responses coming automatically to the fore. "Thank you." She gazed helplessly at the roses he thrust into her arms. It was irrational, but she was afraid to invite him inside. Not afraid of him—afraid of her own too-powerful response to him.

"I...I was on my way out," she began, then stopped in dismay, realizing too late that the words sounded rude. "I mean—"

"Going out to dinner," he suggested equably, his eyes traveling with mischievous intent past her sweat shirt and jeans, returning to linger on the casual wisps of

brown hair that escaped her topknot. She disdained to
attempt tucking them back in, preferring to pretend
regally that disarray did not exist, but his scrutiny did
nothing to suppress the memories of that feverish embrace they had shared the day before. While she hesitated on the porch, the kitchen door downstairs opened
and her mother came out.

"Ellie, do you have any—" Blanché Martinson became aware of Josh's tall frame at Eleanor's door and
stopped short. She smiled tentatively, not used, as
Eleanor knew, to the sight of a strange man on her
daughter's doorstep. Still in the grip of her automatic
social responses, Eleanor introduced them.

"This is Joshua Blackmun, mother. My mother,
Blanche Martinson. Did you need something?"

With a courtesy Eleanor wouldn't have credited to
him, Josh ran lightly down the steps to greet her mother.
"Pleased to meet you," he said politely, no trace of his
inevitable thoughts about Eleanor living with her
parents appearing on his face. "I just stopped by on my
way back from the studio to see that Eleanor came to no
grief yesterday. That was some storm."

His eyes sought Eleanor's for one brief instant that
brought back all the heat of the previous afternoon. She
felt her cheeks go instantly scarlet, and lowered her
head to the roses to camouflage her reaction.

Eleanor's mother murmured a greeting to Josh, and
then turned to her daughter. "I wondered if you had any
Parmesan, Ellie. I seem to be out."

"Sure," Eleanor mumbled. "I'll go get it." She glanced
hesitantly at Josh, but he had already begun an amiable
conversation with her mother. At least, she thought,
racing into her kitchen and shoving the roses into the
sink, she didn't have to worry about inviting him in.
She snatched the wedge of cheese from her refrigerator
and hurried back out with it.

When she reached the bottom of the stairs, her worst fears were realized. Her mother looked up brightly and announced, "Josh can stay for dinner, Ellie. Isn't that providential? I thought he might enjoy attending your father's Group, since he's a writer, too."

"Wonderful," Eleanor agreed hollowly. How could she explain to her mother that it was torture to be next to Joshua Blackmun without letting go and melting all over the floor? How could she bear to spend the evening in the same room with him when all she could think of was taking that craggy face between her palms and kissing him until they were both gasping for air?

She brushed by the two of them and bustled into her mother's kitchen with the cheese, hoping against hope that he wouldn't touch her, lest she blow her usual calm manner in favor of incoherent gabbling.

Dinner went better than she could have expected it to. Her younger brother Robbie, who played bass in a country-western band just beginning to achieve local recognition, was enthralled to meet Joshua Blackmun. He would have monopolized the whole conversation if her father hadn't begun a discussion of the ways in which writing lyrics for music differed from traditional poetry. Joshua was surprisingly well-read on this topic, entrancing her father with several pertinent comments about John Donne's songs.

Eleanor ate without speaking much. She was in a strange state of mind that accepted unquestioningly the easy way Josh fitted into her family's dinner table and his relaxed demeanor with her parents. Though he was seated next to her, he made no effort to impose his physical nearness on her. She was content to let the moment carry her where it would.

She was excused from helping with the dishes on the grounds that she had a guest. "Perhaps you could check that there are enough chairs in the living room," her mother said with a preoccupied air. "Robbie, did you wash out that coffee urn?"

Eleanor ushered Josh into the living room, a low-ceilinged, gracious place with lots of comfortable shabby furniture and a graceful, marble-manteled fireplace. The lamps had not yet been lit, and the room was full of dusky shadows. She bent wordlessly to touch a match to the logs.

When she straightened, Josh was standing close. In the dancing firelight his eyes were dark and amused. "Might as well let it all down," he murmured, reaching for the clip that held her increasingly untidy topknot. Her hair came tumbling down over her shoulders with a silken whisper, framing her wide-eyed, solemn face.

His expression changed. "You've been occupying my thoughts," he whispered, seizing her with a rough desperation that woke an answering urgency in her. "I don't know if I like that or not. I just know...." He fused their mouths together for a scorching moment. His mouth was hot and demanding, plunging her into the dark turbulence of desire. His hand moved down her back, trembling, leaving a trail of fire. "I just know what I want," he groaned against her lips. "And I want you." He pulled her into him, and she felt the hardness of his need for her. For an eternal moment her body melted.

Then a footstep sounded outside the living-room archway. When her father entered the room they were feet apart, Joshua poking the fire, Eleanor making a pretense of straightening the sofa cushions. They hadn't spoken, but the air was charged with the tension of their passion.

Ira Martinson didn't seem to notice. He rubbed his hands together genially. "This will be an interesting meeting," he said to the room at large.

Eleanor groped wildly for something, anything, to

say. "Marigold is coming." She grinned at her father. "Something amiss in chapter 5."

"Good, good." Ira looked around for his notebook and found it on a side table. "That should liven things up."

People began straggling in, the students and younger members making straight for the kitchen where Blanche Martinson had assembled a tray of goodies, the older members getting comfortable and chatting casually. Josh, Ellie noticed as she hovered about being helpful, had found himself an inconspicuous seat and was watching everything with the wary, curious gaze of the perennial observer.

She felt a moment's fierce protectiveness as she looked around the room. Although the Group had its share of successful writers, many of them would never do more with their writing than express their feelings in a private journal. Others were still struggling with the mechanics of their chosen craft. They were vulnerable to the wrong sort of criticism. If Joshua Blackmun was the kind of man who took pleasure in pulling down others' dreams, she would find out from his reactions tonight.

But he didn't put a foot wrong all evening. With attentive courtesy he listened to each reader, even occasionally contributing a helpful suggestion. Marigold's chapter proved to be an icebreaker. In thinking up ways for her heroine to tell the hero about his love child, even the new members of the Group lost their shyness.

Marigold herself was overcome to receive a plaudit from Josh—her excited recognition of him had been whispered around the room, but the Group was too professional to disintegrate into a panting mob, and Josh was left in peace. It wasn't until all the regular members had read that Ira polished his glasses and directed an inquiry to his surprise celebrity guest.

"You've been making some good suggestions for everyone else, Joshua," he began in his rumbling, professional voice. "Maybe there's something we could help you with. Are you struggling with a lyric? Stuck for a metaphor? Everyone here would be pleased to think they had a hand in one of your excellent songs."

Eleanor looked at her father suspiciously. She could have sworn that prior to this evening he'd never heard one of Joshua Blackmun's "excellent" songs. Josh was clearly taken aback.

"Well," he said slowly, "as a matter of fact, I have been kicking some words around in my head for a while. I can't put my finger on what's wrong, but it doesn't all hang together." He pulled a small notebook out of his shirt pocket. With a challenging look at Ellie he read:

> "You look like sweet sincerity,
> You got the 'come here' in your eyes.
> But though your body tells me truth,
> Your words are telling me lies.
> Come here, woman.
> You don't seem to understand.
> Come here, woman.
> I want to be your man."

There was a silence, and Ellie's father nodded his head slowly. "I see what you mean," he said quietly. "It seems to lack focus. A little nebulous, maybe."

Ellie was still analyzing the significance of his scrap of song. She found that she didn't much like the sassy, demanding chorus and the implication that the woman was lying to him. Was the woman supposed to be her? Was she lying as a woman? As a publicist? Without thinking, she blurted out, "You make it sound as if the woman has no choice in the matter. It's so...caveman...or something."

Josh's expression was enigmatic. "Caveman," he said. "Maybe that's what I need." He made a few notes and smiled at Eleanor. "Good suggestion, Ellie."

His smile was disturbing, mocking and sensual, making it clear to her that she was the subject of the song. Eleanor caught a few knowing glances from members of the group and bit her tongue. She wanted to object to his high-handed method of wooing. But part of her was flattered that he had transformed their elemental stand-off into words and music. She didn't want it to go further, though. Words and music could be powerful weapons for a man to use against a woman.

When the rest of the Group straggled off she bade him a cool good-night, her body warring with her mind's decision to back away from the challenge he presented. He took her farewell with a sharp gleam of laughter in his disconcerting gray eyes and disappeared into the night.

As she helped her mother load the dishwasher, Ellie began to regret the lost opportunity to know Josh better. Rinsing coffee cups, she carried on an argument in her mind. *So what if he's writing a song with lyrics about you? He's interested in you, and you're interested in him. You were a fool to let him walk out of here.*

Her mother unconsciously echoed her thoughts. "That Joshua Blackmun is very charming, isn't he?" She sent the crumbs on the cookie platter down the disposal. "For someone who has been in public life, he's quite natural and unspoiled."

"Mom!" Robbie's voice was shocked. "You make him sound like a cheese or something." Robbie had been exhilarated by his contact with the big-time singer. The country-western band he played with was just one stop on the road to fame and fortune, as far as he was concerned. Meeting Josh had made that goal seem more achievable.

"A big cheese, no doubt," Eleanor muttered. Her family's approval was somehow irritating, as if it pointed out her stupidity in being so unfriendly to Josh.

She said good-night and plodded wearily up the steps, her body drooping tiredly. It had been a long and tortuous day, and she was ready for it to be over.

But Joshua was not. He was sitting on the top step, waiting for her. "Hello," he said as she stared at him in numb amazement. "I thought we might talk."

3

WORDLESSLY, ELEANOR PASSED HIM on the tiny porch, conscious as she went by of the warmth of his body, the male scent that filled her nostrils for one heady moment. She thrust open her door and stood aside, inviting him to enter with a grave inclination of her head. Her mouth wanted to curve in a grin, but she already wondered, *What happens next?*

Joshua stood for a second just inside the door, giving the cheerful, quiet room a sweeping scrutiny. His eyes ended at Eleanor as she closed the door, and a broad smile crept onto his lips. "You look nice in here," he said. "It's a nice room."

So do you, she thought, but didn't say the words. She had the feeling that she didn't need to, that he knew what she was thinking. Their eyes held for a moment, and she felt it quicken and heat her blood in a sudden leap of desire. Hoping, fearing, that he would kiss her, she moved away. "I'll get us something to drink."

At the kitchen door she paused and turned. "Why don't you—" he had been right behind her, and she nearly bumped into him "—put on a record." She didn't want him in the kitchen with her. She needed to catch her breath. Without trying, without even touching her, he overwhelmed her.

Obediently Josh headed for the stereo and she made her escape. The kitchen was full of the scent of roses— Josh's flowers lay in the sink, the scarlet buds beginning to open. Eleanor spent a few abstracted moments stuff-

ing them into the largest container she could find, an old
silver pitcher of her mother's, battered but still graceful.

She put water on to boil and hurriedly rinsed a teapot, moving with furtive swiftness. Somehow it had
become important to finish the series of homey little
tasks before Josh was free to come looking for her.
Cups, honey, milk and a fragrant herb tea were assembled on a tray in record time. She sighed impatiently as
she waited for the water to boil.

A draft from the ill-fitting window over the sink
brought the scent of roses to her again, and she studied
them as if they could give her a clue to Josh's behavior.
She moved over to the pitcher and rearranged a couple
of buds, her fingers lingering on the silky petals. Im-
pulsively she lowered her face to the flowers, inhaling
their voluptuous perfume. When she straightened, Josh
was standing in the kitchen doorway, watching her.

She summoned her poise with an effort. "Thank you
for the flowers," she said, pleased that she could main-
tain her self-possession. "I was just telling them hello."

"Do you greet everyone like that?" His gravelly voice
was bantering, but there was a caress in it that brought
back the clutch of desire in her. "Because if so, I think I
missed out."

"Only plant life," she assured him breezily, thankful
that the teakettle chose that moment to sing. "I'm much
more selective with mammals." She poured water into
the pot and carried the tray into the living room. Josh
had chosen an album of David Grissman's mandolin,
and the crisp, staccato phrases glittered in the empty
room.

He turned the stereo down a little as she put her tray
on a low table before the couch. He sat in one corner of
the couch, not crowding her, his legs stretched comfortably in front of him. She poured tea into the cups
and handed him one. "I'm sorry. I didn't ask what you'd

want to drink. Perhaps you would rather have had coffee, or a beer or something."

He accepted the cup politely. "Not at all. I don't drink before driving anymore. And I rarely drink coffee."

"I see." The veiled reference to his accident three years ago intrigued her. But she stifled it, not wishing to pry. Instead she said, "You like the mandolin?"

He set his cup down and relaxed further into the couch, his eyes never leaving her face. "I'm learning to play it. Grissman's a lot better than me—so far, anyway. But I'm getting there. It's an instrument with a lot of subtlety." He waved one hand toward the stereo. "You've certainly got a broad range of albums there." Again came the smile that transformed his face. "Everything from *A* to *Z*—the Amazing Rhythm Aces to Frank Zappa."

Eleanor shrugged. "I enjoy music recreationally, though I couldn't even play a kazoo. Several of the agency's accounts are with Peter's recording artists, so I get to spend a lot of evenings in the local clubs listening to music and pretending it's business."

They spoke of performers they had seen, comparing notes and getting involved in a heated discussion over the long-term importance of salsa as opposed to reggae. Despite his self-imposed seclusion, Josh had evidently kept up on the local music scene and been in touch with former colleagues. People that were just names to Eleanor were friends of Josh's—some of them good friends.

"I realized a couple of things after the accident," he remarked, when she asked him about it. "One was that real friends are worth keeping. Some people fell away from me when I stopped pursuing fame." His mouth hardened briefly, and at once Eleanor wondered if he still loved Vivienne Santos, despite her well-publicized defection. She felt a pang of some strong, primitive emotion, and realized with surprise it was jealousy.

Josh's love life was none of her business. *Not yet, anyway.*

His eyes were fixed on the van Gogh reproduction that hung over her bookcase; his voice was matter-of-fact. "I got bitter and surly after the accident. I guess you know about my smashup?" He glanced at her and she nodded. "I made myself kind of unpleasant with everyone for a while. But there were some good people who refused to let me toss away their friendship. That's come to mean a lot to me."

The record ended, charging their momentary silence with significance. Ellie knew Josh watched her as she added more tea to her cup. She felt nervous, unsure. There had been many dates and many male friends since her divorce, but she'd purposely kept the level of intensity low. It had been years since she'd experienced this sort of heightening of her emotions. To break the spell, she spoke at random. "Was Peter one of those friends?"

Josh stirred on the couch. "Hardly. He's an old army buddy I hadn't seen in years. We ran across each other at the Keystone in Palo Alto several months ago and got to talking. I liked his attitude toward recording and his list of artists, so I let myself be talked into making an album with him."

He looked back at the van Gogh and appeared to be memorizing the artist's rendition of a sidewalk café at night. "I didn't mean to say anything about our...talk yesterday. But since we're on the subject, I was at Trax this afternoon throwing a fit of artistic temperament." His smile was tight. "Peter didn't buy it. I thought at first that you were the one who'd sold him on cashing in on me, but I owe you an apology. He told me quite frankly that he's behind all the hype."

Eleanor's conciliatory instincts came to the fore. "Now, Josh," she said, her voice automatically assuming the soothing tone she'd found worked well with wounded performers. "Peter doesn't mean to be callous. He's—"

Josh interrupted her with a savage laugh. "He's decided to go after the big time, and he thinks I'm the one who can get him there. If I'd understood that, I might not have signed a contract with him. But I did, and I don't want the hassle of fighting it. The situation could be worse. At least I have total artistic control, and besides, Peter's a good producer."

He paused, then spoke again, unwillingly. "And you were right yesterday when you said I needed to get back in front of an audience. I have sneaked in a couple of performances in the past six months, but they've just whetted my appetite. I never want to play those stadium gigs again, but—" he smiled wryly "—the smaller nightclubs are a different story. I've been writing my brains out for the past year and a half, and I was never meant to create in a void. If I don't let some of it out, I'll overload."

Ellie nodded understandingly but didn't speak. Again the silence stretched between them. "I've been doing all the talking," Josh said. "It's your turn now." He waited, and when she didn't respond, he moved impatiently. "For instance," he prompted, "what makes you live with your parents?"

Eleanor blinked, startled by the direct question. "I mean, you're a big girl now," he added. "Aren't you?"

He seemed to be enjoying her discomfort. That prodded her into replying. "It's convenient," she said evasively.

His eyebrows rose as he digested this. "Hard on your boyfriends, though, isn't it?" His voice grated on her ears. "Having to creep downstairs in the middle of the night. Or maybe they just stay all night—"

"Stop it!" Eleanor held his gaze for a moment, struggling to control her irritation. "Why don't you just ask

me what you want to know," she said levelly. "There's
no need to be childish."

He took a deep breath and pushed the straight, untidy
locks of dark hair off his forehead. "I didn't mean to be
rude." He sighed. "I don't know what makes me want to
rile you like that." Picking up his cup, he regarded the
cold herb tea absently. "I guess I want to know about
the men in your life." He glanced up, his gaze sharp. "Is
Peter one of them?"

Eleanor choked slightly on a sip of tea. "Peter?" she
gasped. "Gracious, no. We're just friends." She paused.
"What makes you ask?"

"Something he said today," Josh said cryptically. She
could feel his eyes on her as she drained her cup and put
it on the tray. All the secret places of her body began to
respond again, tingling with the force of Josh's presence,
remembering the passionate delight of his kisses. She
kept her own eyes on the tray, knowing they would tell
him more than she wanted him to know. The room
seemed full of their unspoken thoughts. So the shock
was greater when Josh broke the silence with a huge
yawn.

"Gotta get going," he said, stretching his legs out
briefly. "It's a long drive back up to La Honda."

Masking her bewilderment, Ellie stood. "I enjoyed
talking with you," she said, not realizing she'd assumed
the casual, charming manner of the office, knowing
only that her pride demanded that she salvage something by pretending they met only as publicist and
client. "The next time we speak, I hope to have worked
out a publicity schedule you can live with."

Josh stiffened momentarily, but the movement was so
fleeting she thought she had imagined it. The next instant he was yawning again. "This couch is too comfortable," he mumbled. "Give me a hand up?" He extended
his hand, and Ellie grasped it helpfully. She was un-

prepared for the strong tug he gave, meant to tumble her onto his lap. But her body responded automatically; she somersaulted over the couch instead, landing on her feet behind it. She still clasped his hand, and the momentum of her roll brought him out of the couch's embrace and over its back in turn. Ellie dropped his hand to avoid completing the self-defense move of flipping him to the floor. He staggered for a moment but regained his balance. Panting slightly, they confronted each other.

"What the hell was that about?" Ellie noted that Josh sounded more curious than angry.

"It was a reflex," she explained lightly, turning away to switch off the stereo. The realization that she'd almost thrown Josh on the floor made her tremble. He probably didn't know how to fall properly. He might have hit his head on a table corner or something else equally damaging. *I might have hurt him*, she thought.

Josh gave her a wary smile. He rubbed his shoulder. "Just out of curiosity, was it personal at all? I mean, I can take a hint."

His words wrenched an unwilling snort of laughter from her. With lessening anxiety she told him, "I do judo as a sport. After a while, the responses are pretty much programmed. I'm sorry it happened. I don't want to reinforce your caveman ideas of courting." She blushed at his slow smile. "Or whatever it is you're doing."

He narrowed his eyes. "So you admit that we're involved in that age-old game. For a minute I thought you wanted to pretend there's nothing between us."

She was too honest to deny his words. "What's between us," she said finally, "is bewildering to me. I won't deny that something exists, but I don't know if I want to encourage it." Her laugh was shaky. "You're a very good kisser, you know."

She stole a look at him and was riveted by his fierce, eager expression. "So are you," he said softly. "I was going to get you on the couch and verify our abilities in that direction to the satisfaction of us both." He rubbed the back of his neck ruefully as he shook his head. "But you sure put the kibosh on that. Seems like maybe you don't want to be my woman, after all."

Bemused, she watched him walk to the door. He opened it, then paused. "And I'll let you in on a secret, honey. I still want to be your man."

She was still rooted to the floor when the door closed quietly behind him. His footsteps plunked down the wooden stair treads. A distant motor sprang to life and roared away. With a start, she looked around her empty living room. He was really gone.

ELLIE MOVED ASIDE the half-full beer glass to make a place on the tiny table for her elbow. It was Saturday night; party night in Santa Cruz. Her brother Robbie's band was opening for a moderately well-known country-western group at the Barber Shop, one of the live-music dance clubs that catered to the party atmosphere. The small table in front of Ellie, overflowing with glasses and ashtrays, was surrounded by a tangle of chairs and people. Robbie's girlfriend was there, singing and clapping in time to every song, though she couldn't be heard over the general uproar; so was Grady Williams, a huge, heavily bearded, philosophical photographer and graduate student. Grady was discussing the political scene with Marigold, who, though she drank nothing stronger than mineral water, liked to soak up "atmosphere" for her novels. Also present were several other longtime friends of both Ellie's and her brother's. Because it was Robbie's band, they were sitting right down front, applauding like crazy after every number, creating a nucleus of cheerful chaos.

The noise was so great that Ellie didn't notice the new arrivals until she felt a tap on her shoulder. She glanced up into Peter's smiling, mustachioed face. Peter was an attractive man in his late thirties with a head of golden-brown curls and a compact, stocky build, but tonight Ellie paid no attention to his twinkling blue eyes and well-tended handlebar mustache. Because behind Peter stood Josh, eyes both warm and watchful as he waited for her to notice him.

His sudden appearance brought a grin to her face. Then, with an impulse toward discretion, she turned the smile on Peter. "How nice to see you! Are you here to offer Robbie and the boys a recording contract?"

Peter perched on the nearest spindly chair, huddling close to her to be heard. "They don't sound half-bad tonight," he remarked judiciously, cocking one ear toward the stage, where the band enthusiastically pounded out "White Line Fever." "Give them a little more time and they just might hear from me."

He jerked his head back toward Josh, who still stood, subjecting the people around him to the wary curiosity she'd noticed in him during the Group meeting. "I brought you something," Peter said, his eyes knowing. "We've been to two clubs already tonight, but I'm willing to bet we stay here for a while."

Ellie smiled kindly at Peter, masking the elation his words created. "I can see you think you've done me a favor. If you really believed that, you'd vacate that chair right away so Josh could sit in it."

Peter blinked. "Uh, right," he mumbled. He got to his feet and clapped Josh on the back. "I'll go get a couple of beers," he shouted jovially. "Be back in a minute."

Ellie smiled at Josh, allowing her pleasure to show. She pointed to the chair and he obeyed promptly, pulling it closer to her and laying an arm lightly along the back of her chair once he was seated. Putting his lips to her ear, he breathed, "I've been wanting to see you. Wanting you, really."

A shiver of delight coursed through her. *He's not wasting any time*, she thought, and then didn't try to think anymore as his lips nibbled her earlobe hungrily. "Who are all these people, anyway?"

She pulled away a little and took advantage of a lull in the music to introduce her friends. Marigold melted visibly when Josh, shaking her hand, remarked that he needed no introduction to her, since they'd already met.

"Fancy you remembering," Marigold gushed, "when you must meet so many people."

"Not many who write romances," he said lazily, smiling with what Ellie considered to be completely superfluous charm. "Can't wait for it to be published, so I can find out how it ends."

Pink with pleasure, Marigold would have told him then and there if Robbie's girlfriend hadn't dragged her off to the ladies' room, sending a sympathetic grin toward Ellie. The band announced another song, and Josh listened attentively. Ellie saw that Rob had noticed Josh's presence. He would be thrilled, she knew. At the end of the song Rob looked at Josh, who smiled and sent a thumbs-up salute, followed by an inquiring gesture toward the stage. Ellie didn't realize what was going on, but Rob did. His face broke into a huge grin and he bounded toward the microphone.

"Ladies and gentlemen," he announced happily. Ellie turned to watch Josh, who got up and made his way toward the edge of the stage. "We are privileged, very privileged, to have with us tonight a man who's always been one of my personal music heroes. He doesn't follow the trends—he makes them!" Josh vaulted lightly onto the stage and took the guitar one of the awed band members handed him. He strapped it on and stepped up to the microphone as Robbie finished his introduction. "Ladies and gentlemen...Joshua Blackmun!"

There was a collective gasp of recognition from the audience, then a storm of applause. Josh's eyes found Ellie; she felt his smile was all for her. He turned for a hurried consultation with the band, then confronted the audience again.

"Thanks very much, folks. It's nice of Rob and the band to invite me up. We're just going to jam a little bit here to find out what we like to play." He stepped away from the microphone, collected the band's attention, and they burst into a spirited rendition of "Mamma Don't Allow." The song was an excuse for every member of the band to take a solo, and they whooped it up. When it was over, Josh kept the electricity alive, swinging immediately into a plaintive Patsy Cline song, followed by one of his early hits. The band was playing as they never had before, swept along by Josh's energy and stage presence. Ellie felt chills course through her; she found Josh the man and Josh the performer dividing again in her mind. Absently she noticed that Peter had returned with drinks. He poked her gently and said into her ear, "Great publicity, this. How did you talk him into it?"

She moved a little away from him. "Wasn't my idea," she muttered. Josh brought the song to a satisfying end and bowed, first to the audience and then to the band. Applause roared forth again, and he swept his arm around the stage, relinquishing it to the band members. He unstrapped the guitar and disappeared behind the drum set. "Isn't he coming back?" Ellie couldn't help the forlorn note that crept into her voice.

"He'll be back. Just wants to throw everyone off the scent so they won't mob the table." Peter shot her a quizzical look. "Ellie, are you getting involved with Josh?"

She evaded his eyes. "I don't know what you mean. And if you mean what I think, no I'm not."

"Good." He leaned back in his seat and sipped his beer. "He's going to be hard enough to handle without you getting personally wound up with him."

She sat up straighter. "Is this the same man who told me a few days ago to do whatever it took to bring Josh Blackmun around?"

Peter sighed. The band began a driving rendition of a Jackson Browne song, and he had to lean close to be heard. "I didn't mean for you to fall into bed with him. Blackmun isn't famous for fidelity, and I know you, Ellie." He smiled at her with almost brotherly fondness. "You're not the fooling-around type. You could get hurt."

Touched by his concern, Ellie patted his hand. "Thanks for the warning, Peter, but you know how even the best advice is often ignored." She glanced wistfully at the spot behind the snare drum where Josh had disappeared. "It's probably too late anyway," she whispered.

"Where's my beer?" Josh suddenly came up behind them, and Peter offered him the chair next to Ellie with a grandiose gesture. Josh drank thirstily while Peter made an amiable offer to buy the next round. Ellie's friends closed protectively around the table, hiding Josh's distinctive profile and murmuring their compliments on the music. Josh was charming to them, but Ellie could sense that something in his attitude had changed. He drank two more beers in quick succession. Robbie's band finished their set and came to cluster around the table, shaking Josh's hand with reverence and thanking him for playing with them. He kept a good-natured smile pinned on, but when the volume began to rise he pulled impatiently at Ellie's hand. "I need to get out of here," he said in her ear. "Come on."

He led her around the stage and down a short, empty corridor. Through a partly open door she glimpsed the headlining country band that was to play next. They were passing a bottle of whiskey around. Josh pushed open the exit door and ushered her out. They stood for a moment, taking deep breaths of the clear, cold night air. "The smoke in there was so thick you could cut it with a knife," Josh muttered. Ellie silently agreed. They walked around to the parking lot; she paused by her car.

"So...what are you doing down here on a Saturday night?" She tried to keep her voice careless. Josh leaned against the car and watched her. The streetlight cast a bar of shadow over his eyes; she couldn't interpret his expression.

"We were working at the studio. Peter's eager to get the album finished, and I don't see any point in drawing things out. We worked late, and afterward I wanted to see you."

The directness of it took her breath away. "Well," she managed. "You've seen me."

"Don't play coy, Ellie." Josh took her arm firmly, his hand warm through her sweater. "Come on. Let's go."

She watched, bemused, as he climbed into the passenger seat of her car. He leaned over and opened her door. "Are you going to stand out there all night?"

At a loss for words, she got into the car. "Do you mind telling me where we're going?"

His eyes glinted at her. "To my place."

The sheer effrontery made her chuckle. "Thanks for the gracious invitation, but—"

He moved closer, his words interrupting her. "As I told you before, I don't drive after drinking anymore. So if you don't want to drive me to my place, we can go to yours. I'm not particular. But I don't intend to spend the night in the street."

She frowned at him. "You had three beers. You're not drunk."

He leaned back in the seat and closed his eyes, apparently considering the battle won. "We had a couple of drinks at the studio after wrapping up," he said casually. "I came over here with Peter. And like I said, I never drive after drinking anymore. Young Rob mentioned that you nurse the same drink all night, so I know you're sober enough to drive." He yawned and opened one eye. "Can we get going?"

Ellie threw up her hands in disgust and started the car. "I know I shouldn't let myself be manipulated like this," she grumbled, "but I'm sure not taking you to my place. It's no skin off *my* nose if you have to hitch a ride back here for your car."

It took almost an hour to make the drive up Highway 1 to the turnoff and another twenty minutes on the twisting mountain roads to his secluded La Honda cabin. They drove in silence, although Ellie knew that Josh merely feigned sleep. She tried to lessen her tension, allowing the dark highway and silent hills to occupy all her consciousness. But when he spoke to prepare her for the turn into his driveway, she jumped.

"You nervous?" There was mischief in his voice. She ignored it as she maneuvered past the pile of logs that was all that remained of the downed tree. Pulling up in front of the house, she put the car in neutral and waited.

He reached over and turned off the engine, pocketing the keys. "You're coming in, of course."

She shook her head tolerantly. "You're too bossy. Give me back my keys, please." They stared at each other. The small confines of the car began to seem almost claustrophobic. He drew the keys out of his pocket and leaned toward her. After inserting them into the ignition he wrapped one large, warm palm around the back of her neck and drew her into the kiss.

It started out sweet and as gentle as the eucalyptus-scented breeze. His lips were so soft, almost yielding, she thought hazily. They drew her deeper and deeper, and suddenly she was caught in a maelstrom of passion. Fierce desire rose in her, igniting a physical longing she was unable to resist. His hand moved down her back and under her sweater, finding the silky skin eagerly. When he brushed her breast she began trembling, and knew there was no going back.

Josh tore his lips away from hers with an audible gasp. "Please," he whispered in her ear, his ragged breath arousing her even more. "Please come inside. Please don't go home now."

"Yes," she said shakily. "Okay." She opened her car door and got out, hoping she could make it to the house on legs that suddenly seemed made of jelly. Josh came around the car and pulled her tight against him. They shared another slow, seductive kiss, prolonging it until neither of them could take any more.

"Ellie?" She knew what the question was. She drew back and looked at him searchingly. With devastating suddenness all the doubts and insecurities, all the reasons she'd avoided romantic encounters for the past five years, came flooding back. Sensing her uncertainty, Josh loosened his hold slightly and assumed a watchful expression. He waited silently.

Finally she whispered, "I don't want to lead you on, Josh. So I feel I should tell you that, while I generally enjoy kissing, and...and whatnot, when it gets right down to it, I haven't wanted to make love for a long time—not since my divorce, as a matter of fact. If you think...if you expect...." She stumbled over her thought, and was relieved when, after staring at her for a moment with an unreadable expression, Josh pulled her back into his arms.

"I'll take my chances," he growled into her ear. He

guided her up to the front door. "We'll go into the living
room, *not* the bedroom."

There was a dim light burning in the long room. Josh
went to start a fire in the big stone fireplace. She glanced
around the room and realized suddenly that the skylight
above was made of clear glass. The room seemed roofed
in starlight.

She looked at Josh as he knelt on the hearth and
found him watching her. "Do you give all your dates
that very daunting speech?" He came toward her as he
spoke, leading her to the big down-cushioned couch
that sat facing the fireplace under the skylight. She sat
nervously in one corner, and he promptly sank into the
other one. She was grateful for the space.

"I've never let it get this far before," she admitted,
glancing at him and then fixing her eyes on the flames.
"In fact, maybe I'd better. . . ."

Her attempt to rise was foiled by Josh, who moved
instantly to cover her body with his, crowding her
into the soft down. "I promise not to get angry if you
don't want to go to bed with me," he whispered beguil-
ingly, starting to nibble along her jawline between
words. "So why don't we indulge in a little kissing and
whatnot?"

"Well. . ." Ellie began weakly. Then his lips found
hers, and she didn't want to talk anymore. Slowly she
lost herself in the waves of sweet sensation that swept
her as Josh fused their mouths together in a fiery explo-
sion. She couldn't help the small, satisfied sound that
escaped her when one of those big hands drifted down
her side, the rough callouses on the tips of his fingers
catching on the soft cashmere of her sweater, his thumb
and open palm moving deliberately over her breast.

He found the bottom of her sweater and the shirttail
that was tucked into her jeans. His hand dug under these
obstacles to encounter the smooth skin below, and re-

versed its journey, gliding upward till it found what it sought.

Ellie sighed tremulously and let his hands ignite her while their lips drank passion from each other's heat. She began to move restlessly against the length of his body, quickly finding the evidence of his arousal. That knowledge sent a fresh quiver of desire through her.

Feeling her shiver, Josh gasped and almost desperately pulled his mouth away. Ellie turned her head, her lips seeking his, and finally, reluctantly, opened her eyes. He was looking down at her as he crushed her body warmly to him. The raw desire and hunger of his gaze captured her, kindling her further.

"Do you feel this, too? I can't be feeling it alone!" The harsh intensity of his voice was unbelievably sweet to her ears. "Lady, you're too much temptation. We'd better stop now if I'm going to keep my promise."

"No!" Ellie couldn't help the plaintive cry. She didn't want to stop. The depth of her apparent need was too startling, too demanding. With some confusion, she realized that although she had succeeded in burying her sensuality after her divorce, her emotions were not dead. She had never experienced so primitive a desire for the comfort to be found in lovemaking.

Licking her lips hesitantly, she glanced up at Josh under her lashes. He was waiting for her decision. "It is really too soon, you know," she said softly.

He shrugged impatiently. "In terms of minutes, hours, days, perhaps."

His words unlocked a sudden rush of wonder at the rightness of her feelings. With the sensation of making some inexorable, unavoidable bow to fate, she put up one hand to caress the lean planes of his face. When she brought his mouth down to hers, a tight coil of passion seemed to unleash itself in them, sweeping away all possibility of retreat.

But still Josh let her set the pace. Boldly she trailed her fingers down his chest, finding and unfastening the buttons of his flannel shirt. Beyond the driving force of physical need there were other, deeper motives for her behavior. Dimly she realized that she had to exorcise the demons that had plagued her for so long. But she turned a deaf ear to the voice that whispered of a more-compelling reason to let herself be carried away.

She caught Josh's flaming glance as her hand reached his waist and paused. His breath came in deep gulps; he seemed to be trembling. It was intoxicating to have so much power over a man's body. Licking lips suddenly gone dry, she touched his belt buckle.

Then he moved, his lips igniting hers, his hands hungrily finding her tender places and bringing fevered moans from her mouth. Ellie was lost in the sensuous vortex he created around her, hardly noticing as he stripped away their clothes.

His hands and lips seemed to be everywhere, caressing, teasing. She let herself react with voluptuous abandon, loving the feel of him beneath her questing palms; the hard, muscular frame belied by smooth, silky skin.

She retained just enough common sense to whisper, "Josh...I don't have...I didn't bring...."

He stared down at her for a moment, then smiled with great tenderness, sending another jolt to her overloaded sensory receptors. "Right," he said, his voice a gritty purr. "I can take care of that." He looked around at their clothes scattered over the floor, at the dying fire. "Let's go to the bedroom," he whispered tantalizingly in her ear. She used her teeth to pull gently on his earlobe, enjoying the way it affected his speech. "I've been... fantasizing for days about...getting you back on my Navaho blanket."

It was a long trip to the bedroom, with many pauses for feverish caresses. "I'd pick you up and carry you there," Josh mumbled when they'd made it to the living-room doorway, "but I'm afraid you'd slug me." She crowded gently against him and he groaned. "Ah, lady...."

"It's all right," she managed to say. "I can walk on my own two feet—barely."

He guided her into the bedroom and rested her gently on the rough cover, pausing with narrowed eyes to drink in the sight of her lush body against the faded colors. His obvious pleasure in looking at her did away with any self-consciousness Ellie might have felt. She found within herself an abandon that was totally new to her and yet seemed as natural as breathing.

Raising one knee slightly, she opened her arms to Josh, beckoning him to join her with imperious haste. He drew in his breath sharply and came to kneel between her legs on the bed, letting the hard, heavy weight of him brush tantalizingly against her moist valley. She sucked in air, and his hands came to poise over her breasts. Wonderingly he watched the nipples pucker and harden before he touched them. "You are so fine," he whispered, his fingers gently brushing over the nipples, around them, finally cupping the rounded ripeness of her breasts. Ellie's eyes drifted shut at the exquisite pleasure as he lowered his head and took each nipple in turn into his mouth, sucking and nibbling, letting his tongue flick with maddening slowness over the hard, aching tips.

Her hands began to wander, over his back, around to his chest, down the trail of rough black hair that led to the smooth, thick column of desire. The feel of it sent her needs spiraling out of control, and she tugged gently at his body, arching her hips, trying to take him into her where she needed him so much.

His body stiffened. "Ah, Ellie! I can't—" With a groan, he collapsed on top of her, letting her guide him, thrusting hard and deep in uncontrollable hunger.

At last their bodies joined on the Navaho blanket, dissolving in the heated combat that was no combat, the amorous dance that could for a short time fuse the disparate halves, male and female, into a total being, mystically complete. Somehow, on the ancient coverlet, the act of love was like a sacrament for Ellie. There was no hesitation in her as she took him in and found almost unbearable pleasure in the tumultuous meeting of their flesh. At the end, when they shook together with the final dissolution, she realized with wonder that a burden she'd been carrying for far too long had finally vanished. And then she found it necessary to quit thinking altogether.

4

SOMETHING COLD AND WET nudged Eleanor's bare arm. She woke slowly, taking in the darkened room filled with unfamiliar shadows. Again came the peremptory nudge, and she turned her head to find gleaming eyes fixed on her. Bertha stood beside the bed, an eager expression on her doggy face.

Ellie managed a feeble pat. "Good dog," she mumbled, her mind still crusted with sleep. "Go away now." Bertha paid no attention to this poor-spirited talk. She took a friendly swipe at Ellie's face with her long, wet tongue. "Ugh!" Thoroughly awake now, Ellie stretched under the covers and came up against a warm body.

Josh lay on his stomach, his face turned toward her. In spite of the stubble on his chin and the powerful, naked shoulders that showed above the sheet, he had a defenseless, boyish look in sleep. Ellie stared at him for a long moment, in the grip of a sensation she didn't want to acknowledge. But the reality was hard to ignore.

She was in love with Joshua Blackmun. A more wildly inappropriate lover for her would have been hard to find. Mentally she listed the negatives. He was famous; he was used to having his own way; he was in a profession that demanded an outsized ego for survival. She shook her head at her own folly, but with a sense of resignation. Upon meeting him, it had all been inevitable. The sensible thing to do was to take the future slowly and enjoy it while it lasted. There was no use borrowing trouble

As if her thoughts had been audible, Josh stirred and rolled over. His eyes found her immediately. "Good morning." It was impossible not to respond to that sexy, delightful smile. "If it is morning. What are you doing awake so early?"

His eyes slid like a lingering caress down her bare torso, approving of the full, rounded breasts, the strong contours of shoulder and belly. She fumbled for the sheet, but he beat her to it, keeping her from pulling it over her nudity.

"You're beautiful, Ellie. Don't hide your beauty from your man." His hand drifted with lazy possession down her shoulder until he was cupping one breast. He moved suddenly and she found herself lying on her side, tucked into the warm curve of his body, her back to his front. He yawned again, still toying with her breasts in a very distracting way.

"What time is it, anyway?"

"About five, I should say." Ellie nodded toward the bedside. "Bertha woke me."

Josh stretched his legs, bringing her buttocks into close contact with his groin. A fiery dart of desire pierced her. "Checking up on me." The dog padded silently around the bed. Josh spoke to her without ceasing the arousing movement of his hands on Ellie. "Good girl. Go away now."

"Don't you need . . . need to let her out?" Ellie found it difficult to talk with the hard length of Josh's body burning hers and his hands spreading fire.

"Not now, that's for sure." His voice thickened, and he moved one hand from her breasts to glide down her stomach and probe the delights he found there. She sighed and parted her legs, the languorous pleasure of his knowing touch making her feel oddly paralyzed.

"I want to attack you," he growled in her ear, his fingers plunging into the warm cavern of her desire. "I wish I could have woken up already making love to you. I need you, my woman." He surged against her, and she could tell he spoke the truth.

She felt like purring, like being caressed. "I can't stop you," she whispered, rolling a little further onto her back and arching into his tormenting hand. "I seem to be...helpless."

He picked up on her mood immediately. "You are my helpless woman," he murmured in her ear, pulling on her lobe with his teeth. "You are totally in my power, and I will do with your nubile body what I wish."

"Oh, my." She twisted seductively, managing to rub herself against him where she thought it would do the most good. "I can't escape. Help, help."

"I'll help you, all right." His breath was as ragged as hers. "I'll drive you crazy like you're doing to me. Ellie—my lady!" She found one of his nipples and plucked lazily at it, her other hand slipping over the bunched muscles of his derriere, around the hair-roughened length of his thigh. The fires he'd started in her were beginning to rage out of control. "That's no way to defend yourself."

He grasped her hands and held them above her head, enjoying the sight of her as she lay, quivering, on the verge of laughter. "Josh! What do you think you're doing?"

"I'm getting ready to have my way with you, my proud beauty." He lowered his mouth to hers, and she gasped at the hot current that flowed between them. "But first I need to kiss you everywhere. I need to know you want this as much as I do."

His lips moved down her throat, saluted the peak of each aching breast, moved along the curve of her stomach. Ellie writhed against the restraining clasp of his hands.

"Josh—please—now, Josh!"

He let go of her hands so he could hold her quivering thighs, probing with fingers and tongue, gently at first, then more deeply as he responded to her moans of pleasure.

"Tell me what you want, Ellie. Tell me what you need."

She couldn't find words in her disordered brain, but her body reacted with all the strength she could muster. Freed of her sensual languor, she twisted strongly away from him, tumbling him flat against the pillows and climbing on top. "I'll show you what I need," she growled at him, enjoying her momentary mastery of the situation. In one swift motion she completed their union, grunting in satisfaction as she watched his pleasure-drenched face. Teasingly she bounced a little, her own raging desires held in check for the purpose of drawing out Josh's enjoyment.

"Lady—" his voice was hoarse "—I can't. . . ."

"You're helpless," she whispered, leaning over to brush her breasts against his chest and dropping a playful kiss on his lips.

He seized her head, his lips fierce against hers, sending her soaring again as his body rocked against her. Leaving the game, she moved with him until their fervid cries of satiation mingled in the early dawn.

Later they lay drowsily side by side. Ellie was nearly asleep again when Bertha came back into the room, this time announcing herself with a bark. Josh jerked into wakefulness.

"Okay, girl." He gave Ellie one last apologetic squeeze and got up. "If you say so, it's morning."

He went to let the dog out, and Ellie got up too, hunting in the closet till she found the velour robe she'd worn before. She stumbled down the dark hall to the kitchen and banged her shins on a wide board that was unaccountably set across the bottom of the doorframe.

With a muffled curse, she stepped cautiously over the piece of wood. Her bare foot encountered a wiggly, furry mass. "What on earth?" Groping for the light switch, she finally flooded the room with brightness. The squirming mass at her feet became three roly-poly balls of fur, tumbling blindly over one another and emitting small cries of distress at the absence of their mother. Homing in on Ellie's bare feet, they scrambled over her toes, their tiny claws and teeth tickling all the sensitive places. As she attempted to get to the stove without stepping on a puppy, several more of them spilled over the side of a low basket set by the back door. One of the puppies at her feet found her little toe and began sucking on it enthusiastically.

"Help!" Ellie bent and scooped the puppies into her arms just before the second wave of them found her feet. "I am not your mother," she said firmly, her fingers nonetheless caressing the wriggling, silky bodies. Scuffling her feet along the floor, she reached the basket and began pouring puppies into it, only to have them squirm out as fast as she put them in. Josh found her there, kneeling by the basket, laughing helplessly as the puppies crawled over her.

He grinned as he caught her eye. "Gone to the dogs already," he said, shaking his head. "How quickly it happens."

Bertha leaped over the board propped across the kitchen door and settled herself in the basket. The puppies clambered all over one another to get to her. Ellie stood to meet Josh's embrace.

He had stopped in his bedroom to pull on a pair of drawstring pajama bottoms, but his chest was still bare. Ellie found her fingers running with sensuous pleasure over the resilient planes of muscle and the curls of dark hair. He made a noise low in his throat, his lips nibbling at her neck under her tousled hair. "We don't have to get up this early," he whispered, punctuating his words with lightning darts of his tongue. "Let's go back to bed." He gave her a naughty grin. "I don't think we got it quite right before."

Ellie's middle began to melt, but she summoned her willpower, stronger now in the kitchen confines. "It'll have to do. I have a long drive in front of me." She leaned away from his torturing mouth and said generously, "Get dressed and I'll give you a ride back to your car."

"That's not the offer I was looking for from you." His fingers went to the belt of the velour robe. Ellie batted them away. She was already beginning to regret her offer to drive him to Santa Cruz. Although the feel of his hard body sent a fresh rush of arousal through her, she was in need of time alone. What had happened between them had been unexpected, unsettling. She felt as if she'd been lifted out of her calm, orderly existence by a whirlwind. Now she needed to find the quiet center of the storm.

As if he sensed her withdrawal, Josh intensified his embrace. "Honey child..." he began, his voice a lazy drawl.

Eleanor thrust him away. "Don't," she said tensely. Hurt, he drew back. They regarded each other for a moment. "Don't crowd me, please, Josh." She felt open and vulnerable, and the feeling made her apprehensive.

"All right," he said finally, watching her. His mouth smiled without changing his other features. "Tell you what. We'll stop along the highway and find something for breakfast." The smile began to reach his eyes. "You are hungry, aren't you? Or are you going to trample that sacred tradition into the ground, as well?"

She stepped away from his arms and he made no move to detain her. She felt an absurd sensation of relief. "You mean the theory that making love makes you hungry? Don't you know that's just an old wives' tale? Not a word of truth in it." She could hear the edge of hysteria in her inconsequent babble and forced herself to take a deep breath. Meeting his eyes, she attempted a genuine smile. "What it really does is make you . . . energized." His sudden crack of laughter encouraged her and she let her eyes sparkle up at him. "Yes, I feel convinced I won't miss my morning run today." She sidestepped a couple of warm little puddles on the floor to reach the kitchen door, looking back to see Josh pick up a solitary puppy that still cried around his feet.

"Poor little baby," he crooned to it. She felt her throat tighten. He squatted down by Bertha's basket and carefully found a vacant teat for the tiny creature. Noticing Ellie's eyes on him as he straightened, he explained matter-of-factly, "The runt. Seems like there's always one that has to scramble harder." He came closer, his eyes taking obvious pleasure in the sight of Ellie as she stood, tall and straight against the doorway. "Now what's all this nonsense about jogging?"

Ellie shook her head mournfully, stepping over the board and striding down the hall. "Don't you jog? You must not be a Californian." She smiled over her shoulder as he followed her. "Well, maybe we can find something to take the place of jogging. This morning, for instance, I'll bet you're so invigorated you could walk all the way to Santa Cruz without needing a ride." He reached for her, smiling, as she came out of the living room with her clothes in her hand. She avoided him nimbly and shut the bathroom door in his face.

"Be out in a minute," she called airily, and then started the shower to drown any comments he might have to make. If she kept moving, staying one jump ahead of him, everything would be easier.

The air outside was fresh and cold and barely tinged with dawn when they left his house. They drove in silence for the first few minutes. Then Josh spoke. "Will your parents be worried or something? Is that why you're going back so early?"

Ellie shook her head. "I've often stayed out all night on the weekends." She stole a quick look at him and was surprised that he didn't react to her provocative answer. He caught her glance and smiled smugly, dropping one hand to her knee as she drove.

"You can't make me jealous that way," he said. "I'd already deduced that you hadn't made love for a while. I'll bet you were staying with one of your women friends."

She laughed ruefully. "Right you are. But mom and dad wouldn't make a scene even if they guessed I wasn't at a girlfriend's house last night. I've told you before, I don't live there so they can run my life for me. I like being near them, and we enjoy one another, but they wouldn't think of asking me to account for my time. They trust me to make my own choices."

He was quiet for a minute, digesting that. "Then why are you going home so early?"

She kept her voice light. "You're so smart, figure it out for yourself." There was a restaurant at the side of the road, and she pointed to the sign that proclaimed it was open. "Do you want to stop here?"

It was the kind of restaurant where all the seats were booths and the food was tasty if uninspired. After the waitress had bustled off with their breakfast orders, an uneasy silence ensued. Desperate for a topic of conversation, Ellie groped for something to say. "I talked to Milo Connors on Friday," she remarked, naming a prominent San Francisco pop-music critic.

Josh looked up from his coffee cup. The expression on his face gave her a sinking feeling, but she plunged on. "He was interested in hearing about your new album. There might be a note about it in his Sunday column.

And I set up an interview for you next week, if that's all right."

He didn't answer. With her usual calm deliberation, Ellie added lemon to her tea and waited for him to speak. When he didn't, she couldn't help filling the ominous silence. "Peter seemed to think it would be okay, anyway. He's ecstatic, needless to say."

Josh set his coffee cup down in the saucer with a crash. The sound gave Ellie a bad case of internal shivers, but she didn't allow it to show on her face. At that inopportune moment the waitress returned with their food.

With a show of hearty appetite Ellie poured syrup over her waffle. Josh waited for the waitress to finish fussing around the cups and plates. When she walked off he leaned over the table. He didn't raise his voice. With the amount of quiet rage he could fit into a whisper, he didn't need to shout.

"You're going to go ahead and make a media event of me? Even after last night? I can't believe I'm hearing anything so...so cold-blooded, so callous, so...unwomanly."

Ellie quit making methodical inroads on her waffle. She laid her knife and fork down and looked at him for a long minute. *Please*, she was thinking, *don't let me be in love with him. I don't want this kind of trouble.* But it was too late for such thoughts. It had been too late the first time they kissed.

Finally she spoke, maintaining her calm with difficulty. "Josh. If you thought I would neglect my professional responsibilities because you and I went to bed together, I'm very sorry. I don't intend to stop doing the job I'm being paid for."

His face wore incredulity for a moment. "Do you mean...? You can't mean that you want to be paid off before you'll quit! No, Ellie—"

Now she was angry. "Don't be a jerk, Blackmun. I'm
saying Peter hired the agency to promote your album. If
you equate that with promoting yourself, so be it. I intend to do a good job—the only kind," she added arrogantly, "that I know how to do. If you took me to bed
to get me off your case, you're out of luck. I'm not quit-
ting."

"Talk about jerks!" He flung some money on the table
and pulled at her arm. "I have some things to say to
you," he muttered between his teeth, "that are best said
in private. Let's go."

She refused to budge. "I haven't finished my waffle,"
she pointed out calmly. He glared down at her as she cut
another bite and chewed thoroughly. "Your eggs are
getting cold," she mentioned after she'd swallowed.

"I don't want the eggs." But he did drop back into his
seat, watching every forkful she took with angry impatience. It took all her poise to finish the waffle, drain her
teacup, then find the right change to pay for her food
and tip. Josh pointed to the large bill he'd thrown on the
table, but Ellie shrugged.

"Under the circumstances I'd rather pay for my own,"
she told him evenly. "I'm ready to go now."

She unlocked the car door for him and slipped behind
the wheel. But she didn't start the engine. If there was to
be shouting and recrimination, she'd rather not have to
give any of her attention to driving.

Josh pulled her around to face him. "Let's just get
straight who's trying to manipulate whom. I don't have
ulterior motives for making love to women. I didn't
have one in your case, God, who needs an ulterior mo-
tive to make love to a fascinating, desirable, sensual
lady?" It took Ellie a few seconds to realize that he was
talking about her. She blinked, momentarily side-
tracked from her grievance.

"What I discovered in your arms was...special to

me," he continued. "I had the foolish notion that you felt the same. If you had, you could never talk so calmly about serving me up to the media like some kind of trussed chicken." He stopped for breath, and his face changed. With a groan he gathered her close. "Don't do it, Ellie. Please."

His touch was like flint to her tinder. His lips ignited flames on her neck, her ear, her jaw. Blindly she glued her mouth to his, yearning for the blaze of sweet passion their kisses could kindle so easily. Her thoughts whirled incoherently. Was it worth it? Shouldn't she help him? Wasn't it cruel of Peter? She barely felt the stickshift digging into one thigh, since Josh's hand trailed quivering fire up the other one. Sighing, she became pliant and leaned against him, her arms coming around his neck.

Josh broke off the kiss and took in her softened, dreamy face. "Does this mean you aren't going to do it? You mean the goddess has capitulated?" She raised her eyebrows in smiling reproof, about to tell him not to jump to conclusions. But Josh didn't wait for her to speak. "So you want to be my woman after all. Well, darlin', you're goin' the right way about it."

Ellie stiffened. His laughter seemed suddenly arrogant, territorial. Her movements calm and deliberate, she removed Josh's arms from around her. Sliding back behind the steering wheel, she buckled her seat belt and started the car. She didn't look at Josh.

They were on the highway before he spoke. "I blew it, didn't I?"

Lips pressed tight together, she nodded.

"You intend to publicize me to the hilt."

She risked a short glance at him. He was looking straight ahead, his own mouth grim. "I will promote your album. You will naturally be involved in the promotion."

His voice rose. "Because of that dumb crack I made

you're going to condemn me to being interviewed and badgered, my privacy invaded, my mistakes dug up and waved in front of me, my most intimate feelings paraded for every gossip-hungry moron to discuss?"

She winced, but nodded. "Not because of your extremely stupid remark. Not because of the unpalatable facts it reveals about your idea of our relationship. Simply because that's what I'm supposed to do." She pounded the steering wheel gently with the palm of one hand. "You don't seem to understand, Josh. If I quit, do you think Peter would give up the idea of promoting your album? Of course not. He'd just hire someone else to do it—probably some aggressive city firm that wouldn't even understand your objections, let alone pay any attention to them."

"You don't understand." His voice was harsh. "You couldn't do this to me if you understood."

No, she wanted to cry. *You're wrong. I do understand. Oh, how I understand.* But now wasn't the time to bring up the past.

"I'm sorry," she said instead. "I'll do my best to smooth things for you, Josh. But I can't quit."

"Can't—or won't?"

"Won't."

For the rest of the way to Santa Cruz, there was silence.

THE INTERVIEW ROOM at the San Francisco *News* was isolated from the deafening clatter of the newsroom. But with the door closed to shut out the noise, the tiny glass-walled room was overheated. Eleanor edged her chair as far as she could from the ceiling vent and bumped it into the rickety table in one corner. The room was full with just her in it. When everyone was present for the interview, the tiny space would overflow. She glanced at her watch, worry etching her forehead. Peter and

Josh were supposed to have met her there. They were late.

Milo Connors breezed in, tape recorder under his arm, note pad clutched in his hand.

"Hello, sweetie," he caroled, setting the tape recorder down on the table. Ellie stood to meet his engulfing hug.

"Hi, Milo." She had accompanied other clients to interviews with the music critic, and knew that his effervescent, slightly ladylike charm masked a keen insight into the characters of his subjects and a sometimes malicious sense of humor. She would have preferred to avoid turning him loose on Josh, but there was no one in the Bay Area music scene whose approval could be more valuable. Without notice from Milo Connors, favorable or otherwise, a musician had scant chance of receiving attention from more-important East Coast critics.

She accepted his kiss on the cheek good-naturedly. He was only a little taller than she. "Thank heaven you didn't wear heels, darling! Think of the injury to my ego if I had to go tiptoe to say hello."

"Heels are so uncomfortable." She sat down again and grinned up at his freckled, little-boy countenance. He had a thatch of nondescript sandy hair and a stocky build, which gave him an innocuous appearance that was totally misleading. She found herself speaking her thought aloud. "How can you always look so...so fresh?" She ran a hand through her own brown hair and wished that the dark circles beneath her eyes weren't so obvious. "I feel positively haggard next to you."

"My sweet, you look blooming." Milo pulled a chair next to the table and sat, his knees nearly touching hers. "How long has it been? Months, anyway."

"George's," Ellie said, naming a publicist for a big San Francisco firm. George was in the habit of throwing lavish and indiscriminate parties in his Victorian flat, which were attended by people from all levels of the music industry.

Milo made a face. "That dreadful party. It was so crowded, I started to leave five minutes after I got there and couldn't find the door again for two hours!" He opened his note pad. "Charming as it is to chat, sweetie, we do need to get on with it. Where's the boyfriend?"

For a moment Eleanor was speechless. Surely her relationship with Josh couldn't have found its way to Milo's sharp ears in the scant time they'd been seeing each other. "Boyfriend?" she croaked.

"Peter Macguire, my dear nitwit, and his new prize." He tilted his head, inquisitive. "Peter was with you at George's," he pointed out. "I thought there was something between you."

The relief made Eleanor giddy. "There is," she retorted. "Friendship. Peter and I are friends, that's all." Milo looked disbelieving, and she sighed in exasperation. "Surely you've heard of friendship, Milo darling." Her voice was sweet. "It's in all the dictionaries."

"Don't be catty, darling." He was unruffled. "And you've missed my point. Where is he, whatever he is?"

Eleanor glanced at her watch again. "I don't know," she admitted, trying not to sound as nervous as she felt. "They were supposed to meet us here a few minutes ago. Must have run into some traffic."

Milo plugged the recorder in and checked the tape. "I've got a very heavy schedule today, so I can't run overtime."

"Got an interview with Mick Jagger?"

"No, that's tomorrow." He finished fussing with his equipment and turned briskly back to Eleanor. "Lay some background on me. Why's Blackmun coming out of the woodwork like this, after hibernating for three years?"

Ellie answered promptly, her mind automatically

finding the most-flattering way to present her client, smoothing down his resentment of the media without blunting the impact of his sudden return to recording.

But while she gave easy, practiced answers, her stomach began to churn with anxiety. She hadn't seen Josh since their disagreement three days ago. She hadn't been able to stop thinking about him, either. She wanted to see him again, but not as his publicist. The ambivalence of her feelings kept her in constant turmoil.

The wall phone next to the door buzzed, and Milo interrupted his questions to answer it. "Call for you, love," he said, turning back to her.

It was Peter. "Ellie, you'd already left when I tried your apartment this morning. I can't make it today."

"Do tell." Eleanor heard the exasperation in her voice. Peter responded to it with a flood of excuses.

"Those Japanese money men—you remember I told you they were thinking of investing? They picked this morning to show up bright eyed and bushy tailed, and they expect me to spend the day with them." She let an impatient sound through her teeth. "Sorry, dear. I got hold of Josh and told him to go on by himself. He should be there any minute. I know you can handle it."

"You know more than I do, then," Eleanor muttered. But Peter wasn't listening.

"Thanks, doll. I knew I could count on you. Stop in later and tell me how it goes." Peter paused for a moment, then spoke hurriedly. "Listen, I have to go. Good luck."

She hung up the phone slowly. Good luck indeed. Taking a deep, silent breath, she turned back to Milo's curious gaze. "Peter can't make it," she said casually. "Had to take some investors around. But Josh will be here any minute."

"I'll arrange for someone to escort him up here from

the lobby," Milo replied, reaching for the phone again. Eleanor stopped him.

"That's not necessary." Standing by the glass door of the interview room, she could see down the hall. "He's here already." She swung the door open. "Hello, Josh. Come and meet Milo Connors."

"We've met." Josh stood in the doorway, his expression as harsh as his voice. "Connors."

Milo nodded in return. "Blackmun." He was cool now, and wary. "As I recall, the last time we spoke you were with Vivienne." Ellie felt her face go rigid. Knowing the facts about Josh's former love did not, she discovered, stop her from experiencing a surge of primitive emotion whenever she heard Vivienne Santos's name. "That must have been—"

"Three and a half years ago," Josh answered bluntly.

"And does Miss Santos know you're back in the studio these days? Will she be recording with you or anything like that?"

Josh's face darkened; he didn't answer. At last he turned to Eleanor. "I thought this interview was for the purpose of discussing my new album." When he looked at her his eyes were cold and bleak. She wrenched her own gaze away quickly.

"Mr. Blackmun doesn't wish to discuss his private life, Milo," she said, her clear voice matter-of-fact and soothing. "I know you'll understand and respect his wishes."

"Of course." Milo's answer was courteous, but he glanced speculatively at Josh. "So did you bring me a tape?"

Ellie clapped her hand to her forehead. "Oh gosh. Peter was supposed to—"

"I've got the tape." Josh dug in a pocket of his worn leather jacket. "Two songs. You'll have to play it now, I can't leave it with you."

Milo's eyebrows went up farther. "I really need some time to listen—"

"Sorry." Josh was curt. "I can't spare it. No one else but Peter has even heard the final mix yet." His brief smile showed teeth. "This is one album that isn't going to be sneaked ahead of time. We're keeping close tabs on all the preliminary tapes."

Eleanor prayed that Milo would choose to be amused instead of affronted. For a long moment it was a toss-up. Then Milo managed a giggle.

"You are being secretive. Well, all the world loves a mystery. Let's hear your stuff."

He rewound the interview cassette and replaced it with the tape of Josh's songs. The first cut was sharp, gritty rock 'n' roll with tight, pointed lyrics about being the runt of the litter. Ellie glanced involuntarily at Josh and found his eyes on her, their expression opaque. She looked away. Milo was making notes on the lyrics while his foot imperceptibly tapped the beat. That was a good sign, anyway. She smothered a nervous smile.

The second song was the one he'd been polishing the night of Group. Eleanor stiffened. Set to a bouncy, impudent rhythm, the song was like a thrown gauntlet, signifying a new assault in the eternal war between men and women. There was a second verse now.

> "Do I have to drag you off,
> By the hair on that pretty head?
> Take you back to my cave,
> And my saber-toothed tiger fur bed?
> Come here, woman.
> I'll make you understand.
> Come here, woman.
> You want me to be your man."

Josh's voice was drawling, impertinent and seemed to taunt her. She didn't like the tone of the song. And beneath her dislike she could sense a rising flood of memories of a man in her past who had hurt her—hurt her badly with a song.

The tape stopped, and Milo rewound it. He tossed it back to Josh, who fielded it one-handed and put it in his pocket. "Great tunes," Milo commented, radiating sincerity. "Are you releasing them as singles?" Josh shook his head and Milo pressed on. "Well, when will the album be out?"

Josh considered for a moment. "That's really for Peter to say. Early next year, at a guess."

Milo put his interview tape back in the little recorder and spun it forward to where he'd left off. "Now tell me, what made you pick a small label like Trax for your comeback album? Wasn't your old label interested?"

Eleanor held her breath, ready to jump in if Josh refused to answer the question. "I didn't ask them," Josh growled. "I'm really only recording this album because Peter is an old army buddy of mine. He asked me, and I said I would." He closed his lips tightly, as if any further utterances would have to be pried out.

Milo didn't exactly pry, but he did manage to extract a creditable amount of information. With Eleanor intervening to smooth out the rough spots, the interview began to go well. She was almost relaxed when the bomb fell.

Milo had finished an intelligent series of questions on the continuity between Josh's new album and *Narwhal*, the last one he'd recorded. Josh had unbent and answered with a freedom that in him was close to garrulous.

There was a slight lull in the conversation. Josh stretched his legs out in front of him, waiting for the next question.

Milo smiled engagingly, and Ellie tensed, well aware that he was at his most dangerous when he was charming. "You know," Milo began in a conversational tone.

"I was in L.A. last weekend and I happened to run into Vivienne." At the sound of her name, Josh straightened, his eyes going cold again.

Milo chatted vivaciously on, his sharp eyes noting every sign of discomfort in his victim. "When I told her I was interviewing you this week, she had a few interesting things to say about your relationship in the weeks before your accident. She also told me that the songs on *Narwhal*, particularly 'Lot's Wife,' referred to your feelings for her. Can you confirm that?"

There was silence again, but this time the tension twanged through it like an out-of-tune E string. Then Josh stood up, the anger and disgust plain on his face.

"I don't suppose," he bit out, "that in this century it's possible for a man to be known for his work without having to provide a constant supply of gossip for the tabloids. Make up your mind, Connors. Are you a music critic or a gossip columnist?" Milo bridled, an angry flush drowning the freckles. "Either way, I don't want to talk to you anymore." Josh wrenched open the door and strode off.

"Well, really!" Milo punched the Stop button on his tape recorder with a petulant click. "The man's got a real bee in his bonnet about privacy, doesn't he?"

Eleanor opened her mouth to smooth things over. "You shouldn't have asked him that, Milo," she said instead. Milo began to look huffy. She pinned on a placating smile. "We did agree, you know," she said soothingly. "Do you want me to go try to get him back?"

"Heavens, no!" Milo folded his note pad shut with finality. "I hope you know what you're undertaking, trying to get that one good press," he added meaningfully.

Eleanor summoned all her poise from years of dealing with people who felt a temperament was the visible manifestation of artistic ability. "Milo, darling. I'm sure

Josh was on edge because he was nervous. After all, being interviewed by you—well, it's pretty important that it go well."

Milo directed a look of deep suspicion at her. "Is that sarcasm I detect, sweetie?"

"It's the truth and you know it." She grinned at him, to all appearances her usual relaxed self. But her hands, with their tense betraying knuckles, she had thrust into her pockets.

"Josh doesn't put on an act for the press," she went on casually. "He is what he is: an intensely private, incredibly creative man who doesn't want the pressure of being turned into a superstar. You have what amounts to an exclusive now, since I doubt he'll consent to any more interviews."

She leaned forward, noting Milo's sudden look of speculation. "Please go easy on the personal stuff. I know you like to give the public what they want to read, but if they want any other Joshua Blackmun albums, they'll have to put up with the scarcity of information about what he eats for breakfast."

"Do you happen to know what—well, never mind." Milo checked himself, looking somewhat sheepish. "I tell you, darling," he added confidentially, "sometimes *I* don't know if I'm a music or a gossip columnist." They stood, and he gave her another hug. "I'll go easy on your client," he promised. "Catch you later."

Ellie pushed through the *News* building's revolving glass doors and wrapped a plaid wool scarf tightly around her neck. The wind whistled down the narrow caverns of San Francisco's downtown business district, cold and damp with the sharp tang of salt from the bay.

She was preoccupied with going over the interview in her mind, trying to decide if it had been a total failure or not, so she didn't notice the tall figure standing by her car until she nearly bumped into him.

"Josh!" He leaned back against her car, his hands in the pockets of his jeans, a forbidding expression on his face. She stood facing him, her shoulders braced against the wind. Just seeing him made the treacherous tremors of excitement roil through her. But his expression left little doubt that it wasn't love he had on his mind.

"I thought you'd already left." She said it to be saying something, to fill the silence that stretched too thin between them.

He folded his arms across his chest, his hands looking big and rawboned against the worn leather jacket. "Were you skulking up there to avoid me, or to give a few more juicy details to your buddy?"

It was an unkind speech, and she flinched under it, but it served to get her armor into place. "I was trying to undo the damage. No thanks to you, I don't believe you'll be pilloried in Milo's Sunday column."

"No thanks to you, you mean," he growled. "I didn't ask to come within ten feet of him." He took a step closer, and she fought down her impulse to retreat. "Now do you understand my objections to this sort of thing? Now will you let up?"

Ellie prided herself on her calm even temperament, but she could feel the rare beginnings of anger stir. This man had no idea how hard she'd have to work to get decent publicity for him that wouldn't raise the specters of a past he seemed to dislike talking about. Instead of helping, he was actively hindering her efforts. And now he was going to hector her, as well. To complicate the whole mess, she had made the mistake of getting emotionally involved.

"Let me tell you something, Blackmun," she said evenly. "And try to get it through your thick skull, because I'm not going to tell you again. Until Peter calls me off, it's my responsibility to promote your album. If you want to make it hard on yourself, and if you want to see a lot of negative articles about you that bring up your past as an excuse for the rotten way you behave now, you're going about it in exactly the right way. And now—" she glanced at her watch "—if you'll excuse me, I have to go set up a photo session for you, so you can scowl and snarl your way through it."

For a moment he was still. Then he stepped closer, crowding her against the car door. "You have enough moxie for two, did you know that?" There was male frustration in his voice, as well as something else. She gaped at him and saw that he was trying to keep from laughing. "In case you've forgotten," he added, his words coming out in a gritty purr, "I know you're not as tough as you act. I know that underneath this Wonder Woman exterior—" his hand came out and slid around her back, pressing her even closer to him "—you've got a heart of gold."

His arms folded around her in slow-motion seduction. Helplessly she watched his mouth lower until she had to close her eyes. The touch of his lips fanned the turmoil within her into red-hot sensations that concentrated, for the moment, in her lips. He moaned deep in his throat and his tongue licked along her lower lip, pleading, demanding. Their mouths seemed to fuse together, moist and heated, making an electrical contact that charged every particle in her body. Then he was breaking away, drawing great heaving breaths. She felt the cold salty air inside her throat and realized she, too, was gasping.

He raised one hand and let it rest briefly on the fabric of her jacket above her breast. "A heart of gold," he said again, gazing intently into her bewildered eyes. "I'm counting on that."

He was halfway down the block before she could summon her wits. "Blackmun," she called loudly, but he didn't turn. A few people glanced curiously at her. She put a finger to her lips, expecting them to be swollen, and walked around to climb shakily into her car. She kept her eyes on his tall, spare figure until it was lost in the crowded distance. "Blackmun, you rat!" Her lips curved in an unwilling smile as she started her car for the long drive home.

5

THREE DAYS LATER, Eleanor parked in front of the converted lumberyard that housed Trax Records. She got out of the car and stood for a moment, inhaling the sharp, clean breeze off the ocean. Behind her, traffic rumbled down Highway 1. Before her were the hummocky swells of chaparral that clothed the cliffs of the Santa Cruz Bay. Streets were packed with beach houses, and shops and gas stations interrupted the brush, but nothing could completely suppress the wild aspect of the view. The sun shone fiercely in a cloudless blue sky, taking some of the sting from the cold rawness of the wind.

Eleanor knew that Josh was in the studio, working on his album. The edginess she'd felt since Peter had called that morning to okay the photo session peaked in a rush of feeling compounded of desire and fear. She sighed and lifted her face to the breeze, willing it to blow away her troubles.

Grady Williams pulled his large frame out of her little car with a series of profane grumbles. Grady was an excellent photographer; a meticulous craftsman who possessed an uncanny knack for finding the emotion behind the facade. But his first love was philosophy. He had been attending university for years, taking the courses that appealed to him without worrying about whether they furthered a degree. As a result, it had taken him six years to get a bachelor of arts degree, and he'd been happily toying with a masters in philosophy for the past

three and a half years. Photographing musicians for
Peter supported his academic habit.

Ellie watched, amused, as he loaded himself with
camera bodies and lens bags and ambled toward Trax's
main door like a bear in search of a good place to hiber-
nate. "How long is this going to take, anyway?" Even
his voice was bearlike, a low rumbling monotone that
could go on for hours when engaged in an absorbing
discussion of Pascal or Heidegger.

Ellie opened the door for him and followed him into
the cavernous interior of Trax Records. "Most of the
day, probably," she told him, heartlessly ignoring his
groan of protest. "Peter's paying you very well, so stop
making such a fuss."

He punched her playfully in the arm, almost felling
her. She reeled back helplessly through the crowd of
hopeful, weirdly dressed teenage punk rockers who
were always hanging around at Trax, and trailed Grady
across the shabby lobby to a flimsy partitioned-off corner that was Peter's office.

Peter wasn't there, of course. His desk was piled with
unsteady stacks of promotional literature, records both
in and out of their jackets, large manila envelopes with
cassettes and photos spilling out of them, unopened bills
in their give-away window envelopes. A crazy quilt of
thumbtacked posters and glossy photos glared from the
walls.

A new desk had been shoved into one corner, its top
still free of clutter. Behind it sat a harassed-looking
woman whom Ellie judged to be in her midforties. She
had the telephone cradled between shoulder and ear
while she scribbled on a message pad before her. "Yes,
of course I'll tell him." She glanced at Grady and then at
Eleanor. "Uh, excuse me."

"We're looking for Peter," Ellie said quickly. "He's expecting me. Eleanor Martinson."

There was a loud noise from the receiver, and the woman jumped. "Just a moment, Mr.... uh... er," she gabbled into the receiver. She covered it up again and whispered, "I don't know where he is. This place is a zoo! Already this morning there was a group with orange hair and purple faces, absolutely insistent! I think they're still out there in the lobby. I couldn't get them to leave. And then this whole mob dressed as mushroom clouds! You'll just have to look for him yourselves! Go on out and I'll buzz you through." She turned back to the telephone. "Right. Right. I'll see that he gets the message."

The phone rang again as soon as she hung it up, and Eleanor pulled Grady out the door. "Mushroom clouds?" he muttered as they passed through the cluster of orange hair and purple faces outside.

"The Eves of Destruction," Eleanor told him absently. Her concentration was on the forthcoming meeting with Josh. What would he say? What would she do? She had come armed with an invitation from her mother for Josh to have Thanksgiving dinner with the family next weekend. Whether she issued the invitation depended on Josh's behavior. If he was overbearing, if he again displayed his performer's ego, she had decided that she would start the heart-wrenching process of falling out of love with him.

The punks closed around them, clamoring to see Peter, but Ellie barely noticed. Grady lifted one arm and growled menacingly. "Be off!" Cowed, the punks fell back.

Peter had installed an inner, locked door to keep eager budding musicians from wandering around the recording studios, blundering in on sessions and making a nuisance of themselves. The crowd in the lobby had originated because Trax, as a small, independent label, was uncommonly receptive to undiscovered talent. In the past three years, Peter had added several promising new-wave bands to his list, along with bands representing his primary interests: bluegrass and country music. The Eves of Destruction were currently getting ready for a tour of England, hoping for the big break that would make them famous back in the U.S.

The door buzzed and they darted through before the punks could push after them. Ellie led the way briskly down an echoing concrete hallway. Above their heads some of the lumberyard signs still swung from the rafters: Nuts and Bolts, Tubing. To each side were soundproof walls, behind which were recording studios and rehearsal rooms.

The studios were numbered, the rehearsal rooms lettered. Room A, when they peeked into it, seemed overly full. The five young women who occupied it were wearing improbable wigs styled into wide, flat mushroom-cap effects that ranged in color from pale mauve to midnight purple. Their lithe bodies were encased in leotards dyed to match their hair and decorated with wide lightning bolts down the left side. One of the Eves played idly on an electric piano. The others broke off their conversation. "Hi, Ellie," they chorused.

"Hi, ladies." She yanked at Grady, who was rooted to the floor, and entered the room. "Are you ready for the invasion of Britain?"

The Eves made enthusiastic noises. Grady brought one hand up to smooth his bushy brown beard. He began to smile.

"This is Grady Williams." Ellie made a sweeping gesture. "The Eves of Destruction. You'll be taking their pictures, as well as Josh's, today. That's why they got all dressed up for you."

"My pleasure," Grady said, absorbing the sight of the leotards once more. "My *extreme* pleasure." He unslung his lens case and opened it. A couple of the Eves clustered around.

"Hey, wicked camera, man."

"Yeah, positively Kierkegaardian."

Grady paused in the act of fitting a wide-angle lens to his camera body. "You ladies into Kierkegaard?"

"Nah, I'm more a Hegelian myself."

"Joanne, don't knock Kierkegaard, man. I mean, the dude was *dangerous*."

"You guys are way out of line," broke in another Eve. "Locke is the one who really had it together."

The rest of the group turned on her. *"Locke?"* They spoke in unison, their voices thick with disgust.

Grady ripped open a box of film happily. "I think I'm going to like this assignment." He waved absentmindedly to Eleanor, his eyes on the Eves. "You can run along if you want. I'll just get to know the girls here and then find out what Peter has in mind."

Eleanor left him loading his camera and went on down the hall. There was no one in Rehearsal Room B, but the door of C was faintly ajar, and she could hear voices coming from within. She paused in the doorway, her heart knocking in her throat, her eyes scanning the room for a sight of Josh.

He was sprawled in a folding chair, his guitar resting carelessly in his lap. He was talking to Peter who stood by a tape console. There were other instruments on stands around the room, but the backup musicians who played them weren't in evidence.

Josh looked up and saw her standing in the doorway. For a long moment their gazes locked. Her heart pounded so crazily she wondered if he could see it trying to jump out of her shirt. Then a slow smile spread across his face.

"Well, here she is," he drawled. Tightening his fingers around the neck of the guitar, he played a few chords, which she recognized as the chorus of "Heart of Gold." Remembering the scene in San Francisco, she wondered if he'd managed to bury his hostility. He watched the confusion on her face and his smile deepened. "Miss Ellie," he said in his slow country voice, standing and putting down the guitar. "I'm entranced to see you again. You look real pretty today."

Suspecting sarcasm, she kept her expression bland. "Thank you, uh, Mr. Josh. What is this game we're playing today? 'Beverly Hillbillies'?"

His eyes sharpened and grew dangerous. Peter, ignored in his corner, cleared his throat. Ellie and Josh paid no attention.

"Well," Peter said to the room at large. "What happened to Grady? Couldn't he make it?"

"Hmm?" Ellie tore her attention from Josh for a moment. "Oh, he's in Room A with the Eves of Destruction, deep in photography and existentialism."

A pleased smile crossed Peter's face. "Those young women are going to get great press in England. They can play the socks off any punk rocker." Ellie barely heard him. He glanced from her intent face to Josh's, and cleared his throat again. "Guess I'll go on down and show Grady what I need."

"Good idea," Ellie replied absently. There was a soft click as Peter closed the door behind him, and then silence.

"I was born in Arkansas," Josh said finally. "That gives me the right to resent any implications that my accent is phony."

Ellie smiled slightly. "Having spent some time researching your background, I happen to know that you moved to Salinas when you were three years old."

He had the grace to look ashamed. "Well," he said defensively, "my parents both kept their accents as long as they lived. I like to get in touch with my origins occasionally, you know?"

"Your parents are dead?" The question slipped out,

and she bit her lip in vexation. A man as private as Josh
Blackmun probably didn't want to answer questions.

He didn't seem put out. Moving a step or two closer
he nodded, speaking as if the words were an after-
thought. "My dad died when I was ten. My mother
went the year before my first big success." He sighed. "I
always felt that was a mean trick of fate—to take away
the one person that gold record would have really
meant something to."

Ellie hesitated, but her curiosity was strong with any
client, and in this case she wanted badly to know everything there was to know about Josh. "Didn't it mean
something to you?"

He shook his head, again moving closer until he stood
so near that his breath seemed to stir the hair around her
face. "It was a nice little tune when I wrote it, but by the
time the producers finished drowning it in orchestration
I didn't even recognize it."

The words were commonplace, matter-of-fact; their
effect on Ellie was incandescent. She wanted so badly to
melt into his arms that it was painful to hold herself
aloof. She glanced briefly into his eyes; the burning in-
tentness there told her that Josh, too, was affected by
their closeness. His hand came up to cup her chin and
tilt it so that their eyes once again met and held.

"Do you—" There was a tremor in his husky voice.
He cleared his throat and continued. "If I were to put
my arms around you, sweet Ellie, would you flip me
onto the floor?"

Ellie took a deep breath. "N-no. No, I wouldn't do
that, Josh."

With infinite slowness he brought one arm around her
shoulders. "What would you do?"

She could bear the teasing no longer. "This!" She took
his face between her hands and brought it down so their
lips could meet. For a moment he was still with surprise.

She let the pent-up emotions of the past few days flow out in a searing, burning kiss that forced his response. Their mouths opened simultaneously, their tongues meeting with an exquisite electric shock.

Josh groaned and tightened his arms around her, his hands roaming hungrily over her back. She felt boneless, her whole being melting with delight. He groaned once more and she realized she was moving against him in ancient, seductive patterns. His body surged with need against hers while his tongue flicked lightning along her nerve endings.

Suddenly he collapsed on the floor. Josh clutched her to him so that they lay, with Ellie on top, in a confused tangle of arms and legs. They were encircled by folding chairs, and the thick pad of acoustic carpet cradled them. "Oh, lordy," Josh said with a sigh. "You did it anyway, you vixen. I'll get you for this."

She squirmed in confusion and his smile widened. "That feels good," he whispered. He took her lips again, easing her over until she lay cradled in one arm. His other hand began unfastening her crisp white blouse. The touch of his fingers was mesmerizing. She heard a heavy, ragged sound and realized that it was her own breath.

His lips trailed down the sensitive flesh of her shoulder. She trembled, wanting to feel his caress everywhere, paralyzed with desire. He captured one nipple gently between his teeth, charging the fires within her with urgency. He slipped his knee between her legs, his hand searching out the zipper of her pants. The pressure of his knee created a pleasurable ache that spread through the valley between her legs like wildfire.

Her hand was fumbling for his belt buckle when he sighed and pushed her away. She froze, opening her eyes to find his knowing gaze upon her. His smile was tender and rueful.

"This *is* a rehearsal room," he pointed out. "I believe we're past the point of needing to rehearse, little darlin'."

The endearment eased Ellie's tension. "I don't believe," she said, looking down at their disheveled bodies, hers nearly as long as his, "that anyone has ever called me a *little* darlin' before."

Josh looked, too, evidently pleased with what he saw. "A good, strong woman." He smoothed the firm curves of hip and thigh with a possessive hand and adopted his exaggerated drawl again. "Out in the backwoods, we value that. It can be a long haul uphill from the spring to the cabin, carryin' those heavy buckets of water." His hand closed gently around her right breast, his thumb absently toying with her erect, throbbing nipple. She swallowed, but he didn't seem to notice. "And then there are other things strength is useful for...."

His voice changed and Ellie saw that he was watching his hand on her breast. His hands were roughened with callouses. They looked very brown against the white of her skin. When he looked back up at her, his eyes had darkened with feeling in a way that seemed to collect and intensify her own emotions unendurably.

At last he looked away. She sat up to button her blouse, feeling the absurd threat of tears behind her eyes. Scrambling gracefully to her feet, she found his gaze on her again, his expression disturbingly blank. She could think of nothing to say that would ease the tension in the room.

Sitting easily on the floor, his shirt open to his waist to show the gleaming bronze skin and swirling dark hair beneath, Josh somehow made her control slip. She wanted to pin him to the floor and show him what it was like to be loved by a good, strong woman. Instead she turned away and ran her hands through her hair.

Behind her there was the sound of movement as he

got to his feet. "Ellie?" She couldn't answer. "Ellie, we need to talk."

"Not now." Her voice came out strangled, and she waited a moment before going on. "I don't want to talk about it now." She strove to calm her tumultuous pulse. "Would you...do you want to come over for Thanksgiving dinner?"

He said nothing, and she turned to face him. She hadn't meant to blurt out the invitation like that. She could read the wariness on his face before he masked it.

"Your place?"

"My parents, actually. It was my mother's idea. My family took quite a shine to you."

"They're nice people." He spoke at random. "Yeah, sure. I'd like that."

Peter came in while they were still staring helplessly at each other. He raised his eyebrows at the sight of Josh's unbuttoned shirt. "Too hot for you?" Though his voice held a gentle taunt, his look in Ellie's direction was mildly solicitous. "Listen, Grady will be ready in a minute, Josh. Ellie, you don't need to stay if you don't want to."

"Thanks," she murmured, moving toward the door.

"Oh, wait a minute." Peter smacked his palm lightly against his forehead. "I tell you, I'm totally out of it in the organization department. I think we need more than just a receptionist around here—I need someone in charge of my memory." He turned to Ellie. "I forgot to tell you about the tour."

"What tour?"

"Josh's tour, of course." He looked at her impatiently. "Didn't I tell you Josh had agreed to a tour? Guess not." Ellie glanced at Josh, but his face was impassive. "Those investors were so generous that I can send the Eves to England *and* ship Blackmun here around to a few select cities."

He turned to Josh. "The booking agent said no problem getting your gigs in the smaller venues starting at
New Year's—I gather there's a lot of flu going around in
the East, and a lot of groups have canceled. He's getting
on the advance work right away. I need you to send him
a press kit," he told Ellie. "Get his number from Yvette
in front and give him a call, will you? You can hammer
out the publicity angles between you."

Ellie forced herself to assume a semblance of her normal manner. "Fine, Peter. Be sure to tell Grady to get a
number of portrait-style shots for print-media release."
She pinned on a jaunty smile as she looked at Josh. "I'll
be seeing you around."

He took her hand and raised it lightly to his lips, ignoring Peter's quizzical frown. "Thanksgiving. I'll be
there in the morning. Give your mother my thanks for
the invitation." Fascinated, Ellie at last tore her eyes
away from his. "Goodbye," she mumbled, and fled the
room.

IT WAS FRIDAY AFTERNOON, nearly five o'clock. Ellie
could hear Marigold in the reception room of the agency
typing furiously, anxious to get home and check her
mailbox for news of her manuscript. Any moment Gena
would be coming in for the weekly wrap-up, wanting to
know if they were on schedule for the various promo-
tions they had going.

Ellie sighed with five-o'clock weariness. She felt overwhelmed with arrangements for Josh Blackmun, who
wouldn't agree to play in any concert hall seating more
than three thousand people, and wouldn't hold more
than two interviews per city, and absolutely put his foot
down at the notion of TV and radio talk shows. Ellie had
not spoken with him since their encounter at Trax, but
Peter faithfully relayed all his big ticket's demands, with
pleas for her to look after things so Josh wouldn't get

upset. Ellie respected Josh's objections to certain parts of the promotional ritual, but it made her job all the harder.

She was nearly finished with the press kit. All she needed was proof sheets from Grady, so she could select pictures to accompany the kits—and an extra copy for herself. *For my files*, she told herself, although she knew it was for the memories after Josh had gone. Probably by the time he finished the tour, with his reputation reborn and his album assured of a place at the top, he would have forgotten her.

She dialed Grady's number and waited for him to answer. His deep voice rumbled, "Hello."

"Hey, Grady," she began, then realized the phone was still ringing. Grady was standing in the door of her office, a young woman on each arm. Without their mushroom hairdos and lightning-struck leotards, Ellie almost didn't recognize them as Marlo and Joanne, bass and keyboard for the Eves.

"Thought we'd drop in on our way to Cleo's," Grady said, naming a popular watering hole for Friday happy hour. "I've got some proof sheets for you guys." He stepped back into the outer room long enough to bellow, "Front and center, Gena my dear."

Gena hurried into the room, chic and scented and a bit huffy from Grady's unceremonial summons. But when she saw the proof sheets he was neatly ranging on Ellie's desk her annoyance vanished. "Fantastic," she crooned, picking up a sheet of pictures of the Eves. Grady had photographed them on the beach at sunset, and the evening fog wreathed their leotards. "I've got a meeting with Peter in a few minutes, and these are just what I need. Thanks, Grady. I'll get back to you about the ones we want." She breezed out, leaving Ellie free to examine Grady's photos of Josh.

The ones in which Josh was formally posed were, for

the most part, somber, almost brooding. But there were
two excellent candid shots. In one he was laughing, his
head thrown back, the strong contours of his neck high-
lighted, and in the other he clutched a guitar, trium-
phant at having brought off a really good lick.

"Numbers nine and fourteen," she told Grady. "I'll
want fifty copies by Monday. Okay with you?"

"No sweat."

Ellie turned her attention to the two Eves. "How's it
going, Marlo, Joanne? Aren't you guys leaving Sunday
morning?"

Marlo nodded. "Two weeks in Great Britain. I can't
wait to visit David Hume's grave."

Ellie blinked. "Right. David Hume. Sounds like a lot
of fun."

"Hume, the skeptic." Grady spoke in his best
teaching-assistant's rumble. "The girls here are helping
me with my thesis," he added, beaming down impartial-
ly on Marlo and Joanne.

Joanne leaned forward. "Does this guy know his way
around the existentialists!" Her eyes were wide and
earnest.

"How old are you, Joanne?" Ellie's question was
abrupt, and Joanne blinked.

"I'm twenty-two, man. Thought you dudes at the
agency knew all there was to know about us."

"Gena's handling your promotion." Ellie felt a wave
of fatigue flood over her. She tidied the proof sheets into
a neat stack on her desk and opened the bottom drawer
for her handbag. The Eves projected youth and vitality
on a massive scale. Just contemplating it made her tired.

With an effort she roused herself to display interest.
"Did the philosophy come first, or the music?"

Marlo waved her hands around while she spoke.
"Hey, they were sort of synergistic, you know what I
mean? I mean, we were jamming together, and then

Joanne took a course in the early cats—Descartes, Kierkegaard, all those guys. I mean, the words just started pouring out. We've written some heavy tunes out of the whole experience."

Grady nodded genially. "When they get back, we're going to audit a course on Heidegger," he confided. He glanced at his watch. "We'd better get going if we want to snag a booth. You coming, Ellie?"

"Not today." Ellie straightened her shoulders, hiding a smile at Grady's complacent expression. She had never expected him to fall for all five members of a punk-rock band, but life was full of strange surprises. "You all go ahead. And good luck on your tour, girls."

Her office seemed dull after they were gone. She leaned back in her chair, feverish thoughts surging through her mind: Josh's brown hand on her white skin, his lips on hers, their bodies. . . .

Marigold suddenly appeared in the doorway, ready to leave. "Will you lock up, Ellie?"

Eleanor jumped to her feet. "I'm leaving, too." She had to get away, subdue her thoughts, or she'd find herself on the highway to La Honda.

Instead, she strode briskly to her car, drove home for her *gi*, and ended up at the old Quonset hut that housed her judo classes. For the next couple of hours she astounded the instructor by tossing all competitors around as if they weighed no more than feathers.

"She is ferocious tonight," Omatsu Kinsai murmured to his partner, co-owner of the judo dojo.

"She should be taking karate," sniffed his partner. He stepped forward, bowed solemnly to Ellie, and flipped her decisively to the mat.

Ellie looked up at the metal ribs of the ceiling, with its bare, glaring lightbulbs swinging in the constant draft. She closed her eyes for a moment. It was a relief to have finally been thrown. Having the breath knocked out of her seemed also to dispose of the panic that had been filling her. Now she felt able to confront the circumstances of her life again with dignity. She rose to her feet, bowed gratefully to her *sensei* and his partner, and retreated toward the changing rooms. There were five days to get through before Thanksgiving. It would be hard, but she'd manage somehow.

6

THE FEVER OF ANTICIPATION at seeing Josh was at its peak Wednesday evening, gnawing at Ellie's composure, keeping her awake to toss and turn far into the night. As a result, she overslept Thanksgiving morning and woke with barely enough time for her morning run before her mother would need her help in the kitchen.

She threw on her sweats, laced up her running shoes and headed downstairs. Opening her parents' kitchen door, she stuck her head inside. "I'm just off for my run, mom, be back...." Her voice trailed off incredulously. Sitting at the table cutting up celery was Josh, looking as comfortable and at home as if he'd been there all his life.

"Howdy," he murmured, letting his drawl lengthen as his eyes scanned her. She was uncomfortably aware of the hole in the knee of her sweat pants and the disreputable appearance of her favorite old UCSC sweat shirt. But what she read in his expression made it plain that he was more interested in the long, well-rounded body beneath the clothes. His gray eyes, when they connected with hers, were so full of lazy passion that she caught her breath. She looked away quickly, feeling uncomfortable at fielding such a look in the presence of her mother.

He interpreted her glance correctly, and his smile deepened. "Blanche stepped out for a minute." He got up from his chair and came closer, forcing her out the door with his inexorable stride. Somehow she wound up pinned against the side of the house next to the back door, Josh's hands planted firmly on the wall on either side of her shoulders. He was on the step below her, so their eyes met on the same level. In his the spark of mischief was strong and, she realized, seductive. Seeing him in this playful mood caught at her heart.

"I get the feeling," he murmured, "that you don't want me to kiss you in front of your mother."

Ellie swallowed. His mouth was two inches from hers. She felt an overpowering urge to press the softest, sweetest of kisses onto his lips, to weave a net of promise and enchantment around him that he would be powerless to break. She had a moment's rapt image of him as her captive, hers to toy with, to torture with rising desire as he was doing to her, until finally she took him to undreamed heights of satisfaction.

Then the image shattered. The relationship she wanted was not between captive and master, no matter who held the upper hand. She wanted the fierce and heady satisfaction of equality. She wanted to be so strongly planted in his mind that he couldn't get her out, just as she couldn't get him out of her head night or day.

As if he sensed her thoughts, Josh's hands dropped to her shoulders and tightened. Ellie felt a change in him. The playful light was gone from his eyes, replaced with something akin to anger. The anger saddened her, but she knew instinctively that it was protection.

A soft answer turneth away wrath. Without deliberating the consequences of her action, she let her lips touch his, not with the soft seduction of the secret conqueror, nor with the submission of the captive. The solace of her understanding flowed out, defusing the anger.

His hands relaxed, finally, and she let the kiss end. He sighed and moved back to the door. "You know, you've really worked a miracle, woman."

She looked at him hazily, letting the excitement of his

kiss percolate through her like bubbles through champagne. "Yes." After a second she asked, "How?"

He laughed. "A couple of months ago I would have said there were no publicists anywhere who wouldn't sell their clients down the river for some good ink." He ran a hand through his dark hair, pushing an errant lock off his forehead. "And here I am, wanting to spend all my time with a woman who's not only a publicist with integrity, but *my* publicist." Shaking his head, he took one of her hands and squeezed it lightly. "Guess you'd better go for your run."

She nodded, uncertain of his meaning or his mood. It was a relief when his lips curved up in that lazy smile and his voice assumed its down-home drawl. "No need to hurry." He ran a caressing finger across the vulnerable territory of her bottom lip. "That turkey ain't going nowhere."

"Right." She smiled back at him, the brilliant, sunny smile of a child, and turned to walk briskly down the drive, swinging her arms. At the road she broke into an easy, graceful run. Rounding the corner, she glanced back to see him watching her, an upright figure at the side of the house. Before she got out of sight she looked again, but he had gone back into the warm kitchen.

Holiday dinners were traditionally a time of benign chaos in the Martinson family, with far-flung offspring reassembling themselves for the occasion. But this time Eleanor was aware only of Josh: helping Robbie with the leaves for the table; exclaiming with enthusiasm over the perfect turkey; sharing the wishbone with her in a mock-serious battle over who got the wish.

Throughout the day Josh listened, smiled, enjoyed the excellent meal, and took Blanche's probing questions in good part. Robbie showed a distressing tendency to want blow-by-blow accounts of his entire recording history until Ellie took him out of the room and effectively squelched him. After that Robbie was careful to avoid any topic that might be construed as touching Josh's career.

When it was time to clean up, Blanche excused Ellie and Josh. "You two were cooks," she explained. "You've done your share. Maybe Josh would like a walk on the beach, Ellie."

Ellie looked suspiciously at her mother, but Blanche returned an innocent gaze. "Since it's such a nice day," she added.

"I would like that." Josh kept his voice noncommittal, and Ellie acquiesced. It wasn't hard to agree; she wanted nothing more than to be alone with Josh.

To make him suffer for the smile she'd seen lurking around his mouth when her mother made that artless suggestion, Ellie marched Josh firmly down the hill toward the distant, restless blue of the sea. He cast a longing look at the staircase leading to her apartment as they went past it, but Ellie pretended not to see. If they went to her apartment, she knew what would happen. She wanted Josh. Just the thought of him in her bed was intoxicating. But the very intensity with which she wanted him made her wary of him.

They walked silently along the deserted beach at the high-tide mark, where the sand was smooth and hard packed.

"You have a very nice family." Josh's voice broke the stillness.

"Kind of noisy, though." She glanced at him sideways. "Sorry about Robbie. He can't get over his luck in actually getting to know one of his musical heroes."

Josh chuckled. "You didn't have to put the kibosh on him like that. I don't mind his questions. He's certainly not as nosy as Milo Connors."

Ellie stiffened, but there was nothing in Josh's face except that look of mischief. "That was a dirty crack," she said with a false, pleasant smile.

"What are you going to do? Plant me upside down in the sand?" His taunt held a teasing note. Ellie grinned brilliantly up at him.

"If I wanted to, I could," she taunted back. "You're soft as a grape, Blackmun. One flip—" she made an illustrative movement with her wrist "—and you'd be down for the count."

"Oh yeah?" He faced her measuringly. "Let's see some of this famous judo stuff you're always bragging about."

"Bragging?" She bristled with indignation. "You're riding for a fall, buster." She planted her hands on her hips and stared at him. "Go ahead, come at me. Unless you're chicken."

"I wouldn't want to hurt you," he began, liking the sturdy way she stood with her back to the wind, her mouth set in a firm line.

She snorted at his words. "Not very likely, I should say."

"I guess I should warn you, I picked up a few pointers from Sam before dinner." Ellie's brother-in-law, Sam Ogachi, had sparked her interest in judo as a sport.

She shrugged disdainfully. "I hope he told you how to fall. Do you want action, Blackmun, or do you just want to talk about it?"

"I'll show you action," he growled, goaded. He lunged at her, his hands outstretched for a tackle. Before he could touch her she'd sent him sailing through the air, landing flat on his back in the soft sand beyond the high-tide line. A grin of triumph lit Ellie's face.

"I hope that taught you a lesson," she began. Before she could finish he launched himself at her, bringing her down with his arms around her knees. She collapsed easily enough, but when he moved to get on top of her she brought her feet up and he somersaulted over her head. Again he lay on his back, staring up at the blue sky.

"Had enough?" She plopped on top of him, pinning him to the sand, her eyes alight with victory.

"No need to gloat." He reached under his back and removed a piece of driftwood. "I was just making sure you know how to repel attackers."

Her hands moved to brush the sand out of his hair, and the curve of her mouth softened. She lowered her face until it was tantalizingly close to his. "Say 'uncle,'" she whispered. She'd loosened his arms, and his hands moved cautiously up her back. She could sense the desire surge strongly within him. She could feel the sultry emotions playing over her face. "Say 'uncle,' and I'll give you something."

"What?" His voice came out in a helpless croak. She liked the fascinated way he watched her as her tongue flicked out to run across her lips, leaving a sheen of moisture behind. Somehow knowing he was brought low by her seduction enhanced her own arousal. He rocked his hips slowly against her as she straddled him, and passion flared through her.

"Say 'uncle.' Better yet, say 'aunt.'" Her mouth was so close to his she could feel his hot breath fanning her. He tried to lift up to capture her mouth, but her hands kept his head motionless. He arched against her, not really trying to get away. She rode easily with the motion, her eyes dancing as she swayed against him. He groaned, his body burgeoning.

"I won't say it," he gasped. His hands slipped under her jacket, her sweater. She wore no bra, and his fingers slid over the smooth globes of her breasts, his thumbs brushing the rising thrust of her nipples. Now it was his turn to triumph.

"You say 'uncle,'" he said, gently squeezing the firm flesh he held. "Say it, or else."

"No way." She was breathing heavily, but her knees still held his body in place. Her hands tightened in his silky black hair. She put her mouth against his ear and let the whispered breath of her words sizzle into his brain. "I guess we'll have to call it a draw. . . ."

This time when her tongue darted out it skimmed the sensitive surface of his lip. He drew in a raspy breath. "Do it again."

"Not unless you—"

He moved suddenly, rolling over so she was underneath, her long legs on either side of his, her hands still buried in his hair. She laughed, her whole body alive with sensation. She wanted to make love right there, with the raw ocean wind at their backs.

"Do it like this," he whispered, lowering his mouth. The touch of his mouth went to her head, stronger than any wine, stronger than anything she'd ever felt. Her mouth flowered under his; her body trembled. He sent one hand down the long line of hip and thigh, back up the inside of her leg. "That's where I want to be," he said into her mouth as his hand touched between her legs. Even through her jeans she knew he could feel the heat. "Oh God, that's where I want to be."

She murmured something, she didn't know what. He found the snap of her jeans. "I want to bring you pleasure, little darlin'. I need to know you need me." Their lips joined hotly, eagerly, his hand cupping the heart of her desire as she moved against him uncontrollably. Her soft cries fed his own fierce need, pushing him over the point of control.

She shuddered, her eyes squeezed tight, her body pulsing against him. At last the thud of her heart slowed and she could open her eyes to meet his tender gaze.

"This is a public beach, you know." Her voice was rueful.

He glanced at the dunes behind them, the ocean in front of them, the gulls that cried noisily overhead. "I don't see anybody."

She knew there was high, rosy color on her cheeks. He helped her zip her jeans. "There's probably half a dozen binoculars and telescopes trained on us right now," she muttered, struggling to sit up. She gestured at the distant hills crowned with houses.

He smiled lazily. "Too bad they've got nothing better to do than watch us." When she would have gotten to her feet, he held her tighter, close against his side. "Could they see us," he murmured into her ear, "if we were in your apartment?"

She pushed away and rose to her feet in a lithe movement, combing wisps of hair from her face with her fingers. "We'll have to get back anyway." The wind was turning sharp with the approach of sunset. Already vivid reds and yellows stained the sky.

He didn't answer and she stood over him for a minute longer, her legs planted apart on the sand, unaware that the ocean breeze whipped her hair into a dark nimbus around her head.

"Weren't you listening, Blackmun?" She bent and reached a hand toward him. "We have to start walking if we're going to get back. You know . . . walking . . . as in one foot in front of the other."

He grabbed her hand and surged upward, taking her by surprise, gripping her close. "You are so beautiful." The words were unexpected, seeming to spill out of him. "Out here with the wind and the waves I could write fifty songs, and they'd all be about you."

The effect of his words was immediate. She froze. The warmth in her eyes turned glacial. She was out of his arms as swiftly as if he'd struck her.

"I should have known." Her voice was a harsh whisper.

"Known what?" There was puzzlement in his voice, as well as sudden anger. He grasped her shoulders roughly. "What the hell is happening here? What did I say?"

"Go ahead." Her calm control was completely gone. She twisted out of his hands, her fists clenched, her face white. "Why don't you write a few songs, get them on the radio, mention how easily I came to your bed, how clumsy I was there. It's nothing new for me, I assure you." She brought her hands up to her cheeks to dash away the angry tears. His voice was gentler when he spoke.

"I don't have the foggiest notion what you're talking about, honey."

Her chest heaved as she drew in breath. "Then let me explain," she retorted. "Perhaps you remember a sweet little ditty called 'Ice Woman'? Came out five years ago?" He nodded, his eyes narrowed against the emotions that played across her face.

She took another breath. "It was written and performed by my ex-husband. Garrison Hanley." She barely heard his muffled exclamation of surprise. Turning, she faced the ocean, and he moved closer to catch the words she spoke so dully.

"We were separated at the time. Garrison was under contract to the same big recording conglomerate that I worked for. I was a junior publicist." Her laugh was a bitter, ragged sound. "I figured later he just married me because he thought I'd be able to get him great press. His first two albums went nowhere, and he blamed me for that. We fought, and I kicked him out." She locked her fingers together to still their twisting agony. Josh seemed to want to reach out, to take her hands in his, but stood silent instead.

"It was just my luck that the song he wrote to spite me would be his breakthrough. Maybe it was the only thing he ever did with any true emotion in it. He made it very plain in the lyrics just who and what he was talking about. He did everything but mention my name. All the details of our private life, the not very delicious details of my failure to please him—"

At that Josh stirred, touching her with reassurance. "Ellie, what kind of nonsense is this? You must know . . . surely you know by now there's nothing whatever wrong with the way you respond."

She shrugged him off. "Garrison was good at pretending, too, until it became obvious that marriage to me was not providing adequate strokes to his oversized ego." She faced him defiantly. "I have only myself to blame now. I knew when I met you that musicians were poison. They take your tenderest feelings and spread them out all over the airwaves for everyone in the country to snigger at. I should have known better than to fall . . . ."

Her throat turned suddenly dry. She stared at him, feeling the color drain from her face.

When he spoke his voice was harsh, gravelly. "Than to fall . . . ?"

She spoke the words defiantly. "Than to fall in love with you. That's right, Blackmun. I'm in love with you. What a drag, eh? Another swooning female to worry about giving the polite brush-off to." She gulped some air. "Well, I'll make a deal with you. You don't write any songs about me, and I'll remove myself from your life posthaste. You won't believe how fast I'll—"

"I don't want to hear anymore." There was unreasoning fury in his face. He grabbed her and shook her as if that could stop her words. "My God, you've got a load of poison there. Do you pour it all over every man who comes into your life, or were you saving it for me? No, don't tell me! I can guess." She lifted defiant eyes to his, trying not to show how shaken she was by his attack.

He spoke more quietly. "I won't be cast as the villain, Ellie. I'm not to blame for your stupid ex-husband's criminal lunacy." He brought his face closer. "And I make no deals." He thrust her away and turned toward the hills, running his hands through his hair in frustration. "Did you drive him crazy the way you're driving me? A sane, intelligent man would be getting as far away as possible right now."

The surf pounded and roared behind her, just like the rushing in her ears.

"A sane, intelligent woman would be buying you a ticket."

MARIGOLD BUSTLED in and slapped a folder efficiently on Ellie's desk. "There you are. Itinerary and plane tickets to New York City and points beyond." She sniffed audibly. "It's not that I mind doing things for Josh Blackmun, but I don't understand why Trax couldn't have made the travel arrangements."

Ellie continued to sit with her chair tilted back as far as it would go, her legs crossed on a corner of the desk, her chin propped in her fist as she stared out the window. "Yvette is swamped, according to Peter. Thanks for doing that, Marigold." Her voice was listless. "Why don't you run it by Trax for me? I've got a lot of work to do here."

Marigold was indignant. "So do I. Real work, not 'staring out the window' work." Her eyes turned dreamy. "Maybe Josh could come by and pick them up himself," she suggested artlessly. "I'll be glad to give them to him."

"No, thanks." From the corner of her eye Ellie could see Marigold shrug and leave. She scrutinized the tips of her spectator pumps and resumed her gloomy thoughts.

In the two weeks since Thanksgiving, Ellie had heard nothing from Josh. Not too surprising, she concluded, considering the distasteful scene they'd had. Only two sleepless nights had been necessary to teach her that she didn't truly compare him to her ex-husband. Who should know better than she how painfully full of integrity Joshua Blackmun was? He was nothing like Garrison.

But that didn't alter the fact that when she'd so gauche-
ly blurted out her love, he hadn't said the magic words.
Now, on top of the hurt, she felt betrayed by herself for
the realization that all her anger would probably have
melted into nothing if he'd only loved her back.

Instead his first impulse had been to run. Twenty-four
hours hadn't passed after their fight before Peter was
telling her that Josh wanted to start his tour as soon as
the booking agent could set up concert dates. And as if
it would be some kind of wonderful treat, Peter had
asked her to accompany the tour. Under the circumstances, there was nothing she'd rather *not* do.

She scowled at the ivy that shook its green encroaching leaves outside the window. So let Blackmun run,
then. Let him pass up the best deal on a lover that he
would ever find. She would get over him. She'd gotten
over Garrison. Of course, five years ago she'd been
younger, more resilient. And even in the first days of
their courtship and marriage, Garrison had never pro-
voked the kind of response from her that Josh did.

She swung her legs down smartly to the floor. "Stupid
watering pot of a woman," she muttered crossly. A
shadow fell across her desk. When she looked up, Peter
stood there, regarding her quizzically.

"What did you say?" He looked misleadingly polite.

"None of your damned business." She smiled sweetly.
"Did you need something?"

Peter sighed and draped himself over the chair in
front of her desk. "Another one," he said as if to himself. "Everywhere I go there are horribly grouchy people
snapping my head off for nothing, swearing to themselves. It's enough to make you retire from society."

"Sorry to be such a bitch," Ellie said carelessly, not
really meaning it. "I take it you're here for a reason."

"I wanted to pick up our tickets," Peter began. "Marigold told me—"

"*Your* tickets?"

"You knew we were leaving tonight, didn't you?" Peter frowned at her. "Gena said—"

"Gena told me nothing of this." Ellie didn't mean to snap, but she was nearer to losing her temper than she ever had been in her office. "I was under the impression that the tour started December 29. So why are you leaving two weeks before Christmas? Kindly take it from the top and don't leave out the details."

"Josh and I," Peter said, enunciating carefully, "are leaving tonight. For New York. Where we will do the final mix on some of the tunes that require the services of a certain very famous keyboardist who won't leave the Big Apple. I will return after the New York club dates. Josh will go on to Chicago and the rest of his tour. Why didn't Gena tell you this?"

"I don't know." Distractedly Ellie ran her hands through her hair. "We've both been busy. When did you decide to change the plans?"

Peter shrugged, eyeing her closely. "I thought you could tell me." His smile disarmed her. "All of a sudden Blackmun's hot to get to New York—doesn't want to wait, wants to finish our recording sessions there, can't do anything but work and gripe. And, somehow, I get the idea that you know what's causing all this."

An uprush of elation stabbed through the gloom that surrounded her. So Blackmun was disturbed! She had to remind herself fiercely that it meant nothing to her before she could answer Peter.

"I couldn't say." She kept her voice light and searched desperately for a red herring. "Isn't this going to cost you a lot of money? You'll be running up quite a tab with two extra weeks of hotel bills, studio time and expensive musicians."

Peter closed his eyes in mock pain. "Don't mention the money," he moaned. "It's breaking my heart. But I'll tell you something, Ellie." He leaned across her desk, his face earnest. "This album is going to put Trax over the top. Blackmun is fantastic! They'll be proclaiming this a masterpiece from coast to coast. If he wants to add a little gloss by getting Keith Redmont to put down some piano and vocal backups, well, it's worth it."

"Keith Redmont!" Ellie stared. "He rarely does guest appearances on anyone else's wax. And isn't he under contract to—"

"Spare me," Peter ordered testily. "I've spent a hell of a week talking to his record company. But they finally consented. As for Keith, Josh spoke to him for a few minutes and he committed—just like that!" He snapped his fingers. "Evidently they're pretty good friends. But even for the sake of friendship, Keith wouldn't agree to come out here. He has his own studio, luckily, in this big fancy co-op apartment. In fact, Josh is going to stay there, so the cost won't be as bad as it could be."

"Umm," Ellie agreed. Her mind was still dwelling on Josh's imminent departure. It meant nothing to her, of course, since she wouldn't see him whether he was in Santa Cruz or New York. Still, it left a desolate feeling that successfully squashed the remains of elation. Gradually she became aware of quiet in the room and saw Peter watching her expectantly.

"Uh, I beg your pardon," she mumbled.

Peter sighed. "I'm used to it. I said, I wish you'd reconsider and show up in New York for the *Rolling Stone* interview." Getting Josh ink in the prestigious national music-review magazine had been a major coup on Ellie's part. "No matter how good the press has been to date— and considering Josh's attitude it's been surprisingly good—if he blows it with *Rolling Stone* he's blown it in a major way. I'll go to it with him, of course, but I have no substitute for your famous tact, Ellie my love. If you were there I'd feel more comfortable."

Gena appeared, knocking lightly on the open door. "Not in conference, I hope?" She turned to Peter, a frown marring her perfect forehead. "Peter, what on earth is—"

"Not right now, Gena darling," he interrupted hastily. "I was just trying to convince Ellie to go to New York, after all. In fact, I could probably get back four or five days earlier if I didn't have to be there to hold Josh's hand for the first gig. Ellie could do that just fine. Can't you reschedule her projects so she can leave?"

Gena transferred the frown to Ellie. "I thought she was going. I requested she go. Ellie, *dear*, what is this all about?"

Ellie moved uneasily in her seat. She'd told Gena in no uncertain terms that she wouldn't go on tour with Josh, wouldn't even accompany him to New York for the *Rolling Stone* interview. Gena had merely replied that she thought Ellie should go. And that, for Ellie, had been the end of it.

Now Gena was going to act the boss, and Ellie would be put in the invidious position of making it clear that she'd rather look for another job altogether than brave the hazards of New York—and Joshua Blackmun.

Peter stood, obviously wanting to escape the inevitable scene. "You settle it between you. And Ellie, if you decide to go, give me a call so I can rearrange my schedule. We don't leave for the airport till eight o'clock tonight." He walked out the door, then whisked back in, a lidded wicker basket in his hands. "I almost forgot." With a mischievous smile at Gena, he flipped open the lid on the basket and set it on Ellie's desk. "I was asked to deliver this present to you." With a broad smile he strode out.

Bemused, Ellie stared at the basket. Two silky paws appeared on its rim, followed by a quivering, wet nose and big brown pansy-shaped eyes in a furry brownish-red face.

"It's a puppy!" Gena sounded dazed. "What on earth...?"

The puppy jumped eagerly, trying to clamber out of the basket. It had a wide, happy mouth and a little pink tongue with which it began to wash the hand Ellie held out. She plucked the little round dynamo of fur out of the basket and held it to her cheek. The puppy squirmed in ecstasy, trying to lick her face, her hair, anything it could reach.

"It's so cute!" Gena chattered on. "Where do you suppose it came from? And why did Peter give it to you?" There was an odd note in her voice, but Ellie was too dazed to analyze it.

"I know where it came from." She cradled the puppy in her arms. "It's a girl. Bertha's sweet little daughter."

"Bertha?" Gena sounded edgy. Ellie glanced at her in amusement.

"Don't worry. If Bridget has an accident, I'll clean it up."

"Bridget?" Gena was momentarily diverted from her grievance. "Is that what you're naming her?"

"It seems to fit." Ellie hugged the little puppy again, then tucked her back in the basket.

"Ellie." Gena sat determinedly in the client chair. "You will go to New York."

Ellie looked at her. "I've already told you my feelings on the subject, Gena. I'd rather not go into it again."

"You have to go!" Suddenly Gena was crying, her shoulders heaving as she searched her pockets for a tissue. "Now he's giving you gifts. It gets worse all the time."

Ellie thrust a box of tissues into Gena's hands and stared blankly at her. "I don't understand. Why should the fact that Josh gave me a puppy make things worse?"

"Josh?" Gena stopped sniffling, her eyes alert. "It wasn't from Peter?"

"Of course not." Ellie perched on her desk and looked speculatively down at her employer. "I think you'd better tell me what all this is about."

Gena let loose a flood of eloquence. She was in love with Peter—had been for months—and wanted him more with each passing day. But he treated her as a friend and business associate, nothing more.

"It's because you're around, of course," she said with a hint of resentment in her glance at Ellie. "You're so big and *vibrant*, it's easy for us tiny ones to get overshadowed." She smoothed her dress complacently over her slight figure as she spoke.

Ellie repressed a sharp retort. "You know that's bull," she said calmly instead. "You're twice as attractive as I am in a feminine, ruffly kind of way, so don't hand me any of that garbage. Peter cares nothing for me romantically, and the feeling is reciprocated. You have a clear field."

Gena narrowed her eyes. "You may care nothing for him," she replied, "but he'd only need a little encouragement to fall for you. I can tell. Well, if he's ripe for anyone, I want to make sure it's me." Her face softened, and she put one hand pleadingly on Ellie's sleeve. "Please, honey, just go for two weeks of the tour. You don't have to do the whole thing—skip L.A. if you want. Just give me a couple of weeks without competition, and I know I can have Peter where I want him."

"That's revolting!" Ellie paced over to the window and looked out at the encroaching tendrils of ivy. "You make it sound as if Peter has no options."

"He doesn't." Gena spoke with confidence. "I'm going to be the best thing that ever happened to that man. And he's going to be the best thing that's happened to me since Hal died. All I need is a little time."

"But Gena—" Ellie broke off helplessly. She turned back and saw Bridget's basket rocking vigorously back and forth. There was a note tucked into the wicker that she'd overlooked. Pulling it out, she felt a quiver at the sight of Josh's bold scrawl on the single folded page.

"Bertha sends her compliments and one of her offspring," he'd written. "She demands visiting rights, schedule to be negotiated after tour. Josh."

Ellie stared stupidly at the paper for a moment, then crumpled it in her hand. She realized Gena was speaking.

"You're an intelligent woman," Gena was saying. "You can see my side of it—"

"I'm a foolish, foolish woman," Ellie interrupted her. She smiled and stroked the puppy. "I'll call the travel agency." She glanced at her watch and saw with surprise that it was past five o'clock. "I'll call them tomorrow. Better yet, I'll let Marigold call them since she has a copy of the tour itinerary. If I leave December 28 or 29 I'll be there for the interview on the thirtieth." She thumbed through her desk calendar, making a few notations. "That gives me time to wrap up everything I'm working on here. And it lets Peter get back here by Christmas, so make your plans accordingly."

"You mean—"

"I don't promise to do the whole tour, but I will be gone at least two weeks. Is that okay with you?" She picked up the puppy basket, her handbag and briefcase and brushed past Gena, who stood stock-still with surprise.

"Ellie?" Gena's voice was plaintive. "What's going on here? You change your mind just like that—" she snapped her fingers "—because someone gives you a puppy? I don't get it."

"Don't waste your time on my motives," Ellie murmured, gazing radiantly down at Bridget's wriggly body. "You have your work cut out for you, after all." She paused with her hand on the door, clearly waiting for Gena to leave so she could lock her office.

"I don't understand," Gena mumbled. Then her face

brightened. "I'll tell Peter about your change of plans," she volunteered. "Perhaps he'd like to have Christmas dinner at my place." Her face turned dreamy.

"Whatever." Ellie gestured impatiently. "I need to get Bridget home now. See you tomorrow."

7

NEW YORK WAS A COLD, noisy, dirty city. That was Ellie's initial impression. Her cab ride from the airport had been terrifying; her hotel room, although horrendously expensive, was just the littlest bit seedy. When she rested her hand on the windowsill to look out at the congested streets, it came away gritty with black city dirt.

Nevertheless, she continued to gaze out through the faded brocade draperies. Peter had grandly insisted that she stay right in Manhattan, close to Keith Redmont's luxurious penthouse and not that far from the Music Hall, the nightclub where Josh would be performing. He had wrangled an invitation for Ellie to stay at Keith's, too, but she'd refused.

She wanted to see Josh with a burning urgency, but she was afraid, too—afraid that her feelings were stronger than his, that he would feel fettered by the love he knew she carried for him, that the first time she saw him again might be the time their relationship ended. So she stood at the window, watching the traffic with blind eyes, waiting for the evening.

It was three days before the end of the year; tonight would be the first of Josh's three New York concerts. The booking agent had been lavish with Ellie's press kit. Local papers were carrying the story prominently in their Entertainment sections. Peter, during his recent stay, had guided Josh through two newspaper interviews, which had come out well, all things considered. As a result, all three concerts were sold out.

Peter was back in Santa Cruz now. He'd left just before Christmas, having wrapped up the recording sessions. When she'd spoken to him on his return, his enthusiasm had overridden her doubts about the need for her to go to New York.

"It's going to be a fantastic album," he told her over the phone the day before she left. "I'm getting it out as fast as I can. We ought to be shipping by the time the *Rolling Stone* interview comes out. If that goes okay, we're home free."

The *Rolling Stone* interview was set for the next day. Ellie had sent Josh a polite little note before she'd left, reminding him of the interview. She'd sent a similar letter to Claudette Cort, the *Rolling Stone* reporter, confirming their schedule and gently reiterating Josh's position on personal questions.

Now she could feel the jitters rising inside her. She'd never been in charge of so important an interview before. She'd never met Claudette Cort. "I'm just a hick publicist from the far-out fringes of California," she muttered aloud. Certainly that was how the reporter would see her.

She pressed her forehead to the cool, reviving glass, forgetting about the dirt. *Please don't let me screw it up*, she prayed. Then she put her suitcase on the bed and began to unpack. She would be in Manhattan four days; she might as well make herself comfortable. She would unpack her sweats and jogging shoes and go for a run in Central Park. That would make her feel better.

She had lifted the last of her clothes from the suitcase when she heard a knock on the door. She swallowed, then walked over to open it. But it wasn't Josh. It was the bellhop carrying a big florist's box. He lingered while she opened it.

"Nice roses." He spoke with the offhand voice of someone who's seen everything. "I'll get you a vase."

Ellie barely heard him. She was staring at the red, velvety petals that filled the box. They took her back to a battered water pitcher filled with blossoms that could have been the twin of these. She opened the card with numb fingers.

Welcome to New York. Meet me backstage tonight after the show. And don't kiss the flowers unless you're willing to do the same by me.

It was unsigned, but she knew that arrogant scrawl. Smiling tremulously, she picked up one perfect bloom and brought it to her lips. There was a cough from the door, and she turned to see the bellboy watching her blandly.

"Here's your vase, ma'am."

She thanked him vaguely, then realized that his continued presence was due to her failure to tip him. She grabbed a bill from her handbag and thrust it into his hands, almost pushing him out the door. In a happy daze she arranged the roses carefully in the tall, slightly tarnished silver vase, setting it on the wobbly writing table by the window.

Bundled up in sweat pants and long underwear, she left her key at the desk and went out into the wintry afternoon. From her fourth-story window she had seen Central Park's vast green-brown oasis just two streets away. She headed toward it, fascinated in spite of the cold wind that nipped her nose, at the variety of people thrusting past her on the sidewalks, the chic stores and brightly decorated windows with their Christmas motifs. Everyone seemed smartly dressed and self-assured; she felt out of place in her exercise clothes. She was relieved when she was finally in the park, trotting along the paths, letting the raw air burn a path into her lungs.

By the time she got back to her hotel it was dusk. Her excitement built as she rode the elevator to her floor. She felt cleansed of her earlier confusion. Taking the place of the leaden doubt and anxiety that had been weighing her down was a fresh anticipation of the evening.

She would need a shower; she would want some dinner. There were hours to pass before she would see Josh. There was something piquant in the torture of waiting, of knowing that he, too, was waiting, thinking about her presence in the audience that evening.

She had a sandwich sent up to her room, signed the room-service check, and smiled slightly at the thought of Peter's face when he saw how much this was costing him. The money from his investors must be burning a hole in his pocket. Otherwise he would never have insisted that she go along for the duration of the tour.

The New York concerts would culminate in a New Year's Eve show with Keith Redmont. Then three nights in Chicago, two nights in Houston, two nights in St. Louis and two more in Portland, before a return to California and the four Los Angeles concerts.

The whole thing would take three weeks. And now she allowed herself the exquisite pleasure of dwelling on how far a relationship could go in that amount of time.

She dressed carefully, if casually, in a hand-knit wool sweater and well-creased cords, her warm fur-lined boots and long quilted down coat fortifying her against the cold. Even so, when she stepped out the hotel door she abandoned the idea of walking the twelve blocks to the concert hall.

Summoning a cab, she berated herself for forgetting to bring a hat or a scarf. All her winter clothes had been bought for ski trips, and most were unsuitable for so urban a winter setting. The fur-lined boots and the down coat were the best she'd been able to do.

The Music Hall was a cavernous former movie palace on the fringes of Greenwich Village. With judicious renovation that brought out its former art-deco glory, it had metamorphosed into a huge nightclub, and rows of small tables and sturdy chairs stretched across the terraced floor. The entire back wall was a long, mirrored bar, which conducted a lively standing-room business for those who didn't have tickets or arrived too late.

Ellie was almost one of the latter. The Music Hall, it turned out, was a popular watering hole even before the show. She was there a good half hour early, but every seat was taken. The man at the door shook his head when she presented the pass Peter had given her.

"Don't know if we can honor that, ma'am." She could barely hear him over the noise inside. She stood in the tiny vestibule looking in amazement at the four-deep crowd around the bar. "You can pay the standard cover charge and stand up at the bar if you want to. But we're sold out tonight—no seats left."

Ellie began to protest vigorously. She had no desire to join the skirmish around the bar, especially since she was alone. Although the crowd was a trifle more formally dressed than it would have been back home, the mood was the same: free spirited, hedonistic and not about to take no for an answer. She didn't feel like fighting off cruising males all evening.

So when her effort at convincing the doorkeeper to let her in was interrupted, she directed an unfriendly glare at the man who stood by her elbow.

"Miss Martinson?" He spoke directly into her ear, the only way to be heard. She turned, surprised that he knew her name, and he added, "We're saving a seat for you down front." He glanced at the doorkeeper. "Stamp her hand, Howie."

Howie, a tall pugnacious-looking fellow who probably doubled as bouncer, hastened to oblige, and Ellie was led away.

"I don't believe I know you," she began cautiously.

"I work for Keith," the man told her. He was dressed in cords and a preppy-looking sweater over a discreet white shirt, but his light brown hair waved to his shoulders, offsetting the sedate clothes. "Chuck Green." As he spoke he led her down a center aisle through the sea of little tables. On the stage, the warm-up band had begun pottering around their sound equipment, loosing occasional shrieks of feedback that were greeted with cheers by the crowd. "Josh asked me to keep an eye out for you, show you our table."

"But how did you know—" Ellie stopped. Obviously Josh had described her. She didn't know if she wanted to hear what he'd said.

Chuck Green grinned at her in a friendly way. "He said you'd be head and shoulders above any other woman in every way."

"Did he indeed." Ellie blinked and plowed into Chuck, who'd stopped for a second. Soon he began threading his way through the tables toward one of the boxes that was left from the movie-palace days. The side walls were thick velvet curtains; their lavish draping gave partial privacy to the box's occupants. Chuck gestured for Ellie to enter, and she saw that the box had been equipped with a luxuriously upholstered banquette that curved in a right angle around a big table. The effect was secluded, private, with an excellent view of the stage.

There were six or seven people crowded around the table. One of them, Ellie realized breathlessly, was Keith Redmont.

Redmont had been a force in the music world for ten years, a charismatic performer and gifted songwriter whose albums were produced with clockwork regulari-

ty. His following was immense, his gold records count-
less, and his last album had been declared a masterpiece
by the critics. It was no wonder she felt dizzy at the
thought of meeting him.

Five minutes after he'd pulled her down beside him on
the banquette, Ellie had lost her dizziness. Though he
viewed the world through eyes that drooped cynically
at the corners, Keith Redmont had long ago come to
terms with his prominence and had developed ways of
dealing with fame. It was well-known that he gave no
interviews except at his own instigation. He had surrounded himself with a loyal staff who took care of en-
suring his privacy. Those who tried to invade that
privacy were swiftly repelled. But those who were
drawn within the magic circle found it a warm, friendly
place.

Ellie was introduced to Jennifer Magnusson, Keith's
longtime girlfriend, whose sparkling brown eyes and
straight, shiny brown hair were far removed from the
glamour Ellie would have expected in a superstar's con-
sort. The other women at the table were the wife of
Josh's bass guitarist and the girlfriend of the drummer.

Jennifer leaned over Keith, her gaze intent. "You
know, Ellie," she said, her voice barely audible above
the surrounding uproar, "Josh has talked so much about
you I knew you instantly when you walked in the
door." She smiled, but her eyes were serious. "He thinks
a lot of you. You're more than a publicist as far as he's
concerned."

"I should hope so—" Ellie laughed a little shakily
"—considering how he feels about publicists."

"If you two ladies are going to gossip," Keith interjected mildly, "I suggest we rearrange the seating. The
way it is, I get the uncanny feeling that I don't exist."

Jennifer punched him lightly in the stomach. "You exist all right," she said affectionately. "In fact, there's too

much of you to ignore. Ellie and I can talk after the show."

Keith raised his eyebrows. "If that's what you think," he murmured, "you've forgotten Blackmun. I don't believe watching you and Ellie talk is what he has in mind for after the show."

Ellie felt the heat rise in her face and was thankful that the warm-up band chose that moment to break into song. Their music was loud and a little rough, getting the crowd into a good mood. In minutes the minuscule dance floor in front of the stage was jumping with dancers.

The din made it possible to assume a state of suspended animation. Ellie waited for the set to end, sipping the mineral water Chuck had procured for her. She wished that she could be waiting backstage with Josh, or that he could be out front with them. As if he heard her thought, Keith shouted into her ear, "The backstage at this place consists of two small dressing rooms and a storage bin. That's why we're braving the hordes out here."

Sitting in the audience really was brave of Keith, Ellie realized when the warm-up band finally left the stage. The noise level abated very little, because the free-drinking audience simply increased their collective decibel level two or three notches. But the houselights came up, and that was a signal for several people to approach Keith's box.

Most of them held pens and papers—notebooks, cocktail napkins, even a sheet of suspiciously perforated tissue. Chuck intercepted them before they could get too close, taking a stack of small cards from his shirt pocket and passing them out. "Keith signs a bunch of cards before we go anywhere," Jennifer explained. "If people want an autograph, that's what they get." She put a protective hand on Keith's shoulder. "There are too many crazy people out there," she said, the worry plain in her expression. "I don't like letting anyone get too close."

"You just want to keep the women away from me." Keith's voice was teasing, but his smile at Jennifer was tender. Ellie blinked and looked away. It was true that most of the autograph hunters were women who gazed longingly at Keith as they morosely accepted the cards Chuck handed out.

But several of the people crowding around the perimeter of the table were carrying cameras and small tape recorders. Their eyes scanned the table, avid for any detail. Chuck shook his head decidedly and herded them away. One man slipped through his net and flung himself at the table.

"Mr. Redmont! Keith! Is it true that you and Miss Magnusson intend to get married very soon?"

Keith turned away to avoid the bright flash of light from the reporter's camera. Ellie watched, fascinated, as the camera was exchanged for a microphone with what amounted to sleight of hand.

"Mr. Redmont!" The man's voice was demanding, insistent. He strained closer, shoving the microphone past Ellie to reach Keith. "Is it true that Miss Magnusson is pregnant? Is that why you're going to get married?"

Ellie saw the distress on Jennifer's delicate face and Keith's expression of aversion. The reporter was practically clawing his way across Ellie's body to get at his quarry. Keith wasn't her client, but Ellie felt the protective instincts rising.

"That's enough," she said authoritatively. Her hand came up and chopped through the air, knocking the microphone out of the reporter's grip. Ellie stood, turning away from the table, her imposing five feet ten inches forcing the intruder into the aisle.

"My microphone," the reporter shrieked. Ellie reached for the cord, planting her foot firmly on the small cylinder that rolled on the floor. She yanked with all her strength. The cord came up frayed at the end to which the microphone had been attached.

The man glared at her and groveled around on the floor until he found the mike. "You'll have to reimburse me for this," he snarled.

"I don't think so." Ellie stepped back to let Chuck take over, since he'd dispatched the other media scavengers. He escorted the reporter away and she sat back down.

There was a short silence at the table. "Wow," Keith said finally. "I don't know what Josh is worried about."

Ellie saw Jennifer's elbow connect meaningfully with Keith's ribs. "Thanks, Ellie." Her eyes were admiring. "You were swell to help." She grimaced. "That sort of thing happens to us all the time. We should have put more people with Chuck for security tonight."

Ellie was wildly curious to know if the reporter's questions had been based on fact, but she restrained herself. Keith touched Jennifer's face tenderly.

"You want to hide out backstage?"

Jennifer repressed a shudder. "Heavens, no. It's like the Black Hole of Calcutta back there. We're safe enough. Josh will be on any minute, and then no one will be interested in us." She glanced at Keith. "You gonna sit in?"

Ellie caught her breath. If Keith played during Josh's concert, he would be guaranteed good press coverage in all the newspapers. But Keith shook his head.

"This is Josh's show. If he wants, I might do an encore with him." He saw Ellie's disappointed face and explained, "The man needs to know that it's all due to his own efforts."

The houselights went down and Ellie turned to the stage, all her senses burgeoning to awareness in the instant before she saw Josh.

He stood in the middle between the bass guitarist and

the rhythm guitarist, drums at his back. He looked lean and dangerous, dressed all in black—tight-fitting black jeans, black leather vest, long-sleeved shirt with a slash of white tie pulled askew beneath the open collar of the shirt. His dark, rumpled hair fell over his forehead. His face was a blade of purpose.

He settled the guitar strap around his neck in the quick gesture she remembered, then his eyes moved in a challenging sweep across the crowd. The hall was eerily silent; even the ever-present clatter of glass died down. Then he spoke, that long-voweled, gritty drawl amplified to fill the room.

"Well, folks. . . ." He paused, and a slow smile did devastating things to his face. "I'm back."

He lifted the neck of his guitar into the air. On the downswing he struck a resounding chord, and the band exploded with him into a fast-paced, tight rendition of his first big hit, "Let the Lady Decide." Immediately the crowd was singing, jumping, clapping along.

Ellie was unnerved by the strength of her own response. She wanted to leap up onto the stage, turn that impersonal gaze into something intimate, just for her. Gripping her hands, she willed herself to sit calmly in her seat. Only the broad cheek-aching grin she wore betrayed her true feelings.

Reading the rowdy crowd like a book, Josh let them tire themselves out with half a dozen driving tunes in a row. Then the band faded quietly away as he pulled a tall stool out from the side into the pool of light at the front of the stage.

He exchanged his Stratocaster for a big-bellied acoustic with a pickup on it. His hands wandered up and down the neck and over the strings with such lazy precision that it was hard to believe he was the only person playing.

Letting the golden notes ring out for a few bars, Josh

smiled at the audience with easy friendliness. "Bass and treble at the same time!" There were some admiring shouts. The music gradually coalesced into "Backwoods Blues," another of his big hits. The crowd applauded boisterously, then quieted to listen with respectful attention to his gravelly voice with its astonishing upper register.

Allowing no time for applause, he swung directly into "Lot's Wife." Ellie remembered Milo Connors's remark that Vivienne Santos believed this song had been written for her. The lyrics were ambiguous but haunting: "You never thought the time would come to flee. Don't turn around, don't try to look at me. . . ."

Although the concert lasted another hour, Ellie could not regain her earlier euphoria. She knew that Josh was playing extraordinarily well, letting the emotions shine through the music like sunlight through water. She knew he had the crowd in the palm of his hand. They went wild over "Runt of the Litter," which she remembered from the demo tape he'd played for Milo. They loved his old songs and his new ones. She could see him opening to them, letting their approval heal some of the wounds he'd been carrying for the past three years, and she was glad. . . . But her heart was afraid again—afraid of the risk she'd taken by giving her love to a man who had the kind of power to hurt that Josh Blackmun had.

"He's working 'em like a master," Keith muttered beside her, clapping enthusiastically after an especially good rendition of "Not Fade Away." "Lordy, the man should have been shot for hiding all this time."

"He needed it," Ellie found herself replying. "But now he needs this."

Onstage, Josh brought his final song to a roaring conclusion, bowed and walked off. But the crowd wouldn't take it as final. They were on their feet, stamping, clapping, whistling, shouting. At last he came back out, followed by the band. He held up his hand for silence.

"Thanks."

A few rowdies in the crowd shouted back, "You're welcome!"

He smiled. "I've got a couple of things to say. This is the best return audience any musician could possibly want, and I surely do appreciate your enthusiasm."

This called for a few more minutes of enthusiasm, and Josh finally held up his hand for quiet.

"Now then. . . Ellie?" He stepped up to the edge of the stage and looked out, shading his eyes against the bright lights that shone on him. Ellie sat perfectly still, her earlier desire for recognition completely gone. But his eyes found her in seconds. "There you are." He stepped back before the audience could locate her. "I just want you to know this one was for you. Every bit of it."

She felt the coldness in the pit of her stomach begin to melt. The sincerity in his voice was unmistakable. Jennifer reached over and squeezed her hand; the gentle touch nearly unloosed tears.

Then Josh motioned to the side of the stage, where a crew member pushed a piano onto the platform. Keith straightened. "Finally," Josh said, raising his voice, "there's someone in the audience who needs a little musical therapy. Keith? You wanna come up here and work out your aggressions with a couple tunes?"

Keith edged along the wall until he could jump onto the stage. Catching sight of him, the audience roared. Josh shouted, "Here he is folks, Dr. Keith Redmont. What do you prescribe, doctor?"

Keith sat down at the piano, ran through a few grandiose riffs, and plunged into "Rock and Roll Music," joined by Josh and the band. Watching the two men, Ellie was conscious of a deep contentment. She had made music publicity her specialty, she realized, because she loved moments like this. Moments when the music connected in so many ways that it generated a tangible excitement.

But the music was only a manifestation of her euphoria, not the cause. The cause stood on stage, lost in the magic he and Keith were creating. Elated at his words, at the public avowal of his feelings, she let one thought run through her head over and over. *He must love me, he has to love me!*

The concert was over before she came out of her trance. Jennifer hustled her to a nearby steel door that opened onto the backstage while the audience was still thundering their approval of the encore.

The tiny backstage was crowded with milling crew members, band members with towels around their necks and a few enterprising reporters. The air resounded with congratulatory shouts and backslaps. Ellie looked around and saw Josh at the same time the reporters did.

They advanced, cameras and note pads at the ready, questions pouring out of their mouths. "Mr. Blackmun! Mr. Blackmun! Will Keith Redmont be touring with you?"

"Was your reception all you hoped it would be?"

"What are your reasons for coming out of retirement now?"

"Will you be moving back to L.A.?"

"Who is 'Ellie'?"

"Who's your current love interest?"

"What's your current record label?"

"Do you have anything to say about the accident?"

Ellie elbowed her way through the crowd with determination. Josh stood penned against the wall, sweat still glistening on his face despite the towel around his neck. He held his body with an angry tautness she recognized. She pushed through the reporters and whirled, facing them like a tigress defending her young.

"No questions." She didn't bother to raise her voice, but the high, clear tones could be heard throughout the room. Conversation stopped. "Mr. Blackmun will give no interviews tonight. If you want interviews, have your editors call me tomorrow at the Clarendon. Ms Martinson, representing Trax Records, Mr. Blackmun's new label. Have you got that?"

The reporters scribbled furiously, then began attacking again. "If you'll just answer one question, Mr. Blackmun. If you'll just tell our readers—"

Josh's voice sounded behind her, hoarse and even more gravelly than usual from exertion.

"You heard Ms Martinson." He stepped forward a little, and Ellie could see his strained profile. He smiled thinly. "I'll give one statement." She moved involuntarily, but he paid no attention. "Someone asked about my accident. My accident was caused by drinking and driving. If you're going to drive, don't drink. Now, if you'll all excuse me?"

The reporters sent up an even more hysterical babble as Josh began to move toward the door. Ellie reached out to the most vociferous one, removed the pencil from her hand, and broke it gently under the woman's nose. "Mr. Blackmun is through talking," she said quietly, but with the unmistakable hint of steel in her voice. "You are all excused." Chuck Green came up to stand behind her, his presence a silent, muscular threat.

Cowed, the reporters began drifting toward the door, muttering among themselves, appealing to the crew and band members they passed to grant interviews. No one took them up on their offers, and they finally filed out.

Keith clapped Ellie on the shoulder, popping out from the minuscule dressing room where he'd been hiding. "Great work, lady. We should all have such understanding press agents." He threw his other arm around

Josh's shoulders. "Let's blow this firetrap. The party's laid on at my place. Meet you there?"

Josh nodded, his eyes never leaving Ellie's face. She felt that burning gaze ignite the want that had been simmering in her since their last meeting. She ached for him. Without him she was empty and would never be full.

"Hey, you two." Keith shook them gently, his face full of laughter. "Listen, forget the party if you want. Just try to find someplace a little more private if you're going to look at each other like that. You're getting everyone around you all steamed up, too."

Ellie blinked and looked around at Jennifer's understanding smile, at the grinning faces of the crew members. Josh didn't allow her time to take it in. "Catch you later," he growled, pulling Ellie from under Keith's arm and hustling her toward the door.

It was drizzling outside, cold icy drops that seemed to lack the energy to be sleet. Ellie barely noticed, however. Josh swept her past one remaining, forlorn reporter, who pattered down the alley after them until they reached the street. "Mr. Blackmun, Mr. Blackmun. . . ."

Josh stood impatiently at the curb, looking for a cab. The reporter caught up with them. "Mr. Blackmun, have you—"

Ellie shook her head tolerantly, noticing the water that dripped off the reporter's hat. "No more questions," she said. He was young, togged out as if Edward R. Murrow was his hero, and his crestfallen expression touched her. "Listen—" she leaned toward him with a conspiratorial wink "—Keith Redmont is still inside. But you'll have to look sharp or you'll miss him."

"Hey, thanks! Thanks a lot!" The young man bounced back up the alley, all thoughts of the cold rain evidently banished. She turned to find that Josh had secured a cab and was holding the door open for her.

"The Clarendon," Josh told the driver. A thrill of desirous anticipation ran through Ellie. He crowded in next to her, the hard length of his body more warming than the down coat. She shivered, and his arm came around her, bringing her closer. "That was a dirty trick," he murmured into her ear, causing another shiver.

"You mean turning him loose on Keith?" She couldn't keep the shakiness out of her voice. It was dark in the cab, and there was the pungent odor of wet wool and old upholstery. In the passing glow of headlights and streetlamps she could discern Josh's gleaming eyes, still watching her with that unnerving, passion-stirring look of hunger.

He gave a crack of laughter. "Keith won't be going out that way. His people will take care of him. That boy is going to have a long wait."

Ellie couldn't find it in her to be very concerned about a nameless reporter when Josh was so close. She was on fire with impatience for his touch. But although he held her fiercely he made no move to kiss her. She tilted her head up to his and moistened her lips invitingly. His eyes took on a feverish glitter, but still he remained aloof. "I've been working night and day, little darlin', but I couldn't stop thinking about you for an instant." Though he didn't touch her, his expression was a caress. "I've missed you."

She brought her hands up to cradle his face. "Josh," she whispered, "I have to confess. I kissed the roses."

He hooted with laughter and brushed his lips over hers, but when she tried to deepen the kiss he moved uneasily away.

"What's the matter? Do I have bad breath?"

He shook his head and stared down at her with heavy-lidded eyes. "Of course not. There's some other reason, but I seem to have forgotten it. . . ."

The heat in his voice rasped over her. She pulled his head down until his lips hovered a fraction of an inch above hers.

"Guess I'll just have to take the responsibility myself." She punctuated her words with velvety nibbles, taking a tiny bite of his lower lip, running her tongue between his lips, moving her mouth softly against his. He shuddered.

"Ellie...we have to talk." His words were a tortured groan. She smiled serenely at him, letting her feelings shine in her face.

"We will talk," she promised as the cab stopped in front of the hotel. "First thing tomorrow."

8

"COZY LITTLE PAD."

Josh stood just inside the door of Ellie's hotel room, eyeing the faded drapes critically. Ellie could tell that the trip from the cab to her room had brought back Josh's defenses. She would have to turn the temperature up if she wanted to wake with him in the morning.

She went across the room to the bureau and pulled a bottle out of one of the drawers.

"It's not too bad for a hotel." She showed him the bottle. "This is illegal, so I hid it in a drawer. I smuggled in some California champagne in my luggage."

Laughing, he crossed to examine the wine. "You can get this stuff in any grocery store across the country," he protested, taking in the undistinguished label.

"I know." Ellie wrinkled her nose at him and unwrapped the sanitized glass. "It's a good thing I didn't spend much money on it, since we're going to have to drink it warm."

He shook his head, easing the plastic cork out of the bottle. "You should have put it out on the windowsill before the concert. It would have been a block of ice by now."

"This weather is so cold that warm champagne will taste great." Ellie shivered and huddled closer to Josh. "There's only the one glass, too."

The cork popped out, followed by a gush of the effervescent fluid. "Any glass!" Josh grabbed it from her and tried to catch the overflow, tilting the bottle to halt any further loss. He held the glass up with a flourish. "Here's to my little darlin', the only woman in the world who'd risk being busted for a bottle of $2.98 champagne!"

Ellie chuckled and snatched the glass after he'd sipped from it. "And here's to you, Josh." She took a sip and ran her tongue deliberately over her lips. "A great singer, a fine songwriter and the best lover I've ever had." She gazed steadily at him, and it was as if she'd lit a fire in the middle of the room. His eyes turned molten.

Ellie set down the glass and drew the heavy knit of her sweater over her head. Beneath it was a thin cotton undershirt. She could feel her nipples firm and harden under his hot stare.

"Ellie, are you sure? I don't want to hurt you." His voice was a hoarse whisper. As if he had no power over it, his hand reached to smooth the silky skin of her shoulder.

She smiled at him, not concealing her love, but not verbalizing it. "Don't worry." Her smile turned shaky. "If you were to reject me now, that would hurt." Heavens, why had she said that? She wouldn't plead for his love. But she could work a little to make sure he gave it to her. Slowly she sank into a wing chair and held out one booted foot to him. Making her voice throaty, she purred, "Take it off, please."

He laughed unsteadily and pulled off her boots, managing to invest the simple service with a wealth of suggestion. She stripped off her heavy wool socks and frowned at the cable imprint they'd left on her feet. "This isn't very sexy. Would you want to make love to a woman with striped skin?"

Kneeling beside the chair, he took one foot in his warm hands and smoothed the ridge marks with his calloused fingertips. "If the woman was you," he murmured huskily, "I'd make love to her if she had skin like a zebra."

Ellie let the heated words flow over her. The rasp of Josh's hands on her feet was amazingly sensual. He slid his palms up her corduroy-clad legs until he reached her waist. Pausing, he looked up at her.

She put her own hands over his, pressing them to her. The currents flowing between them strengthened as they held each other's eyes. In his gray-tweed gaze she could see the doubt, the need. Deep inside her something flowered and grew—more than desire, more than tenderness. She wanted to give to him without reservation, because only with that giving could she have a sense of wholeness.

He must have read something of her openness. His hands, hesitating on her belt buckle, began to move again.

"I want to play lady's maid for you," he whispered. "I want to do everything for you, little darlin'."

He undressed her with tender thoroughness, easing off her cords, pulling her upright so he could strip off her panties and T-shirt, until she stood naked under his igniting gaze. He touched her lingeringly, smoothing the satiny flesh of her belly, dipping his hands into the hidden valley. "Beautiful," he breathed, his eyes meeting hers, melting hers. With trembling hands he began to remove his own clothes. Ellie hastened to help him.

They tumbled onto the bed, seeking each other eagerly, tongues and lips twining, hands moving with feverish haste. Their union was like a meeting of elements, gathering all the power and energy of their beings into one blaze of passion that flared brighter and brighter until, at last, it consumed them both.

THIS TIME THERE WAS NO BERTHA to announce the morning.

Ellie woke with the disoriented sensation of being in a strange place. She sat up swiftly, noting the soft sunlight that came through the brocade drapes, the busy tick of her traveling alarm clock and her own nudity. Then remembrance rushed back. Half-afraid there would be no one there, she looked at the other side of the bed.

Josh slept isolated on the big mattress, his face buried in the pillow, strong shoulders showing above the rumpled sheet. The utter relaxation of his body was just as profound in sleep as was his energy-charged aura when he was awake.

She picked up the clock and squinted at it. They had meant to go on to Keith's party last night, but it was obviously too late for that. She smiled, picturing Keith's face if they were to show up at his plush penthouse at nine o'clock in the morning, expecting to be entertained. Her smile deepened, remembering what had detained them.

She wanted to touch Josh, to smooth his shoulders, brush her hair along his back, if only to remind herself more deeply of the tenderness they'd shared last night. Heroically she restrained herself. He needed to recharge, and she needed to get some exercise. Some *real* exercise.

She dressed quietly in her sweats, laced up her shoes, waiting for some sign of wakefulness from him. But he didn't stir, so she scribbled a hasty note before stepping softly out the door.

A cold wind pushed her along the paths in Central Park, but today the sun shone in weak, fitful gleams, washing the fronts of the buildings with evanescent glory. The city was magically enhanced, its weary grimy facade somehow transformed into cheerful sophistication.

She ran for the joy of using her body, stretching muscles, drawing the biting air into her lungs and making its oxygen hers. She had meant to use her running time to analyze her ambivalence where Josh was concerned, to figure out what kind of relationship they were having. But the rational part of her mind wouldn't operate. Instead it gave her small, delightful pieces of sensory information about her surroundings: the smell of the frozen earth; the sparkle of sunlight on the water of a small lake; the familiar cry of gulls in the distant East River.

She walked back to the hotel along Fifth Avenue, letting her heartbeat slow gradually to normal, watching the faces that hurried past her intent on Saturday-morning business. Tantalizing aromas from a side street lured her, and she bought a sackful of knishes to take back to the room, their crisp golden-brown outsides promising succulence within.

When she got back to the hotel, Josh was still sleeping, his position unchanged. But now she was too eager to share the day with him to let him sleep. She opened the curtains to let in what light there was, and went to shower, leaving the sack of knishes on the bedside table.

She was rinsing the shampoo from her hair when Josh appeared in the shower door, wearing nothing but a twinkle in his eye. He was munching a knish, and he crammed the rest of it into his mouth as he stepped into the enclosure.

"Thanks for breakfast," he mumbled, crowding her into the corner of the stall. He managed a mighty swallow and smiled crookedly down at her. "Why didn't you tell me it was time to get up?"

"Why didn't you ask?" She wrinkled her nose at him and pushed him away. "I need to rinse the shampoo out."

He ran his hands down her sleek, wet curves. "Too bad. I wanted to scrub your back for you, but since you're done, I don't suppose. . . ." He presented her with a washcloth and a wistful look.

She took it with a secret thrill of pleasure, which she

felt obliged to mask in grumbles. "Fine thing! I get you breakfast, I wash your back. Next thing I know, you'll be asking me to dress you or something."

He turned and pulled her into his arms, rubbing their slippery bodies together, provoking instant arousal in hers. Then he let her go and snatched the washcloth from her hand.

"Now you're all dirty again," he growled low in his throat. "Especially here...." His hands soaped her breasts slowly, lovingly, weighing their fullness. He guided her until the shower spray sluiced off the bubbles, his forehead furrowed in concentration as he gently manipulated the rounded globes. "Uh-oh. Missed a spot." Bending, he made lazy swipes with his tongue at each rosy tip.

Her nipples swelled and strained, their longing ache joining with the tumult in the pit of her belly, making all the blood leave her extremities. She leaned weakly back against the tiled wall, its cool surface a welcome shock to her heated skin.

Josh still held her breasts, his gaze on them like lingering flame, though his voice came out in a judicious drawl. "They seem nice and clean now." His thumbs rasped gently across each turgid nipple before he removed the warmth of his hands. He swished the cloth across her stomach, one hand going behind her back to support her. His other hand found the juncture of her thighs and probed gently, knowingly. She drew a deep, shuddering breath.

"Josh!"

"Now don't interrupt me." His drawl was turning husky. His eyes met hers, heavy lidded, sensuous, catching her passionate heat and returning it tenfold. "Interruptions make me lose my place.... I just have to start all over...."

He turned off the water and wrapped her hastily in a

bath towel, urging her toward the bedroom. She hung back.

"Josh, we're both wet. We'll get everything—"

An impatient oath escaped him. "The hotel doesn't care and neither do I." He let his own towel fall from around his waist and opened hers, his eyes hungry on her full curves, his hands pulling her toward him with trembling urgency, until she could feel the heavy brush of his arousal. His eyes drifted shut; the yearning ache on his face touched her immeasurably. "Please, little darlin', let me pleasure you. I'll go as slow as I can. Not like last night. . . ."

She chuckled breathlessly and twined her arms around his neck. "Last night was incredible and you know it." Their bodies fitted warmly together, his hands touching her with an incendiary effect. His mouth captured hers and swallowed her small moan before it could reach the air.

"Too fast," he mumbled against her lips. "Whenever I'm near you . . . can't keep from wanting you all around me. . . ."

His words struck her with a shaft of unexpected pain; they ran together like the lyrics of a song. The same thought must have occurred to Josh. He pulled away briefly, his eyes darkening at her expression.

"Ellie, darlin', do you know how I get the words to go with my music? I realize that something in my life is so important or archetypal that it will strike the right chords. It might be something as little as the way a puppy looks for a spare teat. Or it could be something as mighty and impressive as the way I feel when I have you in my arms."

Reluctantly he drew away and fastened his towel, turning to find his clothes after one last hungry look at her gleaming body. "We need to talk. I meant to hammer it out last night, but—" His shrug spoke eloquently of what had prevented him.

Ellie wondered for a moment if perhaps she should feel angry, rejected. But what Josh said was true. She made for the bureau where she had unpacked her lingerie and began pulling on the silky undergarments she had chosen as much for their added warmth and comfort next to the skin as for their understated sensuality. Wearing something, even if it was only a deep gold satin teddy, made her feel much more able to face the rigors of hearing her man say the dreaded words, "We need to talk."

When she turned to the closet for other clothes, she noticed Josh's expression. He sat on the bed after putting on his pants, socks forgotten in his hands as he watched her with bone-shattering intensity. "You move like honey." His voice was hoarse. "I just want you to flow all over me."

She wanted to melt in a thousand places. "Make up your mind, Blackmun," she whispered. "Do I put on my clothes, or do I take them off?"

His lips edged up in a reluctant smile. "Put 'em on." She moved between the closet and the bureau, assembling warm knit tights, wool socks, jeans, shirt, sweater. "Although it might take all day. What in tarnation do you want with so many clothes, woman? I may never be able to prospect my way through the layers."

She zipped her jeans and tucked in a shirt before donning the thick wool sweater. "It's winter out there, Blackmun, in case you hadn't noticed. My body is allergic to cold weather." She hunted under the bed for her boots and began stamping them on at the same moment as Josh attacked his. The din was thunderous. They stopped, caught each other's eyes, and laughed nervously. Josh picked up his coat and pulled her toward the door.

"Let's get out of here." He gave a distracted glance around the untidy room and the rumpled bed. "Let's get some coffee or something and talk."

They ended up at a small café near Rockefeller Center.

The windows were fogged inside with warm, slightly rancid steam, but the coffee was palatable. It was served in thick white cups, accompanied by a tin pitcher of cream. Ellie glanced up from swirling a generous pale ribbon of it through the dark liquid to find his eyes on her, the smile in their depths disarmingly tender.

"Cream *and* sugar?" The smile was reflected in his voice as she reached for one of the paper packets.

"I don't normally drink coffee," she said defensively. "But it seems appropriate for confrontations." She glanced up at him. "Is that what we're going to have? A confrontation?"

His mouth tightened. "Not if I can help it." Picking up his unused spoon, he drew an invisible pattern around his coffee cup. "Damn it," he ground out. "This is hard for me to say."

Her throat tightened, trapping an anguished moan. He was going to tell her, gently but firmly, that friendship was all he'd had in mind, and if sex was going to make her want more of a commitment, they had better call it quits. She had dished out a similar speech a couple of times since her divorce, although until Josh she would've had no reason to include the part about a sexual relationship. Now that she was in love, when she ached for him in every way, she was going to get cut off.

Josh exhaled, running a hand through his rumpled dark hair. "I wanted to call you the day after Thanksgiving," he began abruptly. "But I couldn't. What you said then—that you loved me—threw me." He picked up the spoon again and used it with great concentration. "I was almost afraid of you." When he looked up, the vulnerability in his eyes grasped her heart. "I haven't let a woman get close—really close, as close as you were getting. I didn't know if I wanted that, didn't know where it was leading."

Ellie couldn't speak. She was still waiting for the bad

part, summoning her poise to deal with it in dignity. But his expression lit a spark of hope.

"When you said you loved me," Josh went on, evidently a little unnerved by her silence, "I just wanted to flee. I called Peter the next day and urged him to speed things up for the tour. You were getting to me, you were penetrating my defenses, and you weren't even trying to. You didn't ask for anything, you didn't make any demands except my honesty. It was too scary." He shook his head, letting out his breath softly. "Lady, you were blowing me away."

Ellie lowered her lashes, feeling the tears trembling just beneath the surface. There was a small, nagging discomfort in her hands. She looked down and realized she had her coffee cup in a death grip. Forcing herself to relax, she took a sip. When she set the cup back down, it clattered in the saucer as if she had the ague.

Josh reached for one of her hands, running his long calloused fingers around the perimeter of her palm, his gaze fixed on what he was doing as if he'd never seen a human hand before. "First I tried not to think about it, about you. But it was too late. You'd already become too important."

Ellie didn't miss the faint note of resentment in his voice. She began to speak, but Josh cut her off. "I don't mean to sound churlish. I've been a loner most of my life. Before the accident I took everything as my due—super amounts of women for a superstar, etcetera. Afterward I was repelled by anything that reminded me of the jerk I'd been before." He smiled bleakly. "That included women, for the most part, until you."

He closed his hand tighter around hers. "You've taught me a lot in the short time I've known you, Ellie. You've shown me that selling the product I make doesn't have to mean selling myself, unless I let it. You've made me understand that I'm in charge of how far the hype goes."

He let go of her hand and combed his fingers impatiently through his hair. "I'm not making a lot of sense here. What I'm trying to say is that I don't have things figured out. It's hard to reorganize my thoughts around a woman who's beginning to mean a lot to me."

His words caused an incandescent warmth to spread through her, starting from where their fingers had touched, then reaching her heart and melting the icy apprehension that had gripped her.

"Josh," she said gently. "You don't have to tell me this."

"I want to." His voice was suddenly impatient. "I need to tell you. If I knew what it all meant, I could be more concise. I just know I want you near me. I want to be with you. I want to help you train that puppy—"

"She's sweet," Ellie interrupted, allowing her eyes to mist over. "Mom's taking care of Bridget during the tour. I haven't thanked you for giving her to me yet." She squeezed his hand, her eyes more eloquent than her words. "Thanks, Josh. I needed to know you cared just then."

"I've always cared," he muttered. "I just couldn't admit it." He cleared his throat. "Bridget, eh? That's a good name."

"She couldn't have had any other," Ellie said positively. She felt effervescent with love now that Josh had revealed his thoughts. He hadn't said the words yet, but that seemed unimportant. For now it was enough that he had deep and tender feelings for her.

"Ellie," he murmured, his face once again serious. "I've been thinking about us during the past two weeks. Seems to me that we never allowed much time for getting acquainted. You turned me on so powerfully I just rushed you into bed. Sure was great, too." His face wore a fleeting, unrepentant grin. "But now things are different. I worry that I gave you no choice, that it's too soon. I didn't mean for us to get carried away last night." He took a deep breath. "I don't want to feel guilty for taking more than I give. I want to put a moratorium on lovemaking until we get the ins and outs of this relationship hammered out."

"Well. . . ." Ellie was doubtful. "If you really want to stop I'll go along with it." She smiled impishly. "It's going to be hard, though."

Josh groaned. "You're telling me."

The waitress came by and poured more coffee in their cups, diluting Ellie's additives and making the coffee undrinkable. She put down the cup in disgust and caught a glimpse of her watch. "Josh!" Grabbing his hand, she tugged some money from her bag and jumped to her feet. "The *Rolling Stone* interview! We've got to hurry!"

THEY WERE TO MEET Claudette Cort at Keith's penthouse. Josh had been firmly against holding the interview on what he termed "enemy turf," and Ms Cort had not liked the idea of meeting in a public spot. She was waiting in the lobby of Keith's apartment building when they got there, consulting her watch and looking impatient.

Ellie recognized her only because of a sixth sense concerning newspeople. She had expected a hard-edged, keen-eyed, professional woman. Claudette Cort was tiny with big brown eyes and wispy curls of glossy hair. She looked swamped by the leather handbag that held her tape recorder, camera and notebook. The gaily-colored scarf wound around her neck fell nearly to her dainty little feet.

Immediately Ellie felt transformed into a giantess, woolly and clumsy. There was nothing overt in Claudette's manner to cause this. She shared a friendly smile between Josh and Ellie, sounding ingenuous and spontaneous. "I feel so lucky to have drawn this interview,"

she prattled as they walked toward the private elevator
that led to Keith's penthouse. "I've admired your music
for years, Mr. Blackmun."

"Josh." Claudette's hand had somehow come to rest
on Josh's sleeve while they waited for the elevator. Ellie
towered in the background, trying to reconcile Claudette's fluttery, feminine way with the tough, slashing
articles that appeared under her by-line. She wanted to
warn Josh to be careful. He was smiling down at Claudette, evidently not inclined to submit her to the same
tight-lipped hostility he dished out for other newspeople. Fearing that any veiled hints to watch himself
would get the interview off on the wrong foot, or worse,
make her sound like a jealous cat, she assumed her usual
place in the background as they stepped onto the
elevator.

Ellie had been looking forward to seeing the inside of
Keith's penthouse, about which there was a lot of speculation in the music business. She knew that he had his
own recording studio in the huge complex, totally
soundproofed and equipped with the latest in audio
technology. There was a rumored rooftop swimming
pool and other trappings of wealthy rock stardom, but
no bevy of lovely ladies that was usually a feature of
such pleasure palaces. Keith was known to be devoted
to Jennifer to the exclusion of any other woman, though
this didn't keep other women from trying to change his
mind.

But this morning she saw no more of the legendary
penthouse than a small reception room off the elegant
front foyer. Josh ushered them both inside very firmly,
closing the door behind him. Ellie noticed the disap-
pointment that flickered in Claudette's face as the door
shut.

"Couldn't we go someplace with better lighting or
natural light?" She was hauling a camera out of her

oversized bag as she spoke, along with the tiny tape recorder and notebook that no interviewer was ever without.

"We won't need to." Josh still spoke casually, but the steel was back in his voice. "You won't be taking any pictures today." He flashed a brief grin. "Now, if you all had decided to put me on the cover, I might let you take my picture. The way it is, you won't need anything but the publicity shots."

Claudette's eyes widened innocently. "Josh," she began, "I must get a few shots. Some photos taken during the interview are essential. My editor will just slay me if I come back with blank film."

"Better than coming back with no camera."

Claudette spared a glance for Ellie. The reporter's attitude was not unfriendly or patronizing toward another woman. She simply focused her energy and attention where she thought it would do her the most good. Ellie felt a reluctant admiration for the single-mindedness she detected beneath Claudette's ingenue exterior.

"Can't you make him see reason, Ms Martinson? May I call you—"

Josh interrupted before Ellie could answer. "She's already tried, and I've already refused. Trax has a selection of excellent photos, which you should have received in the press packet. You can use those for the text."

Claudette abandoned Ellie and fixed Josh with an imploring look strongly reminiscent of Bertha. Ellie smothered a laugh, which became a cough when Josh shot a glance at her. His lips twitched but he turned his attention back to the interviewer.

"I really thought— I mean, since the interview is in Keith Redmont's apartment, I had hoped to meet and talk with him, as well." Claudette caught her lower lip between pearly little teeth and peered hopefully at Josh.

Ellie's irritation suddenly began to outweigh her

amusement at Claudette's tactics. She wanted to pick up the woman, shake her and tell her to thank her lucky stars she was meeting with an artist of Josh Blackmun's caliber, without trying to belittle his achievement by drooling all over Keith Redmont.

Instead Ellie sat back in the artfully cushioned armchair and pinned a social smile on her face. She was confident Josh would be able to handle Claudette without her intervention. And something about the way he'd interrupted her earlier had made her wish they'd thought to buy a few papers and check out the reviews of Josh's concert. If one of the newspapers mentioned Josh's reference to an "Ellie" last night, it was wise not to make free use of her name. She had no desire to be written up in *Rolling Stone* as publicist-cum-squeeze for Josh Blackmun.

One corner of Josh's mouth lifted. He lowered himself into the other armchair and gestured politely for Claudette to take the small sofa that remained. "Keith can't make it," he said gently. "I'm sure I don't have to remind you what his policy is on interviews."

He reached for the telephone perched on a small table between his chair and Ellie's. Cradling it between ear and shoulder, he punched a button and dialed a couple of numbers. "Chuck, I've arrived with some visitors. You can switch On now." He listened for a moment, laughed, then broke the connection and dialed once more, tossing off, "Keith has more security systems than the Pentagon, I think." He spoke into the phone again. "Martha? Got anything hot?... You lecherous old woman, you!... No, I'm surrounded by lovely women in the lounge here and I wanted to—you know—refresh them.... Aw, thank you, darlin', you're a lifesaver."

Ellie loved the warm smile he wore while he bantered with the woman on the other end of the phone. He seemed to shed a little of his hardness and reserve inside

Keith's door. Despite the looming ordeal of an interview he was relaxed enough to flirt with the staff.

Claudette already had her tape recorder out and running, her notebook at hand for any observations. Having lost the skirmish of getting to interview the reclusive Keith Redmont, she was obviously prepared to go on as if it had never happened.

"I want you to know," she began, "that I don't mean to ask any questions you will find offensive. However, I do intend to ask probing questions that might get your back up. Don't get mad. Just tell me to mind my own business and I'll try to keep from digging." With an engaging grin, she added, "Of course, the parts I want to know about most are the parts you never tell. For instance, what happened between you and Miss Santos just before your accident?"

Josh stiffened, but before he could reply the door opened. Chuck Green appeared, pushing a small serving cart on which sat a steaming pot of tea and a tray of dainty desserts. Ellie jumped to her feet and made a big fuss over the refreshments, pouring the tea and carrying it around, placing the tray of pastries on a low table before Claudette, who completely ignored it. Ellie took an eclair that she was too distracted to do justice to.

"I know you don't like to talk about that, Josh," Claudette continued, "but it was a long time ago and naturally people would like to know if your version squares with Vivienne's. The way she tells it, she threw you out on your ass and you were trying to kill yourself over her when you crashed your motorcycle."

Josh's fingers were tight on the handle of his teacup, but his voice was level. "Our relationship was at an end, certainly."

His lips closed with an air of finality, but Claudette kept at him. "And were you trying to kill yourself?"

He looked at her stonily. "No more than usual."

Claudette waited, and finally prompted, "What does that mean?"

Ellie sat forward in her chair, wondering if she should squelch Claudette or just have a messy and voluble accident with the rest of the eclair. But Josh gestured her back. He was silent for a moment, then he spoke.

"I don't have much to say about my relationship with Vivienne. That's no one's business but hers and mine." He didn't look at Ellie and she felt that horrible sensation in her chest that novelists refer to as a sinking heart. "However, about the accident: I had been drinking, drugging, partying too much for a long time leading up to it. Living that way, it was just a question of time before I'd manage to kill myself. It wouldn't have been deliberate, you understand, but I'd have done it anyway."

He cleared his throat. "I had lots of time afterward to think about how I got into that hospital bed. And when I was done thinking, I knew I didn't want to let my vices destroy me. Doin' things to excess is just that—excessive." His face relaxed a little and he took a sip of his tea. "I've learned the value of moderation."

Ellie had never heard him open up so much. For a minute she was tangled in unworthy emotions: jealousy of Vivienne, of Claudette, of everything in Josh's life that excluded her; and hurt that such important revelations were being elicited in an interview. She wanted to be the sole receptacle of his confidences. But the petty thoughts made her ashamed and she put them from her.

Claudette questioned Josh closely about the accident, about his recuperation and subsequent seclusion, and he answered readily enough for the most part, emphasizing the dangers of driving while intoxicated and lauding the pleasures of solitude. They discussed his music exhaustively, both his former hits and the new stuff. Claudette had been at the concert, and her enthusiasm for his new songs had Josh talking eagerly about the writing he'd been doing, which led to questions about why he had decided to make an album.

Josh was complimentary of Peter Macguire and Trax, making Ellie breathe a sigh of relief. In her conversations with him, he'd often been caustic or downright hostile toward Peter. But to Claudette he admitted that he had enjoyed making the album, and that last night's concert had been a tremendous rush. "In fact," he added, studiously avoiding Ellie, "last night was probably the most intense experience I've ever had."

A glow of pleasure suffused her, and she missed the next few questions, coming out of her golden haze in time to hear Josh snap out a sharp "No comment!"

Claudette leaned forward persuasively. "Now Josh, of course I'm curious, everyone's curious about 'Ellie.' What made you mention her name last night if you didn't want to answer questions about her? Is she with you on tour? Do you have permanent plans?"

Josh got to his feet. "I've enjoyed talking with you, Ms Cort. If you have any further questions I'm sure Trax will be glad to clear things up for you." Without another word he walked out the door.

Claudette shrugged philosophically and turned to Ellie. "Well, I got most of the interview anyway. Given his rep for not opening up to the press, I got further than I thought I would." She gave Ellie a frank, appraising stare, seeming to see her for the first time. "Is that your doing?"

Ellie shook her head, letting the mantle of quiet dignity she assumed on these occasions support her. "You handled him very well for the most part. He does have an aversion to talking about his personal life."

"So I noticed." Claudette looked speculatively at Ellie. "Do you know who this 'Ellie' is?"

Ellie nodded, trying to keep from smiling. It was dan-

gerous to talk to Claudette one second longer than she
had to; it was like asking for exposure, and she certainly
didn't want that. But the humor of the situation was ir-
resistible.

"Well, then—" Claudette's voice assumed the persuasive note she'd used on Josh "—what would it take for
you to tell me?"

"You're wasting time on me," Ellie told her bluntly.
"Whoever she is, she doesn't want to have her romance
plastered all over the tabloids to satisfy some reporter's
lust for blood. You've got a great interview—much better
than any other he's given. Write it up and be content."

Claudette chose not to be offended. "A good reporter,"
she said, stowing her equipment back in the huge bag, "is
never content. If you won't tell me who the chick is, will
you at least steer me around this gorgeous pad a little?
Any one of my esteemed colleagues would kill to be in
my shoes right now. This place is the seventh wonder of
the rock 'n' roll world."

Ellie laughed. "I would be glad to, but I don't know my
way around. I've never been here before. And judging
from what Josh said, security probably wouldn't let us
get far."

Claudette seized a gooey pastry from the tray on the
coffee table and took an enormous bite. "Well," she said
indistinctly, wiping the whipped cream off her upper lip
with a napkin. "Let's get as far as we can."

Finishing the pastry, she rested her hand on the door-
knob. It opened under her touch, and Chuck Green stood
framed in the opening. "Josh asked me to see you out, Ms
Cort," he said politely. Spying Ellie, he smiled. "Could
you go upstairs? Lunch is being served on the terrace."

Claudette began to wheedle Chuck into letting her stay
for lunch, but he was adamant. He swept her out the door
and through the foyer, listening to her pleas with an in-
dulgent smile. "When Keith wants to talk to you, he'll let

you know," he told her, pressing a button beside the ornate front door. The door opened, revealing the plush interior of the private elevator. "I'll take you down, Ms Cort." He propelled her firmly into the elevator and flipped one hand in goodbye. "Back in a few, Ellie, if you want to wait for me to show you the way to the terrace."

Ellie had time to see Claudette's eyes narrow before the elevator doors closed.

9

New Year's Eve in New York City.

Eleanor sat with Jennifer Magnusson in the greenhouse high atop Keith Redmont's apartment. The place was actually more like a solarium, filled with a jungle of climbing plants and flowers surrounding a large circular swimming pool. The roof was an ingenious arrangement of glass panes that could be hydraulically folded back during the summer. Now they were closed, and the weak winter sun warmed the two women stretched on lounges near the pool.

It hadn't occurred to Ellie to bring a swimsuit along on a midwinter tour. Jennifer had loaned her a bikini, which she wore with trepidation. There seemed to be so much more of her than of it—she was used to more staid water attire. However, it covered everything of importance, although her breasts swelled voluptuously above the skimpy top and the bottoms threatened to come off every time she dove into the pool.

She had been spending several hours each day at the penthouse and was thinking that she'd be sorry to leave it behind. Evidently one could get used to living in luxury quite quickly. Perhaps it was because, around Jennifer, the luxury didn't seem to be an end in itself, but merely something to be enjoyed in the intervals between hard work.

Keith and Josh were working in the studio, polishing some songs they'd been rehearsing together for Keith's next album. Ellie had suggested that Josh get some rest before the final concert that night, but he'd shrugged it away.

"Although. . . ." There had been a wicked gleam in his eyes. They stood in the studio, waiting for Keith, and he seized her in a tight embrace. "I might reconsider if you rest with me. Of course, in that case we wouldn't get much rest."

Ellie felt the breath leave her body. They had maintained their agreement of not making love, but the result had been to sensitize her to Josh so finely that sometimes just a look from him was enough to start her body simmering. The night before, after the concert, they had been hard put not to tumble into Josh's bed at the penthouse.

"So soon they forget," she whispered mockingly, rubbing herself against him with slow, sensual movements. "What happened to Mr. Noble Rock Star?"

His eyes half-lidded with incipient passion, Josh stared down at her. "He's getting very hungry," he growled, lowering his mouth to touch hers. "He wants to turn into Mr. Big Bad Wolf Rock Star and gobble you up."

She gave up the game abruptly, twining her arms around his neck and stopping his words with her demanding tongue. His hands found her breasts, her hips pressed intimately into his. Passion blazed between them before Ellie pushed reluctantly away.

"How long?" Her voice was husky with wanting. Josh pulled her close again, cradling her head against his chest with a deep sigh. "How long before you come to your senses?"

"My senses are fine," he whispered raggedly. "It's my head that's in trouble." She had her ear pressed to his chest, and his voice rumbled through her. "I just haven't come to grips with the whole commitment thing."

She tried to draw away but he crushed her closer, his

hands moving in sensual patterns on her back. He watched the helpless desire build on her face. "Please straighten it out, then," she said, gasping for air. "You're driving me around the bend here."

"I'll let you know when I'm ready," he promised, turning to greet Keith as he came into the studio.

Now cradled in the aromatic warmth of the greenhouse, she thought about the night ahead. It was noble of Josh to decide that he had rushed her into bed and should give them both time for second thoughts. Noble, and stupid. She had no doubts herself. Josh had been the first man in a long time to stir her sufficiently to overcome the memory of her fiasco of a marriage. She would never have gone to bed with him if he hadn't meant something to her.

But she hadn't really minded the period of abstinence from Josh, either. Although it had been hard, it had lent a new, if not tortured, dimension to their sensual awareness of each other. Knowing that they wouldn't be making love, each had felt freer to indulge the tenderness behind the driving urges. And the buildup of tension that was inevitable merely signified to her that when the act finally occurred, it would be more explosive than anything she'd ever experienced.

She shivered at the thought. Jennifer, lying next to her, misinterpreted it. "Getting cold?" Her voice was drowsy. She opened her eyes and squinted at the sun. "The days are so short now, it's hardly worth it to try for any sun." She glanced sideways at Ellie. "But sunlight is supposed to be good for pregnant women."

Ellie blinked at her. "Am I to take it that you're pregnant, then?"

Jennifer laughed and nodded. "I haven't told many people—although someone's been gossiping, or that newshound the other night wouldn't have asked about it. But I know you're safe to tell."

"Congratulations." Ellie was madly curious about the other part of the newshound's question, the part concerning Keith and Jennifer getting married. With an effort she kept herself from asking.

"I guess you're wondering why Keith and I aren't getting married," Jennifer ventured.

Ellie flushed and mumbled, "None of my business, I know."

Jennifer laced her fingers together and looked at them intently. "I want to get married," she said at last, her voice low. "But Keith is already married."

"I didn't know that!"

"It's not common knowledge, although he doesn't keep it a secret." Jennifer was silent for a moment. "It's the classic story. He got married when he was nineteen to a very beautiful girl who was fronting the band he played in then—Linda Forman. Maybe you've heard of her."

The name was vaguely familiar. "She had one big hit in the sixties," Eleanor said slowly. "Then she faded away."

"She went nuts," Jennifer stated bluntly. "She was doing lots of drugs and she simply wigged out permanently one day. She doesn't know anyone, doesn't see anything. Just sits and rocks back and forth." Shuddering, Jennifer sat up and hugged her knees. "You know, it is getting cold out here."

"So is Keith...?" Eleanor hesitated. She didn't want to pry into what was obviously a painful topic.

"Is he divorcing her?" Jennifer shook her head. "I suppose the reason why you don't hear more about this is that everyone assumed years ago that he'd gotten divorced. But he...well, Keith has scruples about that. He still visits Linda, although he can't bear to go too often. She doesn't recognize him at all, you see." Jennifer spoke very precisely, as if by focusing on the words she could negate the pain they carried. "I went with him one time. I was wildly jealous of her before, but when I saw her...."

She paused momentarily. "It means nothing to her whether Keith is legally her husband or not," she continued finally. "But it's not something I could feel justified in taking away from her." She met Ellie's glance and nodded. "Oh, I could get him to divorce her if I threw my weight around. But I can't make it be that important. After all, I have Keith, and soon I'll have our baby. She doesn't even have herself anymore."

They were quiet, then Jennifer shook herself out of her dark mood. "So don't you have any interesting revelations to make to me?" Her voice was gently teasing. "Any honeymoons in the offing?"

Ellie shook her head, trying to keep things light. "Not only no honeymoons, but right now, nothing lurid of any kind."

Jennifer raised her eyebrows. "You surprise me." She swung her feet over the side of the lounge and stretched. "We didn't see much of Josh after the accident. He never came to New York, and we didn't get to California that much." She scrutinized Ellie carefully. "It seems that when he's around you it's as if he's been restored to humanity. He's open—and I think very vulnerable. I don't believe you would play with him or do him any willful harm," she added.

"Of course not." Ellie stood, too, and began to fold the lounge. "If you want to know whether I'd marry him if he asked me, I'd have to tell you that I...I just don't know."

Jennifer led the way to the storage area where the lounge chairs were kept. "You're not in love with him, or you're just not sure it's forever? What's the problem?"

Ellie shoved her chair into the storage bin and

straightened to meet Jennifer's candid gaze. "I'm in love with him all right." She smiled wryly. "I guess anyone can see that from miles away. But about his feelings, I just don't know."

"Well, I predict good news on that front in the near future, judging from the way he looks at you." Jennifer stretched again and yawned. "I think I'll go take a little nap before dinner," she murmured. "I get so tired these days. Help yourself to a drink or whatever." She waved her hand vaguely around, encompassing the whole of the penthouse, and left.

Ellie considered following her but decided that one last swim would be invigorating. She dove in, pulling her bikini bottom back up afterward, and tried to move zealously across the pool. But the water in the shallow end was warm and inviting, and finally she propped her elbows against the edge of the pool and floated, closing her eyes and letting the small waves lap gently at her skin.

Josh found her there when his session ended. He entered the greenhouse so quietly she didn't know he was there until his footsteps on the tile surrounding the pool roused Eleanor from a contemplative stupor amounting almost to sleep. She sat up abruptly at the sight of him as he stripped off his clothes and stood poised on the edge of the pool across from her, gloriously and unselfconsciously naked. He dove in and came up in front of her, letting the water slick back his hair.

"What if someone comes in?" Ellie tried to frown in disapproval, but she couldn't stop her eyes from searching busily below the waist-high water for the other half of his body.

"I'll stand behind you." His eyes were as busy as hers. Perversely she sank back down in the water, letting it cover her to her chin. Josh knelt in front of her until his face was even with hers, letting his spread-eagled knees come to rest on either side of her legs. "At least I'm not trying to hide anything." He cocked an eyebrow at the strip of cloth that covered her breasts. "You're not being too successful, you know," he told her mildly. "Looking like that ought to be illegal."

She could feel the whisper of the water over her legs, a stirring, swelling press of excitement that communicated itself to her almost by osmosis. His voice was low and rough, and seemed to catch her own breath and turn it ragged. "It probably is illegal in some states," she agreed, trying to sound normal. "Jennifer is only three or four sizes smaller than me. I'm surprised it fits at all."

"You're too much woman for it," Josh said. Before she knew what he was doing, he tugged the top down, freeing her breasts to the gentle sway of the water. His hands were poised to cup the richness he'd revealed, but he watched her face. "Only if you say so," he murmured.

She closed her eyes briefly to shut out the intoxication of seeing him trembling for the want of touching her. Her hands found his in the water and brought them slowly up until her fullness pressed into them. "You made the rules, Blackmun. Third base, but no further." She gasped as his thumbs rasped erotically over the aching peaks he held so gently.

"What if I break the rules?" His voice was calm, but his arms shook as her fingers traveled up to nest in his hair.

She opened her eyes. "They were your rules," she reminded him. "Wasn't my idea to be so chaste."

Reluctantly his hands slid away from her breasts and met in the small of her back; he supported her in the water. One hand probed along the edge of the swimsuit bottom, finding and toying with the knot that kept it on. "You know why I did it." He looked directly into her eyes, and she was captured by the vulnerability she saw there.

"I don't think I do, really," she whispered. "Tell me, Josh."

He took a deep breath and brought one dripping hand around to finger her wet hair. "At first it was because I couldn't say the words. I felt guilty, knowing you loved me. I...I didn't want to take advantage of your love."

"Josh—"

"No, let me finish." He placed one finger on her lips. "Women have said they loved me before. But it wasn't like your love. There was nothing nourishing in it." He was silent for a moment. "I still can't give you those words, Ellie. I still don't know how I feel. I thought if we didn't make love I could separate the wanting and the needing from us just being together. It's just all too complicated."

She pulled his hand away from her lips and smiled up at him. "You're a complicated man, Joshua Blackmun. That's one of the reasons I'm attracted to you." Her smile faded. "I wish now I'd never told you, but since I did, let me tell you something else. There are no conditions on my love. I offer it freely, and you may take it just as freely. If you find you must walk away sometime—well, I won't bind you." She blinked away the sudden tears that threatened to overflow and summoned a spark of laughter. "We analyze things to death. Why don't we just let it be?"

His face was grave, but her words lit an answering smile in his eyes. "*Que sera sera,*" he agreed solemnly, letting his hand drift down again to the knot on her bikini bottom.

"Do what comes naturally, you might say." She sucked in her breath as the last remnant of cloth floated free of her body. "Oh, Josh...."

His hands began to move with exquisite power over breasts, belly, hips, finding all the hidden sensitive places and bringing them to flower. Once more her eyes drifted shut as an overpowering pleasure began to build in her.

"Let me give you this, Ellie." His voice ragged with emotion, he watched her respond to his caresses. "At least let me be your man. I want you for my woman, my Ellie."

A tiny smile curved her lips and she reached to bring his head down to hers. "Don't talk so much, Blackmun," she murmured. "You've got a lot of catching up to do."

WALKING ON AIR. Ellie had often heard the expression, and now she knew what it meant. She was walking on air as she drifted into the Clarendon to change for the New Year's Eve concert. She had left Josh sprawled on his bed at Keith's, almost but not quite snoring. Thinking of the love they'd made, in the pool, in his room after dinner, she couldn't help the satisfied smile that seemed pinned to her face. Though he wasn't able to say that he loved her, Ellie felt confident that only a man in love could have been so tender in the middle of helpless passion.

She was still floating a few inches above the ground when she carried a handful of phone messages into the elevator and began to sort through them. The professional side of her was gratified at the requests for interviews and photos. "Too late!" she muttered gleefully. "Blackmun is exclusive. He's already talked to everyone that matters in New York."

Then the name Claudette Cort leaped out at her and she froze. She'd been so wrapped up in Josh, in hustling him around for all the promotional events he'd stand for, in finding cozy unplanned hours to spend with him, in parties at Keith's and concerts every night, that she'd all but forgotten the implicit threat of Claudette Cort labeling her for all the world as Josh Blackmun's new

honey. Her mind's eye immediately came up with hor-
rifying headlines. "Publicist Throws Self into Work!"
"Is Blackmun Pressing Press Agent?"

Don't be irrational. She fitted her key into the door
and let herself into her room. No one knew better than
she just how unimportant the media considered an unknown lover of a famous person. She wouldn't be worth
headlines in any but the most desperate-for-news
tabloids.

Moving automatically, she went to the wardrobe and
got the outfit she'd bought the day before to wear at the
concert. The top was luxurious crimson velvet padded
and slashed like a medieval doublet, beaded and quilted
with gold, worn over black velvet pants. She had
thought about some slinky black heels, but the bitter
chill and the sleet that threatened made her glad she'd
decided to wear her fur-lined suede boots. They didn't
look too bad, and the protection they afforded from the
treacherous streets was welcome.

But all the while she dressed and worked on her hair
and put on makeup, the telephone seemed to loom on
the edge of her vision like some small black monster
crouching to pounce. Finally she could put it off no
longer. She picked up the message with Claudette's
number on it and dialed quickly, needing to get it over
with.

The phone rang and rang. She hung up after seven
rings, deciding it made more sense to fail to return
Claudette's call. After all, what could she say if confronted with point-blank questions on the state of her
relationship with Josh? She had also learned long ago
that when you talk to the press about something you'd
rather not discuss, you inevitably end up saying too
much. A journalist of Claudette's stature wouldn't
publish rumor and insinuation as fact.

"Nothing to worry about," she said aloud, stopping

for a last glance in the full-length mirror on the bathroom door. Her cheeks glowed brilliantly with excitement above the brave crimson of her tunic. She had
used the curling iron to good effect, and her brown hair
spilled over her shoulders in well-orchestrated riot. She
made a gallant figure, she decided, raising one hand in a
debonair salute. "All I need is a sword and a cape."
Donning her long quilted down coat she locked the door
behind her.

She was sailing through the lobby, anticipating the
cab drive to the Music Hall, when a voice called her
name. "Ellie? Ms Martinson?"

Caught, she thought, wondering if she should simply
make a run for it. But that would be so undignified.
Turning slowly, she faced Claudette Cort, who sprang
up from the shelter of one of the capacious wing chairs
that dotted the lobby.

"I called earlier," Claudette said, adjusting the ever-
present bag with tape recorder, camera, et al. "You were
out."

"I did try to call you back," Ellie murmured, eyeing
the bag askance. "But you were out also." Was Claudette hoping to take her picture?

Claudette fumbled in the bag. "Why don't you sit
here for a minute?" she urged hospitably. "I would like
to talk to you about a few points."

One look at that determined face and Ellie knew there
would be no way to keep Claudette from getting her
"few points." But at least she could keep her off-
balance, make her work for the fell deed.

"I'll be glad to chat," she assured Claudette with false
breeziness. "But I'm in a terrible rush. We can talk in a
taxi."

Claudette's mouth tightened for a moment. She
stopped fumbling in her bag, and Ellie congratulated
herself silently. It would be dark in the cab. Pictures

would be impossible. She would deal with the problem of what to do with Claudette at the concert.

She would be too early, of course, she realized as a cab swerved to answer the doorman's imperious gesture. She had meant to go first to Keith's apartment, then ride over with Josh. Now she told the cabbie the Music Hall's address and settled back on the musty seat. The traffic was crawling even though rush hour was officially over. "This is going to take a while," she told Claudette. "You can put it on your expense account. Peter would think I should have taken the bus."

"Peter?" Claudette jumped avidly on the name.

"Peter Macguire, head of Trax Records." Eleanor kept the conversation on Peter and the record company he'd built from nothing as long as she could, postponing the inevitable personal questions. "You should think about doing a story on the Eves of Destruction." She finished a long anecdote about Peter's other artists with a plug for the Eves. "They're touring Great Britain right now, selling out their venues everywhere. Those young ladies are going to be important."

Claudette looked interested and jotted a few notes, evidently unhampered by the cabbie's sudden lurches as he tried to weave through the sluggish traffic. "Thanks for the info," she said, looking back at Ellie, "but that's not really what I wanted to talk to you about."

Ellie grabbed her bag as a particularly bad jolt sent everything flying to the floor. "Talk away."

Claudette fished her little tape recorder out of her bag and turned it on. The action had an ominous significance to Ellie. "I really would like to know all about this 'Ellie' stuff so I can see whether it belongs in my article or not."

"It doesn't," Eleanor said positively.

Claudette waited a moment, and when nothing more was forthcoming she sighed impatiently. "Let me be the

judge of that," she suggested. "You're Ellie, right?
You're the one Blackmun dedicated the first concert to?"

"Yes." Eleanor couldn't keep the caution out of her
voice.

"Well, why did he do it? What's between the two of
you? Do you deny that you're having a relationship
with Blackmun aside from the professional one of being
his publicist?"

The questions came with rapid-fire intent that might
have bowled Ellie over if she hadn't glimpsed the Music
Hall facade down the block. "This is close enough," she
hollered to the driver, hopping out and thrusting money
into his startled face. Claudette scrambled out on her
side and followed Ellie to the curb.

"I couldn't stand that musty smell a second longer,"
Ellie said kindly as they moved off down the sidewalk.
She set a brisk pace, knowing her long legs gave her the
advantage over Claudette's short stature. But she didn't
feel guilty. On her own two feet—warm and snugly
clad—she had confidence that she could regain control
of the situation.

Claudette trotted at her side, tape recorder at the
ready. "For heaven's sake, slow down!" she gasped.
"This isn't the marathon."

"Oh, was I walking too fast?" Ellie slowed her pace
minimally. "Thing is, it's cold out here. I'm not used to
this icy weather. Have to keep moving to keep from
freezing." The cold, she noticed with a small stab of
malicious pleasure, was turning the end of Claudette's
cute little nose red. Claudette, the red-nosed reporter.
She suppressed a smile and tried to feel sorry for having
bad thoughts. She didn't try long.

"So...Ellie...how long have...you and Blackmun...." Claudette's words came out accompanied by
labored puffs of breath. *Must not be a jogger*, Ellie
decided, and slowed some more.

"Here we are." She turned in under the ornate portico of the Music Hall, where an aproned boy swept the minuscule lobby. "I'll be with you in a minute, Claudette. Have to make some phone calls. Howie?"

The big bouncer let her into the manager's office, and she shut the door firmly in Claudette's face. The club was just opening, people beginning to drift in and stand around the bar. With any luck she could hide out in the office until close to show time.

She took a deep breath and unbuttoned her coat. Moving to the manager's cluttered desk, she got Josh on the phone. His answering rasp brought a thrill to her senses.

"When are you coming by to get me?"

"I can't tonight, Josh. I'll meet you at the club."

There was a pause, then his voice lowered to a sexy whisper. "I had planned on waiting till you got here to put on my clothes. Thought maybe you'd like to help me."

She lowered her own voice correspondingly. "Are you . . . just lying there in bed, naked?"

"That's right. Wearing nothing but a smile and—"

"Whoa, down boy! Remember this is a business phone!"

There was a short pause. "It is? Where are you, anyway? Why can't you come here?"

"Some details to take care of," she said as lightly as she could. She had decided it would be better not to tell him about Claudette—not before the show, anyway. No sense in getting him upset just before a performance. "I'm at the Music Hall already, so there doesn't seem to be much sense in going all the way back to get you. The traffic is fierce."

"Of course it's fierce, this is New Year's Eve. Arrgh!" There was a swishing sound from the phone, then a thunk. "There, that's better. The sheets were trying to devour me."

The pressure of worrying must have been affecting her, because she felt hysterical giggles sputtering from her lips. "Josh, what are you doing? You should be getting up and getting ready to blow out your fuses for the lucky listeners tonight. Instead you're making love to a sheet or something."

"Wish you were here."

She snorted. "Oh, that's very romantic indeed. If I was there you would abandon the sheet for me. I must really have what it takes!"

"You know the answer to that one." His voice was husky now. "Do you have time for me to start listing my favorite parts of you? Believe me, my dear, you have everything it takes."

Distracted from her problems for the moment, she demanded, "Which favorite parts?"

"Starting with your ear," he replied promptly, "because it's listening to me. That leads me directly to your sensual and charming brain, currently occupied, I hope, by fantasies of what we could be doing if you weren't so busy with business. Your eyes—"

"Enough already." Laughing, she tried to stem the flow. "Really, Josh, I'm sorry I asked. C'mon now, Blackmun, that's quite enough. Josh! My God!"

"Pert and round and delightfully rosy," he went on inexorably. "Your stomach—"

"Is this going to turn out to be an obscene phone call? Because if it is. . . ."

"Okay, I'll stop. See you after the show."

"Right."

She hung up the phone and sat for a moment feeling extraordinarily happy. At last, reluctantly she moved, fishing her telephone credit card out of her bag and dialing again. If she was going to hide out, she might as well accomplish something.

Even though it was a holiday, Peter answered the

phone at Trax. "Don't you ever take a vacation?" She made her voice lightly teasing, and it only took him a second to figure out who it was.

"Ellie!" He sounded glad to hear her, then apprehensive. "There's nothing wrong, is there?"

"Nothing much," she said bleakly. "The concerts have been going great, and we've gotten some very favorable ink in the local rags."

"I've seen it," he replied enthusiastically. "Or some of it, at least. The clipping agency has sent a few of the notices along. So Josh is playin' good?"

"He's dynamite." Ellie took a deep breath. "We talked to Claudette Cort."

"How did it go? Is she as devastating in public as she is on paper?"

Thinking of Claudette made Ellie's hand tighten on the receiver. "She's so sweet butter wouldn't melt in her mouth, but she digs the knife in pretty well." Ellie debated with herself about how much to tell Peter. "She's got this, er, idea that there's something cooking between Josh and me."

"How would she get that idea?" Peter's voice sharpened. "Ellie, are you . . . ?"

"Well, I don't want to go into a lot of detail here, Peter." She made her voice as unconcerned as possible. "I just wondered, do you have any particular way you'd like me to handle it? I mean, if you want I'll just deny it."

"Good grief." She got a mental picture of him running his hands through his hair in distraction. "What did Josh say?"

"He didn't say anything to her," Ellie assured him cheerfully. "But you know what a mystery he makes of his personal life, and you know how a reporter loves a mystery."

Peter's sigh gusted over the three thousand miles of

telephone wire that separated them. "Handle it any way you see fit, Ellie. You're on the ground." His voice lightened a little. "And this is the last time I want you fooling around with my clients. If you wanted to fool around, why didn't you go to the boss?"

"Just...just one of those things, I expect." She stumbled a little over the lame words. The note of sincerity she heard in his voice had surprised her. Recovering, she added, "Maybe you should try going to *my* boss about any problems you might be having in that direction."

There was silence, then Peter spoke, sounding confused. "Ellie? Was that supposed to mean anything? I must have been working too hard lately or something. I thought for a minute there you were implying—"

Ellie spoke hastily. "Nothing, Peter. Not worth another thought." *Not on a conscious level, anyway.* She wasn't a matchmaker, but knowing that Gena was attracted to Peter made it hard not to stick in her oar. "So I'll get back to you again before we hit L.A. We go to Chicago on the second."

"Right. Well, Happy New Year, Ellie. And watch yourself. I don't want to see you get hurt or anything."

"Happy New Year to you, Peter. I won't get hurt."

She hung up and sat with one hand on the receiver, lost in thought. Perhaps it hadn't been a good idea to call Peter. But she felt she needed to tell someone, and he had a right to know how the publicity was going.

The door burst open. Claudette was standing in the opening, hands on hips, her bag swinging at her side. Howie loomed behind her.

"Now look, Ellie." She was clearly exasperated. "If you don't want to talk, just say so! But call off your goon there—" she jerked her thumb over her shoulder toward Howie "—and let me get on with it! Or shall we simply cancel the story?"

"No, no! Now don't get huffy, Claudette." Ellie made her voice placating and gave Howie an unobtrusive signal to melt away. "I've just this minute finished my phone calls, and am at your disposal. Ask away."

Claudette seated herself, eyeing Ellie closely. "You know," she said, taking out the tape recorder but not turning it on, "if you'd just tell me to M.Y.O.B., I would certainly—"

"Mind your own business," Ellie replied promptly.

Claudette blinked, and then slowly began to laugh. "Like that, is it?" She put the tape recorder back in her bag and relaxed into her chair. "Why don't you just talk to me about Blackmun," she suggested. "You be in charge of how much you say. I won't use your name in the article, I'll just quote you as a source close to the subject. Just tell me what you want me to know and leave it at that."

Ellie thought it over and agreed. It was no more than she did at times for a lot of her clients. She knew how to bring up the facts without puffing them, how to skirt past the danger areas. So for the next hour she talked and Claudette listened, taking notes, asking an intelligent question now and again.

At the end of the hour the manager appeared, wanting his office back. Ellie was ready to abdicate. She'd said all she needed to, and was afraid that any further information would simply be babble—dangerous babble, perhaps.

They walked into the lobby and up the stairs to the bar, already crowded although the warm-up band wasn't due to start for another half hour. Ellie bought drinks and they carried them to one of the tables at the back of the hall. Glancing at the box that Keith had occupied each night of the concert, Ellie saw that it was still empty. The penthouse party had not yet arrived.

Claudette caught the direction of her glance and

looked wistful. "I saw you all sitting there the night of the first concert," she mentioned. "You certainly seemed to be having a good time."

"Nothing like a little life in the fast lane," Ellie said airily, ignoring the "doggy wants a bone" expression Claudette had assumed. "I've never been associated with such exalted levels of the rock business before." From the corner of her eye she caught a stir around Keith's box. She stood and stuck out her hand. "Hope the article turns out well. If you need any more information, or more prints of the photos, please get in touch with me. You have my card, and my office will be able to find me on the tour."

Claudette said goodbye, but not without another longing look toward the box, where Chuck Green was now standing.

Keith and Jennifer were just settling into their seats when Ellie got to the box, but Ellie had eyes only for Josh, who stood by the far door, a fire exit that also led backstage. She walked straight to him and his arms enfolded her in a very satisfactory embrace. "Hope your cute little friend out there hasn't got a telephoto lens on her camera," he growled into her ear, nibbling suggestively around it.

"Maybe I should have brought her here where we could keep an eye on her." Ellie looked up at him teasingly. "She wanted to come."

He squeezed her tighter and kissed her once, thoroughly and tenderly. "Don't talk blasphemy, woman. Gotta go sit in one of those closets they call dressing rooms." He sighed and murmured a few blatant suggestions into her ear of things he'd rather be doing than sweltering backstage.

"Really?" She chuckled. "I don't know if that's anatomically possible."

"Neither do I. We'll find out later." With one last hug, he was gone.

Ellie sighed as she sat beside Jennifer. She was becoming addicted to Josh's presence, wanting to be alone with him and the fiery caresses she found so arousing. Instead she got to watch while he sang for thousands. Would each woman in the crowd be imagining that he was her lover? Would they be fantasizing while he sang? She smiled complacently. Let them. She had the real thing. There was no need to fantasize, although his last suggestion....

Keith leaned across Jennifer to poke her. "You're drooling, Ellie."

She blushed and smiled. "Sorry. Blame it on Blackmun." To change the subject she turned to Jennifer. "Did you get a good rest?"

Jennifer nodded, and Keith put an arm around her. "Let me know if it gets too much for you, love. You've had a lot of late nights recently."

"This is the last one for a long time," Jennifer said, not looking in the least tired. "After tonight I intend to sleep for a week."

"Then you don't always live like this?" Ellie thought of the parties every night after the concerts, the endless streams of famous and infamous people that had come and gone in the big rooms high above the city. She had taken it for granted that this was the daily life of a superstar.

"Heavens, no!" Jennifer laughed and snuggled into Keith's arm. "This is the holiday season, so we've been kicking out the jams. Normally though, we're up early. Keith has so many business details to administer to that it's hard for him to get time to write. And I put in a pretty full day with the Foundation." The Foundation, Ellie knew, provided tuition money and living expenses for promising students of the arts. Keith had started it, but many major artists contributed to its endowment.

"We do go out, but it tends to be a drag if Keith gets

recognized," Jennifer went on. "So really, we mostly stay home." She sighed dramatically. "Prisoners of Fifth Avenue, that's what we are."

Keith grinned lazily. "We make our own world, love." He lowered his head to Jennifer, and for a moment they became lost in that world.

Ellie watched with something akin to envy. These two had managed to reconcile all the forces that opposed a stable relationship between a person of considerable fame and notoriety, and a person with none. They were busy, productive, and above all, detached. Ellie had seen wives—and husbands—of the famous try to find meaning for their lives by immersing themselves in their spouse's career. It was unhealthy for both, and usually ended in disaster.

Could she and Josh ever build such a sturdy way of life? She mused for a few moments on what it would be like if they were to live together. There would be no penthouse, she knew, no fast-lane life in L.A. or New York. Josh would more than likely want to keep up his reclusive existence.

And she was a gregarious person who was used to a lot of social contact. There were too many variables to arrive at any conclusion, but she could feel in her bones that there were volatile issues at stake.

Well, this was no time to brood. The warm-up band burst into sound. Ellie settled back in her seat to enjoy the concert. In a couple of hours, the year would be over. She would worry about the new year when it began.

10

THE NEW YEAR COULDN'T have had a better start, until it ran full tilt into Los Angeles.

For many years Ellie had privately considered that city her own personal hex, a bad-luck place where nothing would go right for her.

Listening to Josh on the long, late-night flights as the tour moved from New York to Chicago, to St. Louis, to Houston, to Portland, she came to believe that L.A. was the same specter for him, held the same dread threat. Sitting together on airplanes, lying together in hotel-room beds, they exchanged life histories, finding parallels, discovering similarities. He was reticent only on the subject of Vivienne Santos, and she was too afraid of what she might find out to probe deeply. Instead, she entertained him with her own cheerful stories.

"So there I was, stuck in Santa Rosa with a drunken country-western band on my hands and a crowd of rowdy red-necks just looking for something to fight about—"

"Hey, same thing happened to me once! Except it was Dallas instead of Santa Rosa, and I was the one passing out in my dressing room while the road manager poured hot coffee down my throat."

"Don't you dare try anything like that with me around, Blackmun. I'll just wipe up the floor with your sad body."

"Tough girl, eh? Let me show you what happens to tough broads in the music business today."

"You wanna decorate the carpet or something? Is that it, huh? Got a death wish, Blackmun? Say 'aunt,' now. Say it!"

"Okay, okay, aunt, you sadist. Man, I think I'm fainting. Mouth-to-mouth resuscitation, quick! Ahh, that's the stuff."

By the time they were on their way to Los Angeles, Ellie could have sworn that the understanding between them was as deep and strong as the ocean. Josh wasn't a man for tender words, except in his songs, and she'd more or less forbidden him to write about her and their relationship.

She didn't repeat her vow of love. It was enough that Josh knew it, enough that he showed her in thousands of ways that he felt the same. Often he spoke of the future in terms of the two of them together. There were no firm plans, but Ellie was content to wait on happenstance. When the tour was over they'd talk about it.

That didn't mean that she hadn't reflected on their future together. Being the kind of person who plans everything, she had thought that after the tour they would curl up in front of Josh's fireplace, Bertha beside them, and discuss their future. For now, they were both content to drift with the tides of their passion, to cement their tenuous bonds with an ever-increasing knowledge of each other.

She learned a lot about Josh during those days and nights on the road. With her, with the crew, he was a different person—quick to laugh, genial, not above helping to set up or strike the equipment. He was a man's man, but there was nothing coarse or crude about him. Aside from Ellie there was only one other unattached woman on the tour, one of the crew members. But the male crew members and the backup band followed Josh's lead. There was plenty of laughter and the usual amount of risqué jokes. But the overall atmosphere was one of respect and support.

The Josh Blackmun who kept everyone in stitches backstage was a different creature from the commanding, demanding artist who settled for nothing less than the best anyone had to give during a performance. When the bass player had partied too hard and wasn't up to standard that night, Josh was merciless. Onstage, he was quicksilver, lightning, as blazing as the sun, as cool as the moon. Constantly he refined and reworked, driving the band in rehearsals when he felt it was necessary.

And there was another Josh Blackmun, the one who could treat importunate reporters to icy, savage indifference. "Mercy," Ellie had exclaimed after one of these occasions, when she hadn't been able to head off a local college student hopeful of an interview for his school paper. "I'd hate to be a door-to-door salesperson in your neighborhood. I bet you're positively lethal with 'We don't want any!' "

"They all ask the same questions," Josh snarled. "They all want to know the same nosy things! Why don't they read the interviews I've already given? Why don't they just use the press handout and leave me alone?"

"Because," Ellie said soothingly, "each one thinks that he or she is the lucky one to whom you're suddenly going to unburden yourself, spilling all the lurid details of your life."

"I didn't realize how young he was," Josh muttered. "Shouldn't have come down so hard on him, I guess."

"Oh, I don't know." Ellie made her voice offhand. "At least you gave him a story."

"I did?"

"Sure." She picked a bit of lint carefully from her sweater sleeve. "If you'd just waited until I could get rid of him, he wouldn't have gotten anything but the press kit and a nice smile from me. As it is, he had an epic encounter with famous recluse Josh Blackmun, whose ferocious temper is probably due to drugs or alcohol or congenital mental incapacity."

"You wretch." Josh laughed reluctantly. "Okay, I'll watch it in the future. But if you hadn't let them in, everything would be fine."

"Who am I, Chuck Green?" Ellie frowned. "If you want me to be your bodyguard, Blackmun, get yourself another publicist or pay me more. I don't make enough money to work every living second of the day."

When he pulled her close and used his persuasive lips on her, she saw yet another Josh Blackmun, the one who could look at her and make her feel as soft and liquid as a teenager at a Beatles concert. For this Josh Blackmun she would have done just about anything, although she kept that bit of information to herself.

The astounding responses he could invoke in her had added a whole dimension to her life, one that had never been more than a nebulous shadow before. The more of his loving she got, the more she craved. She had tamped down the physical side of her nature after the failure of her marriage, after the humiliation of hearing herself described as inept in bed whenever she tuned into Top 40 radio stations. Now she allowed her sensuality to blossom, and the result was intoxicating.

"My God, woman, you're wearing me into a shell of my former self. I'll have to take up running just to get some stamina."

"Good idea. You could use some aerobic exercise."

"What is that we just did? Seemed pretty aerobic to me."

"We didn't do it long enough. Gotta get your heart rate way up and work out for a minimum of twelve minutes if you want an aerobic benefit."

"Twelve minutes, huh? Where's my watch . . . ?"

"Blackmun, I thought you were worn out! Shouldn't we get some rest now?"

"We did rest. For at least five minutes. And since we've already got our heart rates way up, we might as well keep going."

"But—oh! Ahh!"

"And some of this, just to keep your pulse jumpin'."

"Mmm, Blackmun. . . . Oh, that feels . . . hey, what are you doing?"

"Just setting the alarm. Don't want to overdo. Now, can you . . . ahh, that's it. Ellie! Oh, darlin'. . . ."

It certainly didn't seem, coming into Los Angeles, that there was any need for worry. She felt high, able to fly without the airplane. Josh was beside her; Josh was talking about a future spent together. What could go wrong?

For a start, the airport could lose three of their amplifiers and Josh's favorite guitar.

Rick, the road manager, caught them on their way to the waiting limousine that was to take them to their hotel. "We're missing some equipment, man." He spoke to Josh, but his words were meant for Ellie, who had become an unofficial tour leader and buffer for all problems. "The dudes here want all sorts of papers filled out and signed, and you know we're running late for the concert tonight. I got to start getting set up."

"I can do it," Ellie said quickly. Josh had already received a few glances from the celebrity-hungry crowd that was omnipresent in L.A. International. "You guys go on. There's no press call this afternoon, Josh, so you don't need to speak to anyone. I'll take the equipment directly to the concert from here. Can you drop my stuff off at the hotel?" She looked at Josh, and he nodded curtly, his body assuming the stiff shell he wore when he felt unprotected in public.

For the first concert in L.A., he had agreed to play a larger venue, a five-thousand-seat outdoor pavilion in the hills near the University of California campus. The open-air amphitheater would make a stark, dramatic background, and Ellie had been looking forward to the concert.

Now she felt tension begin in the muscles at the back of her neck. With one more look at Josh she turned back into the airport to chase down their errant equipment.

Dusk was falling before she managed to get the equipment located, freed of paperwork and crammed into the biggest rental car she could find. She got out the map of Los Angeles the car-rental agent had provided her with and pored over it for a few minutes. It had been a long time since she'd lived there, and she didn't want to waste a lot of time getting lost on the freeway.

She had forgotten that the time you waste on the freeway is not usually because of getting lost. Twenty minutes after pulling onto Interstate 405 for the less-than-ten-mile drive, she was still eight miles away and choking in exhaust. She'd managed to hit the rush hour dead on the noggin.

Creeping along at a rate that could be measured in feet instead of miles, she began to glance at her watch every five minutes. The warm-up act provided by the booking agent had been scheduled to begin at dusk. It wouldn't be long before Josh was due to take the stage. Rick would be pacing and fretting, but she could go no faster.

When she finally pulled into the backstage unloading zone of the pavilion, she was nearly mobbed by the anxious crew members. "Thank God!" Rick said the words fervently. "Five more minutes and we would have been goners. The guy who's opening is just ending his set now. Get those amps out, Karen, Mike! Somebody let Josh know his guitar finally made it."

Ellie moved aside and let the road crew do their job. She wandered closer to the wings. The stage was a crescent of stone with classic pillars supporting the arching roof. On either side of the stage the pillars fronted blank marble facades that contained the dressing rooms, equipment storage and lighting board. A narrow corridor backstage connected both sides, and there was a door leading out behind the previously set-up drum kit.

The first dressing room she came to was empty, its door open. A lingering scent drifted out of it that awoke old eddies in her mind. She hesitated for a moment, trying to recall what made her so uneasy, then shrugged and passed on to the next dressing room. Its door was closed, but she could hear voices and, unexpectedly, feminine laughter. More disquiet.

Her hand was poised to knock when she heard the warm-up singer start a chord progression on his guitar for his last song. Shocked into attention, she let her hand drop and arrived at the edge of the wings with no memory of walking there.

"This is a little tune I recorded some years ago," the singer said in a mock-humble voice. His profile was horrifyingly familiar. Knowing what was coming, she listened numbly. "Some of you may remember it." He played the chords again, the ones burned into her brain through months of painful exposure, and sang the opening bars. The audience clapped dutifully as they recognized an old hit.

> "When I try to love you baby,
> You're like an Ice Woman.
> Your touch is so cold babe.
> Why are you doin' me harm?"

Ellie turned cold herself, listening to the hurtful words through each chorus and verse. She had been so relieved five years ago when the song lost its short grasp on the charts and faded from the airwaves. She had never dreamed that it would surface now, when she'd nearly managed to escape its image of her.

In a daze she listened to the final chords, the polite applause, the singer's attempt to wring an encore from an audience clearly biding its time until the star attraction appeared.

Garrison Hanley took a final bow, shouted his thanks, and exited on the far side of the stage. Ellie stood behind one of the pillars, unmoving, still in shock. She felt rather than saw Josh approaching, surrounded by brightly dressed, gaily talking people, some of them with famous faces. He was clutching the guitar she'd rescued for him, but he didn't see her, though she thought that the quick glance he sent around the backstage before he moved in front of the audience was meant to locate her. She was too paralyzed to respond to it.

Josh's crowd of former friends and hangers-on lingered around the entrance to the stage, exchanging light comments, which gradually began to penetrate Ellie's fog.

"Still looks a little *untamed*." It was a man speaking, a willowy person in casual clothes so beautiful they took on the aura of formal dress. "I mean, that essential rawness that one found so exciting is still there. What do you think, Viv, darling?"

Ellie's heart contracted suddenly. The woman to whom the willowy man addressed his remarks had her back to Ellie; she was looking out to the stage. But there was no mistaking that waist-length, freely curling mane of midnight-black hair. When the woman turned, Ellie already knew how the black eyes would sparkle under their delicately arched brows, how the full red lips would pout and smile at the same time. Vivienne Santos tossed back her glorious hair and smiled a slow, feral smile.

"You're right, Stanley. One does still find him very . . . exciting." Her voice was husky, slightly accented and very charming. Ellie felt her heart slip down around her knees.

Vivienne Santos couldn't see her, lost as she was in the shadows behind a pillar. But Ellie felt as if every word the woman spoke was aimed straight at her.

"Max." The husky voice brought a man jumping out of the crowd to hover eagerly at Vivienne's elbow. "I want to sing a couple of the old numbers with him tonight. Arrange it." Max nodded and spun around, looking, Ellie guessed, for the road manager. "Janie." A woman bobbed up, beautifully groomed but older by some years than Vivienne. "Go find a couple of your tame music critics and start a rumor that Josh and I are going to be getting back together."

"Musically or—"

"Don't be too specific. Just that we're getting back together." Vivienne sent another look toward the stage, where Josh waited behind the drum kit while the road crew finished setting up the recently arrived amplifiers. "Marleen." This time the woman who appeared didn't wait for instructions, but began immediately to smooth the long black hair with a brush, to touch up the bright lips and straighten the immaculate clothes.

Ellie began cautiously backing up, wanting to get away from the carnage in front of her. She had never anticipated Vivienne's reentry into Josh's life, although if she had thought about it, she probably could have predicted its happening. Miss Santos's latest affair with a British superstar had recently come to a well-publicized end, as all her liaisons did. She was probably ripe for a new applicant to the position of lover, one with the qualifications to get her the right amount of media attention.

Wanting only to avoid attracting Vivienne's attention, and thus avoid being assigned some role in the singer's plans to get onstage with Josh, Ellie concentrated on moving soundlessly. If she'd only managed to look where she was going, as well, she wouldn't have bumped into Garrison Hanley at the door to his dressing room.

"What the—" Garrison steadied her by the elbows, then held her off for a closer look. "Eleanor! I can't believe it. Who would have believed that we'd meet again after all this time!"

Ellie had no answer for his hearty platitudes, and the ringing tone he spoke them in was attracting attention from Vivienne's group. With an overwhelming desire to remain totally unnoticed, she replied to Garrison in a feeble whisper.

"Good to see you, Garrison." She glanced around for rescue, feeling hunted, but although the crew was coming back from the stage, their attention was still fixed on the band. A huge disembodied voice boomed, "Ladies and gentlemen, Joshua Blackmun!" Then the audience spoke with its own single, roaring voice, approval and greeting echoing from the surrounding hills.

Garrison let her go for a moment, and Ellie might have escaped then. But she was transfixed by the sight of Josh, isolated with his band in a pool of white brilliance, his dark head thrown back challengingly as he fingered his big Stratocaster. The applause and cheering went on and on until he held up his hand for silence.

"What is this, the hometown crowd or something?" His voice, with its sexy rasp and humorous inflection, brought the roaring monster to its feet. Josh swept the neck of his Stratocaster down and the band erupted with him into the rocking rhythms of "Runt of the Litter." It was the first time he'd opened a concert with one of his new tunes instead of an old hit. Ellie wouldn't have thought that was a good idea, but the audience was with him totally. It was a measure of his freshly renewed confidence in himself as a performer that he had taken such a step, and she glowed with pride for him at the same time as she fretted over her own predicament.

When she could pay attention to her immediate surroundings, she felt Garrison tugging her toward the loading dock and backstage parking area. "Come on, Eleanor, honey. If you look me up after all this time, the least I can do is buy you a drink." He stumbled a bit and she realized he was already well lubricated. "This rotten place doesn't even have a bar," he muttered, lurching against her and almost knocking her off the dock.

"Wait a minute, Garrison. I didn't—"

"C'mon, honey." He raised his voice to a near shout, and terrified that they could hear him on the stage, she urged him down the steps toward the parking lot. "I know a little place where the credit is always good for the guitar man." He raised the hand that wasn't clutching her arm and she realized that he'd brought along his guitar. Well, at least it made a chaperon of sorts.

She sighed and unlocked the door of her rental car. It wouldn't hurt her to have a drink with him and maybe exorcise the specter of that damned song. She didn't particularly want to skulk around backstage torturing herself with the sight of Vivienne working her wiles on Josh.

"I'll drive," she said firmly, pushing Garrison in the front seat.

"Great." He laughed and pulled a little flask from the pocket of his smart-looking white suit. "'Cause I didn't bring my car. If you don't drive, we'll have to hitch. Or else we can just find a cozy nook right here." He seemed to find that thought supremely funny, laughing again as he slid across the seat to her, his arms outstretched.

Ellie sat behind the wheel and surveyed him with disgust. "Listen, Garrison." She tried to make her voice firm but not hostile. "I'll be glad to have a drink with you for old times' sake. But I'm not here because of you, and I don't have a lot of time to spare. So if you could sober up, it would make this whole thing more pleasant."

He blinked at her and attempted to pull himself together. "Sure thing, sweetheart," he agreed placatingly. She felt a long-forgotten mixture of pity and impatience rising in her—sensations that had marked much of her brief marriage. She knew what was about to happen: he would make sweeping declarations of undying love and dependence. She hoped heartily that she could say good-night before the next stage appeared: the truculent, abusive wounded ego that slashed at anything in its path.

By the time she found a small coffee shop and a place to park near it, he appeared to have pulled himself together. They sat across from each other at the Formica-topped table, cups of steaming black coffee in front of them. Garrison began to talk.

Nothing, it seemed, had been any good since she left. Although he'd had a couple of modest hits written off their crumbling marriage, when that material had dried up, so had his songwriting. A thousand times he'd wanted to go to her, to make it up, but he'd never been able to get out of L.A. He missed her. He needed her. He still loved her.

"Garrison." Ellie shrugged helplessly. "It's not me you need. It's taking charge of your own life. I can't get you back on your feet if you can't do it for yourself. Besides," she pointed out, unable to resist the gibe, "as I recall, you were only too happy to see the back of me. I was the bad-luck piece. I goofed up your publicity. And I was rotten in bed—the Ice Maiden. Remember?"

Garrison moved uneasily on the vinyl seat. "You

know I never meant it. Why, we were great together. The greatest I've ever known."

"That's not what you said at the time. That's not how it sounds in that wretched song you sang tonight." She couldn't keep her resentment from showing, and Garrison picked up on it.

"Has that been bothering you all this time? Hell, honey, you should know I didn't really mean it. I was mad at you because you were always nagging me to spend my life in the studio." His voice faltered. "Guess I should have listened to you. But you were so damned self-righteous. And if I had a few drinks you put on that 'perfect virgin' expression when I wanted you to love me. . . ."

"You see," Ellie said gently, "we didn't suit. I was wrong for you. I still am. Let's leave it at that, Garrison."

He wouldn't drop the subject. "Eleanor, come back to me. Help me! You could put me back together again. I could write some more songs, good ones! I could be famous, I could give you anything you want."

"No, Garrison." She tried to pry his hand from its death grip on her arm. "We have different lives now. Everything is different. If you want to be back together, do it yourself. Dry out and work hard. No one can make you do that if you can't do it yourself."

He buried his head in his arms. "You don't understand." His voice came out a muffled wail, and she glanced nervously around. Behind the counter, the waitress stared at her censoriously. "You didn't used to be so cold." He lifted his head and stared at her. "There's someone else, isn't there? Isn't there?"

"For heaven's sake, Garrison, keep your voice down. Of course there's someone else. It's been four years since our divorce. You didn't even wait for that, as I recall. Why should I deny myself?"

"Why, indeed?" He smiled, the petulant, selfish smile

that used to precede a barrage of cruel, wounding words. "Hope your new lover likes a low temperature in his bed. You never did put out much voltage, as I recall."

Ellie waited for the pain, and found there was none. Why had she ever allowed herself to be made miserable by this man? His words were empty of meaning, because he was empty of truth.

"Go home, Garrison," she said, picking up her bag. "Maybe you'll feel better in the morning."

"He likes it cold, does he? Or maybe he doesn't like it at all. That would suit you right down to the ground, wouldn't it?" Garrison's voice began to pick up volume again. Ellie felt her patience recede.

"Actually," she hissed, leaning across the table to deliver her words with close-up impact, "with him, I've finally discovered what a good lover can do. Haven't you heard that old saying, Garrison? There are no frigid women. Just inept men." She took a bill out of her wallet and threw it down on the table. "Take a taxi home and try to keep your nose out of a bottle for a few hours. It does wonders for small talents."

Her righteous anger lasted her until she'd driven a couple blocks from the coffee shop. Then the recollection of his stunned face ceased to give satisfaction. She pulled over for a minute and rested her forehead on the steering wheel. Then she circled back around to the restaurant.

Garrison was still there, slumped at the table. But now he had company. The waitress sat with him, listening intently as his lips moved. Then she patted his sleeve.

Ellie watched for a minute. She would have given him a ride to his house, but she wasn't really sorry for anything she'd said. He was a weak and bellicose man who had always needed constant ego support without wanting to give any back. She had no doubt that the sad story of his abandonment by his cold, cruel wife was a staple in his barroom conversations. If there was anyone to feel sorry for, it was the unsuspecting waitress.

She put the car in motion again and found that she'd taken the route to the hotel. Although it was good to be back in California, away from the inclement weather east of the Rockies, it would be a while before her internal clock was back in order. Jet lag made her suddenly weary, longing for rest and bed. If she went back to the concert it would be hours before she could get away again. And she would have to stand by and watch Vivienne Santos working on Josh.

She could tell herself rationally that Josh loved her, even though he'd never said it. Logically, Vivienne was no threat to her love for Josh. But she couldn't depend on logic to support her if she had to watch the two of them onstage, singing songs that they'd done in their past, looking into each other's eyes with practiced ease. If she had to see that, it would be hard to tell herself that it was only an act, at least on Josh's part.

The hotel was in Westwood, snazzy but not overly high priced. Her room was next to Josh's, though they didn't connect. She put on the nightgown she'd hardly worn since the start of the tour, and went out onto her balcony. A wrought-iron railing separated it from Josh's. His room was still dark.

Of course he wasn't back yet. It could take him hours to disentangle Vivienne's lithe body from his. She brought a blanket from her room and sank down on the padded chaise longue on her balcony. It overlooked the courtyard garden and swimming pool. The air was fragrant with the scents of citrus and early roses. Lights clustered thickly on the nearby hills, and the traffic sounds mingled with the muted, faraway shush and roar of the ocean.

The curtain from inside her room billowed out, and she reached a lazy hand to slide the door shut. When Josh turned on his light, she would know he was back. Meanwhile, it would do no harm to rest her eyes just for a minute.

THE SUN WOKE HER, peering in under the balcony overhang, laying stark fingers of light on her face. She was stiff, chilly and unbelieving. How could she have slept all night on the chaise longue? Why hadn't Josh's light wakened her? She leaned over the railing that separated her balcony from his and knocked lightly on the windowpane. There was no answer.

He hadn't come in last night.

Why hadn't he come in? Was he with Vivienne? The questions battered her but she wouldn't acknowledge them. She pulled on her running clothes and propelled herself out the door on willpower alone. Part of her was pretending, thinking how nice it was to run without long johns and mittens. But beneath this mental monologue was a vast aching sensation, too raw and undefined to examine. Emptying her mind of fruitless anxiety over Josh's whereabouts, she ran, choosing hills over flatlands, trying to ease the hurt with a flood of endorphins, her body's personal answer to painkiller.

Driven at last by hunger, she returned to the hotel. An ornate clock in the lobby chimed the hour as she passed. Nine o'clock. She felt as if the day had been going on for months already, and it was only nine o'clock.

Needing to cool down a little more, she headed for the stairs instead of the elevator. They led past the coffee shop, and she looked in, sniffing the morning aromas hungrily. Then she stiffened, one foot poised on the first step.

Over the top of a cozy booth for two she saw Vivienne Santos. Across from her, his back to Ellie, was a dark-haired man. As she watched, he ran his hand through his hair in a gesture she'd become only too familiar with. Josh.

Frozen into position, she watched as Vivienne leaned toward him, watched the coquettish dark eyes flirt up and down. She couldn't see Josh's face, but she could imagine what his expression must be to inspire such looks from Vivienne.

She was tempted to go in, sweaty as she was. But another glance at Vivienne sent her pelting up the steps, all thoughts of cooling down gone. She might not be as chic or beautiful as a superstar singer, but she could at least look better than she did.

While she showered, dressed, applied mascara, she told herself that the numbness she felt was a consequence of sleeping on a plastic-covered chaise longue four inches too short for her, or of running too far when she hadn't recovered from jet lag. But that didn't account for the odd sensation she experienced of having just been thrown to the mat by a judo opponent twice as big as she.

Though she wanted to take a lot of care with her appearance, she found herself hustling to pull on the only clean clothes left in her suitcase, slim-legged jeans and a cotton sweater. It was hardly glamour material, so she didn't bother blow drying her hair. At least the sweat was gone, and she'd finally managed to catch her breath.

They were still in the coffee shop when she came down. Now there were plates in front of them, she saw as she walked toward their booth. Josh was eating as if glad of the diversion. Vivienne still talked, her omelet uneaten, one beautifully manicured hand poised to touch him occasionally.

Ellie made her greeting cheerful with an effort. "Hi. Mind if I join you?"

Vivienne looked up, her face blank. But Josh leaped to his feet.

"Where the hell have you been all night?" His voice was low, controlled, but the anger licked through it anyway.

Ellie stepped back involuntarily. She took a deep breath before replying.

"I fell asleep on my balcony. Must have been the return to a decent climate or something. I was stiff as a board when I woke up." Josh's expression moderated, and she looked evenly at him. "Slept like a baby, though. Nothing woke me all night long. No lights in the next room, no loud noises. Amazing, isn't it?" She glanced at Vivienne and saw the other woman watching with puzzlement. "We haven't met. I'm Eleanor Martinson, PR and press liaison for Josh's tour. How do you do?"

Josh moved at last, standing aside so that Ellie could slide into the booth, then sitting beside her. "Vivienne, Ellie," he muttered, and evidently considered that the introductions were over. "The sound man told me you left with Hanley last night and you never came back," he went on to Ellie. He still sounded angry.

Ellie felt all her emotions coalesce into one hard, cold ball. Here he was, sitting with his ex-honey first thing in the morning after he hadn't been back to his room all night, and he had the gall to quiz her about her movements. Her jaw began to stick out. "Garrison wanted to have a drink, and he was very loud about it. I went out and had coffee with him and left him in the coffee shop and came back here because I was tired and—" She flicked a glance at Vivienne, whose face wore the avid expression of a soap-opera watcher. "Anyway, I came back here and went chastely to sleep." She paused and let a thin smile flicker across her face. "What did *you* do?"

"Drove around looking for you all night," he growled.

Vivienne evidently decided that it was time to move from audience to participant. "*We* drove around all night," she corrected sweetly. "I didn't realize we were looking for you though, dear." She tossed Ellie a polite smile and said to Josh, "After all, that drink we had at my place—you can't have thought you'd find her there?"

Josh ignored this. "You're supposed to be working for my tour," he admonished to Ellie. "Instead of being where you were supposed to be, you go gallivanting off without a word to anyone. You put me through hell last night, woman. Don't you ever do that again."

Ellie's back stiffened, but she fought down an angry retort. "If you're going to fire me, perhaps you should think about doing it in a less-public place." She felt a small, mean triumph at the baffled rage that filled Josh's eyes. His hands balled into fists. His chest heaved, and gradually his hands relaxed. Vivienne watched this with an interested smile.

"You're so much better at controlling your temper than you used to be, darling," she cooed. She turned to Ellie. "A couple of years ago he would have smashed the table or something. But then," she added, lively malice in her eyes, "he was dreadfully in love with me, poor boy."

Josh surged to his feet. "I want to see you in my room in five minutes," he said to Ellie, biting off the words and spitting them out. He swung around to direct an icy glare at Vivienne. "And I don't want to see you for at least the rest of my life." He strode away, leaving two silent women behind him.

Vivienne was the first to break the silence. She yawned and stretched, as delicate and graceful as a cat. "I take it you're his new lover," she remarked, letting her eyes roam over Ellie with the candid curiosity of a child. "I must say, you're not the least bit what I expected. He always used to go for the glittery type, if you know what I mean."

"Your type?" Ellie kept the animosity out of her voice with an effort.

"Well, certainly not yours, darling." She yawned again, barely catching it behind a pink palm. "I must say I don't envy you. He's amazingly sexy, of course, and a fabulous lover, but to live with...." She shuddered expressively. "So dull! Never wants to go out, never wants to have parties, just wants to work all the time! One must relax occasionally, darling."

Ellie nodded guardedly, feeling her hostility to the other woman begin to seep away. A woman like this could inspire nothing lasting in Joshua Blackmun. "Did you really drive around all night?"

Vivienne flounced petulantly in her seat and picked up her handbag. "He said we were looking in at a few clubs, but they weren't the sort of places I'd go to." She smiled slyly at Ellie. "I did entice him to my house, but he was too stuffy to believe. Wouldn't drink because he was driving, wouldn't skinny-dip with me. I'd forgotten what a bummer he can be when he tries. Too wound up in the work ethic for words."

She made an airy gesture with her hand and stood up. "You can have him, sweetie...if he gets over his mad and wants you back. He doesn't always, you know." A different expression flitted across her face, making it momentarily vulnerable and wistful.

Then it vanished, leaving Ellie in doubt as to whether it had even been there. "Nice to meet you, uh...er." Vivienne looked into her handbag and shrugged prettily. "I seem to have come out without any cash. Could you take care of the check for me? Thanks, darling. I must run."

Ellie sat for a moment, feeling as if a small, elegant

steamroller had just run over her. The thought fed her
anger toward Josh. She had put her emotions on the line
for him. She had opened herself to love, and conse-
quently to hurt and pain. He wanted to lay down the
law and watch her snap to attention. He wanted to take
her love and trust and give nothing in return.

She was confused, bewildered, and she felt very much
alone. "Once again," she muttered, picking up the
check, "Los Angeles chews me up and spits me out, sad-
der certainly, but wiser? Probably not." She looked at
the total and gasped. Typical. In L.A. a broken heart,
like breakfast, cost more than anywhere else in the
country.

She had the check put on her hotel tab, and with no
clear idea of what she was doing, went to the desk and
paid her bill with the credit card Peter had given her.
Mounting the stairs, she summoned the remorseless
clarity with which her anger always invested her. She
became cool and capable, able to withstand overbearing
males with a single cutting remark.

There was no answer to her knock on Josh's door, but
it was open, and when she pushed it ajar she could hear
water running in the bathroom. She wandered aimlessly
around the room, noting that he hadn't unpacked yet,
either. An open copy of the morning paper caught her
eye; it was folded back to a review of last night's concert.

It was a good review, praising Josh's new music and
his performance, favorably mentioning the old stuff.
Trax was also mentioned; that would please Peter, she
thought. Then Vivienne's name leaped out at her again.
Was there no getting away from that woman?

Miss Santos joined Blackmun for the final numbers
of the concert, including a sizzling rendition of his
hit, 'Lot's Wife.' A little bird whispered to this re-

viewer that these two songbirds may be picking up where they left off three years ago. Judging from the way they kissed after the encores, there may be some truth to that rumor.

Josh came out of the bathroom, clad in the brief terry-cloth robe provided by the hotel, rubbing his hair briskly with a towel. She let the newspaper drop from numb fingers as she stared at him.

He glanced from her to the paper. "Typical rubbish publicists put out." His words did little to allay her growing despair. Knowing that he probably spoke the truth, knowing that Vivienne had schemed for that final paragraph, didn't stop her from feeling as if every word of it had found a target in her already sore heart.

There was silence for a moment. Then Josh dropped his towel and came to stand in front of her. "Why didn't you come back to the concert last night?"

Ellie shrugged, letting the icy numbness solace her wounds. It was temporary, she knew, but it would keep her from bleeding all over the floor. "I was tired. I felt like resting."

"I didn't mean to blow up at you just now," he muttered at last. "But you worried me to death! Don't ever do that again."

Something hot and angry was threatening to melt her composure. "Let me see if I've got this straight," she said slowly. "You won't make a commitment to me. You evidently don't reciprocate my feelings for you. But you expect me to be at your beck and call, waiting at your elbow while you toy with your lady friends. Is that it?"

He was watching her steadily. "That's garbage and you know it," he replied, his voice matching the rock-like hardness of his face. "I don't expect any more from you than you do from me. One of the things I do expect is honesty. Do you honestly believe I involved myself with Vivienne last night?"

She shrugged again with bravado, not willing to take the risk of opening herself to honesty. Honesty brought pain. She had enough pain to handle at the moment. "I don't think you planned to," she admitted grudgingly.

He turned away from her, opening a suitcase and rooting through it haphazardly until he found the garments he sought. When he turned back, she saw that he was struggling for control.

"Listen, Ellie," he began. His voice was raw with emotion. She tried to tune it out. "You were the one who was so understanding. You said you gave your love freely, that I was not to feel pressured by it. Well, right now I get the idea I'm being pressured."

She felt a passionate sense of injustice explode inside her. "Heaven forbid," she cried, "that the great Josh Blackmun should feel pressured by his latest love interest." She stalked closer and jabbed her finger into his chest. "Well, let me tell you something, Mr. Blackmun. What I said was true at the time. But my feelings have changed."

He blanched. "You mean you don't. . . ."

"I mean it's not enough now," she told him steadily. "Love for love's sake is very well and good. But I just discovered I've moved on from that stage. I want more. I want your commitment, your love, your life. Without those things I don't want you."

Her blunt words rang between them for a long minute. His eyes slowly darkened and narrowed.

"You're giving me an ultimatum, is that it?" His words came quickly through his teeth.

She felt her anger begin to drain away; desperate, she grasped for it, pulling it back like a shield.

"You can look at it that way if you want," she replied arrogantly.

He stepped closer until she could feel the heat from his body. She moved uneasily.

"You do want me, you know," he said silkily. He opened the robe that was his only covering. His hands moved out and caught her to him, binding her tightly against his body, giving her no room to maneuver herself out of his grip. She stared up into his face, her anger coupling with the sudden flush of feeling his naked body brought to her even through the layers of her clothes. The erotic sensations as his pelvis surged against hers created a rush of passionate excitement greater than anything she'd ever known.

His mouth descended on hers, his teeth and tongue demanding, taking, plundering with all the power that was in him. Voluptuous weakness washed through her, urging her submission, sending wave upon wave of uncontrollable arousal through her. He bit and sucked at her tongue; his hands found their way beneath her jeans, stroking and prodding until she writhed against him, awash with raging desire.

Then he stepped back, not bothering to close his robe, the evidence of his excitement rampant. "You see," he said hoarsely, "you do want me. You can't deny it. It's obvious here—" He touched the hard aching pebbles of her nipples as they strained against her sweater. "And here—" His hand dropped to rub tantalizingly against the soft mound of her jeans. "Don't try to tell me this means nothing."

She realized her jeans were unfastened, so she zipped them, letting the small act restore her thinking processes. "It's not enough." Her voice came out husky, and she cleared her throat. "Don't you understand, Blackmun? I want what I give you—I want your love for the rest of our lives. I want our children." She laughed bitterly. "And all you want from me is sex." She turned to the door, ignoring his muffled exclamation. "I won't be your groupie any longer, Blackmun."

"You're going to take what we have and throw it away?" There was incredulity in his voice.

She stopped and looked back at him. "Is it worth saving?" she asked wearily. "You tell me."

"Ellie, you don't understand—"

"Oh, yes I do," she interrupted. "I should have known better from the first. But I was so convinced I could make you love me! I forgot that a musician will always love his guitar better than any woman. Hope that Stratocaster can keep you warm until you find someone else to supply your needs."

His lips tightened. "You're going to regret you said all this," he whispered menacingly. "When you come back—and you will be back—you're going to have a tasty little banquet of your hasty little words."

Ellie opened the door. "I won't be back, Blackmun," she said evenly. "You're the one who's going to have to come crawling if you start to miss the best thing in your life." She paused on the way out to issue one more warning. "That was a nice turn of phrase there, Blackmun. Just remember our agreement. You write any songs about me and I'll have you in court so fast your pencil won't even have left the paper yet."

He laughed harshly. "I don't give that—" he snapped his fingers "—for our 'agreement,' as you call it. I broke it even before we made it, and I've been breaking it with every song I write. You can't stop me from writing about you, Ellie. You'll just have to grin and bear it."

She stood for a single enraged, impotent moment before slamming the door as hard as she could in his face.

She locked the door to her own room, and when the pounding started a few minutes later, she refused to answer. Moving with the slowness of an automaton, she repacked the few things she'd taken out. She waited for the pounding to stop. When the phone began ringing instead, she lifted her bags and quietly left her room.

The elevator was empty and waiting; she got into it and let the door shut. She walked out of the hotel, slid behind the wheel of her rental car, and got most of the way down Santa Monica Boulevard toward Highway 101 and the Hollywood Freeway before she had to pull over and let the tears spill down her face.

After that she was fine.

THE DISC JOCKEY'S VOICE was maniacally cheery. "And we'll start off the afternoon with 'Come Here Woman,' the latest crossover hit that's sweeping the charts! It's from Josh Blackmun's smash new album, *Runt of the Litter*."

Ellie reached over and snapped the radio off so forcibly the knob came off in her hand. She tossed it across the room and fell back into her bed. Her gaze drifted out the window and up into the blue arch of sky.

It was late February and the window was open, letting the first scents of citrus drift into her room. Outside, the air was soft with spring; inside, her own personal cloud of gloom hovered over her, blotting out the joy of life. She felt limp, listless, unmotivated even to get up and stop the gnawing sound that she knew was Bridget teething on the wooden leg of her sofa.

Brisk high-heeled footsteps tapped up her staircase, followed by a rapping at the door. "Ellie?" It was Marigold's voice. Eleanor didn't move. "Ellie? Aren't you ready yet? Let me in!"

Ellie hoped fervently the door was locked, but a moment later Marigold appeared in the bedroom, Bridget frisking merrily at her heels. "Ellie, it's only half an hour until the wedding, and you're not even dressed! On your feet, girl."

"I don't feel too well," Ellie muttered.

Marigold perched beside her on the bed and placed one cool palm on her forehead. "Nothing wrong with you that a good man couldn't cure."

Ellie winced in irritation. "Really, Marigold. Too hackneyed for a writer of your reputation."

A broad grin wreathed Marigold's face for a moment. "I know. Isn't it great?" Her romance novel had been accepted by a publisher three days earlier, and she was still floating in the bliss of every soon-to-be-published author.

"Sure is," Ellie agreed. She was sincerely happy for Marigold, but right now all she wanted was to be alone. "There must be a lot of people wanting to congratulate you. You'd better run along."

Marigold looked stubborn. "I'm not going without you. Gena sent me to make sure you got to the wedding, and I intend to do so." She walked over to the closet and opened it, falling back in astonishment at the organizational excesses revealed. "Good grief, look at this! The blouses, the skirts—all sorted!" She looked at Ellie in awe. "Is everything in alphabetical order besides?"

Ellie smiled reluctantly. "Had a lot of time on my hands lately," she explained in a mumble.

"What are you going to wear, this pink thing?" Marigold plucked the dress from the closet and held it up. "It's beautiful. You'll look like a spring flower."

Driven by an imp of perversity, Ellie retorted, "I had meant to wear black, actually."

Marigold hung the pink dress on the closet door and looked at the shoe rack until she found pumps to match. "You must have known for days that Josh would be at the wedding," she remarked. "How come you didn't tell Gena you wanted to chicken out if it was going to panic you like this?"

That stung. Ellie sat up. "I'm not panicking," she said coldly. "I just happen to prefer not to see him."

"Should I find you some underwear?" Marigold glanced at the silk kimono Ellie wore.

"Of course not." Ellie ran her hands through her hair. "I have it on already. Listen, Marigold—"

"Let's get moving, then." Marigold was inexorable. "You're the maid of honor."

"I'm *not* the maid of honor." Ellie submitted to having Marigold pull her off the bed, whip off her kimono, lower the pink dress over her head and zip the frothy swirl of silk. "Gena isn't having any of that stuff. They're just going to stand up at some point during the party and get married."

"Right," Marigold said. "And she asked us to stand up with her, and Peter asked Josh and Keith Redmont." She rolled her eyes in ecstasy. "I can't believe I'm going to meet Keith Redmont."

Ellie couldn't even summon a smile at Marigold's transparent enthusiasm. Picking up a hairbrush, she began to work on her hair. She felt a little uneasy at seeing Keith and Jennifer again, since she hadn't answered the concerned letter she'd received from Jennifer after what Marigold referred to as the "Great Los Angeles Dustup." Answering the letter would have meant crawling out of the cave of hurt in which she'd hidden herself. And that she hadn't been able to do.

Ellie put down the hairbrush and picked up a tube of mascara. "You probably won't be able to get near Keith Redmont for all the reporters," she said cynically, applying the mascara with care.

Marigold studied Ellie's face. "You know, you should wear some blush or something. You look kind of washed-out."

"Thanks a lot." Ellie summoned a wry smile and turned to pick up the blusher.

"I saw Josh at Trax the other day when I went to arrange for the tuxedos," Marigold said airily. "He looks washed-out, too. Must be going around this season."

Ellie brushed away the ready tears, bending her head

over the basket that held her makeup. "I don't want to hear about it."

"You know," Marigold continued conversationally, turning Ellie's face to the light and mercilessly exposing her watery eyes, "if this was a romance I was writing you'd be pregnant. You're emotional, easily upset, have lost your appetite—"

"I'm not pregnant!" Ellie snapped.

"Irritable," Marigold went on inexorably. "Are you sure?"

"Of course I'm sure." Ellie slipped her feet into her pumps and looked into the full-length mirror. The dress was the color of a seashell's inside, with a form-fitting bodice and off-the-shoulder neckline that showed off her sleek curves and creamy skin. Below the dropped waist with its old-fashioned sweetheart points front and back, the skirt frothed in several filmy layers, each a different shade of rose or cream-colored silk, stopping a few inches above her shapely ankles. She would do.

Marigold came to stand beside her, regarding herself with an innocent complacency. She wore blue, a different style but the same elegant effect. "We look very nice," she said, preening. "Think we'll outshine the bride?"

"I hope not." Ellie regarded the wedding with misgivings, and had since Gena had announced her plans a month ago. There would be lots of music from Peter's different artists, one of whom would be Josh. In fact, Peter had made vague references the week before to the special song Josh had written to sing during the ceremony.

She thought about having to stand up beside Gena, the target for all eyes, while Josh sang a song that could, if he wished to be vindictive, simply tear her apart. It was frightening.

Marigold must have seen something of what she was

thinking in her eyes. She began to talk, herding Ellie briskly toward the door. "Now where's your bag? Were you going to take this wrap? The garden is sheltered, but if those ocean breezes find their way in it could get cold."

Numbly Ellie submitted to having her hand-crocheted shawl tossed over her arm, her small Japanese silk purse tucked into her hand. She barely noticed when they were on her front porch, Marigold locking the door for her while Bridget cried distressfully.

All she could think about was that soon she'd see Josh, the first time since that fiasco in Los Angeles. A thousand times she had come close to calling him. But his parting shot, that she would eat her words, had stiffened her backbone. Nothing had changed, after all. If he had been interested in commitment, in something long-term, he would have called her.

And he hadn't called.

Her mother was waiting at the foot of the stairs. "My dear," she breathed, reaching a loving hand to tuck a strand of Ellie's hair into place, "you look lovely. And you, too, of course, Marigold."

Marigold smiled understandingly. "I'll have to have my picture taken so my mother can drool over me."

Blanche turned her attention away from Ellie long enough to beam at Marigold. "Have it taken for the jacket of your book. You certainly look just like a romance heroine today."

Ellie wasn't listening; she couldn't have been more tense if she'd been getting married that day. Her mother seemed to sense the turmoil that possessed her.

"Pull yourself together, sweetie," she admonished, squeezing Ellie's hand warmly. "If today is as important to you as you think it is, you owe it to yourself to keep your wits about you."

Ellie's head came up at this bracing bit of advice.

"Thanks, mom," she whispered, bending to hug her mother fiercely, unmindful of her elegant attire. "I needed that."

They took Marigold's car to the site of the wedding, a lavish house in the hills overlooking Monterey Bay. The place belonged to friends of Gena's, who'd lent it for the day. It boasted a beautiful sunken garden, perfect for a wedding. At one end of the garden was a massed bank of rhododendrons and azaleas, bursting into bloom. Peter and Gena would be married against this backdrop.

Ellie took her mother's admonition to heart enough to spare time from her own woes for speculation about the forthcoming marriage. She had felt somewhat cynical about it up to now, knowing that Gena had set out to get Peter with the same single-minded intensity that a tiger brings to stalking an antelope.

But when she saw them in the garden, their faces radiant, their eyes continually finding each other and exchanging tender messages, she began to revise her thoughts. Gena had obviously become important to Peter—he was positively beaming and boyish, and had even left his phone beeper at home. "Today," he told Ellie while his eyes searched for his bride in the crowd, "I have absolutely forsworn business. Except maybe talking Keith into switching his contract to Trax."

Keith was attended by Chuck Green and the omnipresent stack of preautographed cards that succeeded in keeping the crowd around him from mobbing him. As Ellie watched, Keith managed to extricate himself from the surrounding fans, take Jennifer's arm and sweep her away. He was headed toward the temporary stage, which had been rigged near the long white tables of refreshments.

Ellie saw his hand go up in greeting. A man on the stage moved away from the amplifier he'd been working on and returned Keith's wave.

It was Josh.

When she saw him she realized that she'd been searching the crowd for him since they arrived. *Get a grip on yourself*, she ordered herself fiercely. The air seemed to swim and quiver around the distant dark head. She blinked a few times and found she could focus normally.

Josh wore formal clothes as easily as his blue jeans. Peter had drawn the line at the pastel-colored tuxedos Gena wanted. They had compromised on a white tux for him and pearl gray for the two men he'd chosen to stand up with him, Keith and Josh.

Ellie couldn't tear her eyes away from Josh's lean figure. Gena had insisted on tailcoats, and the short cutaway jacket was very becoming over the crisp white ruffled shirt. As she watched, he stripped off the jacket and tossed it carelessly on the piano, where Keith's soon followed. Unbuttoning the ruffles at his neck and jerking loose his bow tie, Josh picked up his guitar. Keith sat at the piano, and other musicians came out of the crowd to find instruments.

Keith spoke into a microphone over his keyboard. "Hey, folks, we're going to have some music for a while before our good friends Peter and Gena tie the knot." There were some cheers from the crowd, who'd been sampling the champagne freely. Keith grinned. "This is just a pick-up band. There are lots of fine musicians at this party, and anyone who wants to can play musical chairs with any instrument. Just keep in mind, we haven't rehearsed."

He nodded to Josh, and they broke into a ragged but sprightly rendition of the Beatles hit, "When I'm Sixty-four."

Feeling safe from discovery while Josh was involved in the music, Ellie moved a little closer, wanting to peruse his face from the anonymity of the crowd.

He was adding his voice to Keith's on the chorus, and

his eyes closed as he reached for a high note. His hands moved as if by instinct on the neck of the guitar, bringing out the notes he wanted. He looked taut and dangerous—dangerous to her heart.

All the emotions she'd kept repressed for the past month came flooding back. She felt again the delirious pleasure of loving him and the stark agony of that last morning in his hotel room. She knew how the straight, silky lock of black hair would feel if she pushed it off his forehead. She imagined the muscular strength of him under the debonair trousers and shirt. She could almost smell the clean masculine scent that could never be captured in a bottle.

Thinking about how good it would feel to hold him in her arms, she let her eyes drift shut. When she opened them, he was watching her.

He sang the bouncy words of the song, but now the message in his eyes was no longer lighthearted. With burning intensity he gazed at her, and when the song was over he didn't wait to discuss the next one with the other musicians.

His hands plucked a gentle, wistful melody that strengthened as Keith and the bass player began to wind counterpoint around it.

> "At first I said that you were wrong, my friend,
> But when I tried to write that song,
> I realized that neither wrong nor right
> Could stand beside our love for long."

She was lost in the depths of his gray-tweed eyes, hearing the plaintive note in his voice. The rhythm changed and warmed as he sang the chorus.

> "I'm waitin' for you, little darlin'.
> Do you really mean to make me crawl?

I've been waiting so long already,
I'm finally ready to take that fall."

Shaken, Ellie turned away. If she watched him any longer, if she stood so close another moment, she would break down. She moved blindly toward the chairs set out at the other end of the garden for the ceremony and ran smack into Jennifer Magnusson.

Jennifer pressed a tissue into her hands. "Here," she said, her voice sympathetic. "You could use a drink." She plucked a glass of champagne off a passing tray and handed it over.

Ellie blew her nose and accepted the champagne. "Thanks," she said gruffly. "I hate being so wimpy."

Jennifer hid a smile. "I would never describe you as wimpy. 'Bullheaded' is more what I had in mind."

Ellie looked toward the stage once more. Josh was still watching her, although Keith was now singing a hoked-up version of "My Girl." At any moment another guitarist might free him to come after her. What would she say? She could sense a confrontation brewing, and she wasn't prepared for it.

"What are you two going to do?" Jennifer's blunt words echoed her thoughts. "You can't go on this way, obviously. Both of you are eating your hearts out over each other, but you're too stubborn to hammer out your differences."

"Josh doesn't—" Ellie began heatedly. Shamefaced, she stopped and met Jennifer's honest brown eyes. "We don't seem too successful at talking about it."

"Have you even tried?"

"Not really." Ellie sighed and used the tissue again. "It's all so complicated."

"It seems that way," Jennifer remarked wisely, "but it's really simple. Do you love each other? Do you want that to matter? If so, you should be able to work things out."

Ellie managed a smile. "Thank you, Mother Magnusson. Does incipient parenthood affect everyone this way?"

Jennifer rubbed her rounded stomach with an expression of contentment. "I can't speak for everyone, but it's made me horribly bossy and sure I know what's best for everyone." She shook her finger playfully at Ellie. "So follow my advice, or else!"

When Ellie looked back at the stage, Josh was pulling the guitar strap over his head, handing the instrument to Annette, the lead guitarist for the Eves of Destruction. He started toward Ellie with an expression that brought her involuntarily to her feet. But before he reached her a nervous-looking little man bent to speak to Keith, who promptly struck the opening chords of the wedding march.

"Take your seats, friends," he shouted into his mike. The little man cringed, and Ellie placed him as the justice of the peace who'd known Gena for years. Evidently he wasn't used to presiding at unconventional weddings. Perhaps it was the Eves of Destruction, whose finery was definitely of the thrift-shop, lace-anklet variety, who made him so nervous. The huge, lacquered beehive hairdos they were sporting did have a kind of mutant appearance. At any rate, he looked so much like the White Rabbit as he followed Keith through the garden to the rhododendrons, that when he groped in his pocket Ellie expected him to pull out a big watch instead of the handkerchief he used to mop his face.

Josh was diverted from her by the necessity of getting Peter and Gena married. She moved to stand at Gena's side along with Marigold, who was fussing around the bride. Gena had opted for sleek simplicity in her wedding attire, garbing her petite figure in a strapless sheath of silk shantung topped by an antique-lace bolero. She

looked happy and poised behind the enormous bouquet
of spring flowers she carried.

Keith and Josh stood behind Peter, talking in low
voices as the crowd slowly settled into the folding
chairs. Ellie's eyes fastened on Josh helplessly. She
couldn't look away, even when she saw him watching
her. Something strange was happening to her as she met
his eyes.

Everything they had shared came back to her. Before
Josh, her life had been a pleasant nothing. After she'd
left him, it had become torment. Without him, nothing
was any good. So why was she standing back from their
relationship? Even without commitment, to be with him
was better than to be without him.

She barely heard the justice of the peace read the
vows Peter and Gena had written. All her attention was
on Josh. At one point in the ceremony there was unexpected quiet. Peter touched Josh on the arm, murmuring
that it was time for the music.

Josh shook himself briefly and she realized with a
secret thrill that he was so involved in their silent com-
munion he'd forgotten to listen for his cue. Moving to a
mike set up a little way from the wedding party, he
perched on the tall stool and took up his acoustic guitar.

"An epithalamium," he said baldly, and then began
playing, the melody lilting and lyrical. He sang the
words straight to Ellie.

"There's the light of your laughter in the morning,
There's the weight of your tears at night,
The walks and the talks you take together,
The sweetness when you hold each other tight,
And the love you share will keep growin', goin' on."

She heard the song through a haze of enchantment,
feeling each word enter her heart. An epithalamium, she

knew, was a song celebrating a wedding. In the words
Josh had written she saw the foreshadowing of another
nuptial.

His eyes never left hers as he sang, as he finished and
handed the guitar away. Letting her love flow into his
eyes, she plucked one of the roses from the corsage on
her wrist and kissed it before tossing it to him.

He caught it and held it to his lips in turn. There was a
sigh of satisfaction from the crowd at this bit of byplay,
and the sound roused Ellie from her single-minded state
of concentration. Blushing, she tore her gaze from Josh's
and tried to pay attention to what the justice of the
peace was saying. But inside she was a mass of fevered
impatience waiting for the end of the ceremony when
she knew Josh would find her.

At last Peter and Gena kissed. Joanne, of the Eves,
who had taken over the keyboards when Keith relin-
quished them, crashed out the traditional recessional.
Laughing, Peter and Gena raced back up the aisle between the folding chairs, trying to dodge a storm of rose
petals. People erupted from their chairs and crowded
onto the impromptu dance floor of the terrace, where a
motley assemblage of musicians was playing big-band
dance music with an enthusiasm that covered up any
awkward phrasing.

Ellie turned and found Josh beside her, the rose
clasped in his hand. For a long moment they just gazed
at each other. She felt Marigold tactfully melt away.

Then Josh reached with trembling fingers to tuck the
rose behind her ear. "Ellie, little darlin'," he breathed.

At the same moment Ellie moved her hand to touch
his. "Josh," she began, "I—"

"Hush, now." His arms came around her in a slow,
beautiful movement. "Thank God you came today. Oh,
Ellie darlin', I've been wanting you so bad. I need you so
much." He looked down at her, his face serious. "Every

day I feel it more. It's either love or something just as terminal. A thousand times I've reached for the phone, driven past your house. I was too afraid to carry through."

She laughed shakily. "Blackmun, I've been so...stubborn." She thought of Jennifer and plunged on. "I was right the first time. Love is something you have to give. It doesn't make sense to try to withhold it."

He pulled her closer, laying his cheek on her hair. "Oh, darlin'. Let's not talk about who's been the most stupid. I'm sure to win." He moved back a little so he could look at her. "I love you, Ellie. I could have said it months ago if I weren't such a suspicious coward. Where you were concerned I didn't have any gumption. I figured I could play it safe, have my cake and eat it, too."

"*Que sera sera*," she agreed solemnly. His lips twitched and suddenly they were laughing with gusto, clasped in each other's arms.

Then his breath warm against her face brought her body to leaping awareness. She could feel him quicken, too, as the electricity began to crackle between them. "Ellie," Josh said, his voice thick with longing, "how long does it take to get married?"

"You just saw how long." She licked her lips and moved slightly in his embrace, brushing suggestively against him.

He groaned. "I meant how many hours or days will it be before we can get married?"

She blinked up at him. "You're asking me these bureaucratic questions at the wrong time, Blackmun. However long it takes, it's too long. I've done all the waiting I intend to."

His look was a quick blaze of passion, but underneath it she saw the insecurity. "Damn it, woman, I'm askin' you to marry me. Can you say yes or not?"

"I can say yes." She grinned brilliantly at him and

reached up to take his face between her hands, pulling him down until his lips were inches from hers. "Now I'm asking you to kiss me! Can you do it?"

"You bet." His voice was a husky whisper against her mouth. His lips met hers in the softest and tenderest of touches before he swept her hard against him and let his lips and tongue ignite her with a quivering intensity.

"Your place or mine?" He pulled her into the circle of one arm and began striding out of the garden. She sent a backward glance toward the happy couple and caught Jennifer's understanding eye.

"Mine's closer."

He pushed past chattering groups without seeing them. "Yes," he growled, sweeping her toward the cars and gesturing to one of the teenagers who was handling parking. "But mine's more private."

He grinned down at her, and she had to take a deep breath at his expression. "And I have the feeling I'm going to want to be private with you," he said, pushing the rose behind her ear more securely. "Very private. For a long, long time."

HARLEQUIN
PREMIERE AUTHOR EDITIONS

6 EXCITING HARLEQUIN AUTHORS
—6 OF THEIR BEST BOOKS!

Daphne Clair
A STREAK OF GOLD

Marjorie Lewty
TO CATCH A BUTTERFLY

Anne Mather
SCORPIONS' DANCE

Jessica Steele
SPRING GIRL

Margaret Way
THE WILD SWAN

Violet Winspear
DESIRE HAS NO MERCY

Harlequin is pleased to offer these six very special titles, out of print since 1980. These authors have published over 250 titles between them. Popular demand required that we reissue each of these exciting romances in new beautifully designed covers.

Available in April wherever paperback books are sold, or through Harlequin Reader Service. Simply send your name, address and zip or postal code, with a check or money order for $2.50 for each copy ordered (includes 75¢ for postage and handling) payable to Harlequin Reader Service, to:

Harlequin Reader Service

In the U.S.
P.O. Box 52040
Phoenix, AZ 85072-2040

In Canada
P.O. Box 2800
Postal Station A
5170 Yonge Street
Willowdale, Ontario
M2N 6J3

PAE-1

EYE OF THE STORM

MAURA SEGER

A powerful portrayal of the events of World War II in the Pacific, *Eye of the Storm* is a riveting story of how love triumphs over hatred. In this, the first of a three book chronicle, Army nurse Maggie Lawrence meets Marine Sgt. Anthony Gargano. Despite military regulations against fraternization, they resolve to face together whatever lies ahead.... Also known by her fans as Laurel Winslow, Sara Jennings, Anne MacNeil and Jenny Bates, Maura Seger, author of this searing novel, was named by ROMANTIC TIMES as 1984's Most Versatile Romance Author.

At your favorite bookstore in March.

EYE OF THE STORM

MAURA SEGER

A powerful
portrayal of
the events of
World War II in the
Pacific, *Eye of the Storm* is a riveting story of how love
triumphs over hatred. In this, the first of a three book
chronicle, Army nurse Maggie Lawrence meets Marine
Sgt. Anthony Gargano. Despite military regulations
against fraternization, they resolve to face together
whatever lies ahead.... Also known by her fans as
Laurel Winslow, Sara Jennings, Anne MacNeil and
Jenny Bates, Maura Seger, author of this searing novel,
was named by ROMANTIC TIMES as 1984's Most
Versatile Romance Author.

At your favorite bookstore in March.

EYE-B-1

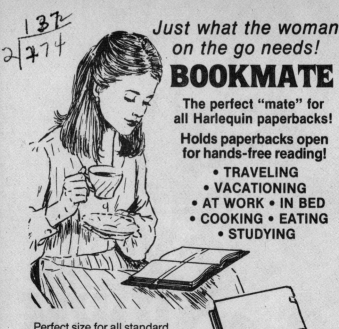